D0957797

Also by Nicole McLaughlin

Maybe I Do
Maybe This Time
Should've Been You
Along Came Us
All I Ask

Maybe for You

Nicole McLaughlin

St. Martin's Paperbacks

This is a work of fiction. All of the characters, organizations, and events portrayed in this novel are either products of the author's imagination or are used fictitiously.

MAYBE FOR YOU

Copyright © 2018 by Nicole McLaughlin.

All rights reserved.

For information address St. Martin's Press, 175 Fifth Avenue, New York, NY 10010.

ISBN: 978-1-250-14002-9

Our books may be purchased in bulk for promotional, educational, or business use. Please contact your local bookseller or the Macmillan Corporate and Premium Sales Department at 1-800-221-7945, ext. 5442, or by e-mail at MacmillanSpecialMarkets@macmillan.com.

Printed in the United States of America

St. Martin's Paperbacks edition / September 2018

St. Martin's Paperbacks are published by St. Martin's Press, 175 Fifth Avenue, New York, NY 10010.

10 9 8 7 6 5 4 3 2 1

One

Alex stepped onto the old wood-and-metal freight elevator in the Stag distillery. The party upstairs was already well underway, leaving her alone to try and recall how her brother, Dean, had taught her to use it. She pulled a small lever, tugged at the door to make sure it had latched, and then pushed the big red button. The well-used gears groaned as it began its ascent.

Conversation and soft music filtered down through the wood floor and stone walls. Alex closed her eyes and took a deep breath. She'd told herself on the drive over that she would not think about how she was supposed to have gotten married here just a couple of weeks ago. Hard to do when she could hear the tinkle of glass and the laughter of people milling about. Just like they did at a wedding reception.

The Stag hosted a lot of events and receptions. Although Alex's brother and his two partners, Jake and TJ, had gone into business to make small-batch liquor, fate had its own agenda, and they'd also ended up becoming one of the most successful wedding and event venues in the Kansas City metro. It was the perfect business model that no one had seen coming. They set up their distillery in a gorgeous old building with an amazing second floor where they could hold events *and* serve their liquor. Nearly every Saturday they earned themselves new customers.

Tonight, however, they were celebrating themselves. After half a decade in business, they were uncasking their signature distilled products. The bourbon and whiskey had been aging in oak barrels for five years, waiting for them to debut it to their customers. Until this point, they'd been selling unaged white whiskey and vodka.

Even Alex, deployed for most of this time, knew they'd been a great success. Tonight was a big deal, and even though her current personal circumstances were nearly crushing her, she was grateful she could be here to celebrate with her brother.

Her left thumb began to roll her engagement ring around on her finger. Someday she was going to have to take it off. But this was not that day. Tomorrow seemed just as unlikely.

Inhaling another deep breath, she blew it out slowly, the sounds of joviality getting louder. Was it stupid to make your first public outing after a personal tragedy a party located in the place that was likely to bring the most pain? Probably, but Alex was nothing if not strong-willed. And after the horrible argument she'd had with her brother this afternoon, she knew it was necessary to apologize and make things right. She also wanted him to see that she was not, as he put it, "too broken to handle life on your own right now."

The elevator ground to a halt and her eyes flew open. She pulled the door open and stepped into the expansive second floor of the Stag. Thank goodness there were so many people for their sake, but the sight of the crowd made her hesitate. Instantly she felt the need to search out her brother, panic settling into her chest.

Taking another step, she decided to focus on the room. It was so beautiful, the imposing antler chandelier sparkling in the center and the massive stone fireplace taking up the west wall. Her heart rate began to rise as her eyes flittered around the room, seeing the centerpieces that Charlotte and Dean had brought this afternoon for the tables. Why had she agreed to let them use things that had been made to decorate her own wedding reception? It had seemed logical at the time, but seeing them now, she realized how silly it had been. Now she had to see them looking exactly how they would have looked on her special day. The temptation to turn around and get back on the elevator was so strong her legs began to shake.

"Alex," a voice called out from the crowd.

She glanced forward to see Jake, one of the co-owners of the Stag, heading in her direction. His grin was only for her, and her entire body sighed with relief at the sight of him. This was what she needed—someone she knew—and she felt a smile form on her lips.

"How are you?" she asked as she pulled him into a hug. The connection felt like being tossed a raft after treading in a deep and lonely ocean. She realized she was incredibly dramatic these days, but she felt justified.

"I'm good," he said as he pulled back and looked down at her. "I wasn't sure if you were coming tonight."

She sighed. "I almost didn't. Honestly, this is the first time I've put makeup on in weeks. I nearly forgot how to do it." Her attempt at lighthearted humor fell flat when his brow furrowed.

"I'm so sorry about what happened, Alex. I can't even imagine what you've been going through."

"Thank you. I'm a bit of a wreck." Would she ever learn how to respond to those sentiments eloquently? When your fiancé was tragically killed, no one showed up and handed you an owner's manual on how to go on. A quick lesson in knowing how to handle the kindness and sympathy of friends without losing your shit would have been helpful.

Sensing her discomfort, Jake nodded toward the huge bar that anchored the north end of the room. "Would you like a drink?"

"More than anything," she said.

He took her hand and led her to the bar. She was glad to see Jen, the bartender, laughing with a man seated at the bar. Although Alex didn't know Jen well, they'd met a few times and she was a familiar face that greeted her with a warm smile.

"Alex, it's so good to see you. And you look beautiful this evening," Jen said.

Alex forced a smile. "Thank you."

Jen made a quick introduction to Jordan, the man she'd been chatting with. He apparently owned a bar across the street. "Can I make you something special?" Jen finally asked.

"Sure. Surprise me," Alex said.

She was grateful that Jake stood with her, quietly telling her who many of the guests were and how the evening had gone so far. Eventually TJ, the third owner, and his date came over to say hi, and now that Alex had her drink, she sipped quietly, drifting in and out of the conversation. Jordan was inviting all of them to his bar the following weekend to hear a band play, and the only thing that Alex could think about was that she wouldn't be in town and wouldn't have been interested even if she was. Coming to this event tonight was hard enough, a bar was out of the question.

Her thoughts drifted to Monday morning, when she would get up early, head to the airport, and embark on her final yearlong deployment. This time to Vicenza, Italy. A beautiful country she should have been looking forward to exploring as a married woman.

Alex was in the Army, Nate had been in the Air Force. The military had brought them together. It was their life until this point. After so many years in the Middle East they'd been so excited about spending a year at Camp Ederle—a final adventure before they came home and settled down into family life.

After Nate's accident, she'd been informed that she could choose to extend her leave or change her orders and stay in the States. Specifically Fort Bragg, where she'd been years ago. At the time the idea had appealed to her, because she hadn't been able to fathom going to Italy without him. Job or no. But the more she thought about it over the past week, the more she realized it was exactly what she needed to do. Nate would have wanted her to see all the places they'd discussed visiting. And to be honest, she had no other plan and staring at the same walls was not doing anything to help her feel better.

Informing her brother of her intentions earlier in the day hadn't gone over well. She knew he was just worried about her, and she couldn't blame him, considering she'd spent the past few weeks in a state of crisis. But could he blame *her*? She'd just lost the love of her life. Multiple weeks of greasy hair and puffy eyes felt absolutely appropriate. But she knew if she stayed here living in her brother's apartment, that's exactly what she would continue to do, and that was unacceptable.

Getting dressed tonight, putting on makeup, doing her hair—all of that had been difficult. Several times she'd had to talk herself out of just crawling back into bed. But now that she was here, looking somewhat decent, interacting with humans—sort of—she knew she'd made the right decision. Moving on, *healing*, required putting one foot in front of the other. Even when it felt impossible. And she'd probably need to keep repeating that over and over again.

A gasp from the bar pulled Alex from her thoughts. She looked up just in time to see Jen darting toward the end of the bar gripping her hand. TJ was calling Jen's name, chasing after her as she headed for the restroom.

"What happened?" Alex asked, leaning toward Jake.

"I think she cut herself."

"Oh no. I hope it wasn't too bad."

"Me too," he said, looking around. After a second, he touched her arm. "I'm sorry to leave you for a minute, Alex, but I'm going to step behind the bar and fill in."

"Oh, of course. I'll be fine."

He made his way around the bar, leaving her standing there with the woman TJ had abandoned without a word. Alex glanced at her—Brooke, if she recalled—and tried to think of something to say. The look of irritation on her face didn't inspire a conversation, so Alex was relieved when she heard a familiar voice call her name. She turned to find her brother.

"I was afraid you wouldn't come," he said.

She smiled. "I couldn't miss this. It's not every day your brother celebrates opening five-year-old bourbon he made with his own hands."

"And it's not every day said brother needs to beg your forgiveness for acting like an insensitive jackass."

Alex's shoulders slumped, and her lips began to

tremble the slightest bit. "Dammit, Bean." She reached out and wrapped her arms around him. "I was trying not to cry here."

"Aw, Buzz. I'm sorry," he said, rubbing her back gently. Using their lifelong nicknames was a sure sign that things would be okay. She'd known that they would be, but fights with anyone she loved made her feel panicky. What if something happened and words of anger were the last thing that had passed between them? "Please don't cry. Just tell me you forgive me."

"Of course I do. I forgave you the minute the conversation was over." She could feel the tension leave his body and she pulled back to look up at him, wiping at her eyes just in case.

"You sure? Because I was really out of line."

"Yes, you were. But in your defense," she said, smirking at his look of surprise, "I know I surprised you with my change in plans."

"Very much so." He nodded. "I was looking forward to finally having you around."

She pushed the tears back once more. "It's only a year, Dean. I know you only want what's best for me."

"Always."

"But you've got to let me figure that out. Even if it ends up being the wrong decision. Or I get hurt."

"I know that, Alex. And everything you tried to tell me earlier makes perfect sense now that I've thought about it. It *is* best for you to stay busy, to keep doing what you're good at. And what better place to heal a broken heart than a beautiful country like Italy? You're a strong and intelligent woman, and I was being selfish wanting to keep you close so I could make sure you're okay."

Her lips quirked. "How many times did Charlotte have to repeat all that until it sank in?"

"About twenty," he said, looking unsurprised that she'd called him out. "And she'll probably have to keep saying it for the first couple of weeks you're gone."

Alex shook her head. "You're hopeless. But I love you for caring so much about me."

Before he could reply, they were interrupted by TJ. "Jen cut herself. I need to take her to the Emergency Room."

Dean's brow furrowed as Charlotte walked up beside him. "How bad is it?" Dean asked.

"She's okay," TJ clarified. "But she needs stitches."

"Where is she?" Charlotte asked.

TJ nodded toward where he'd just come from. "Men's restroom."

Charlotte's eyebrows went up, but she took off without questioning it further.

"I don't know how long this will take," TJ said to Dean.

"Don't worry about it, man. We can handle this."

"I'll stay and help also," Alex added.

TJ nodded and then stepped forward and gave Alex an awkward one-armed hug. "Thanks, Alex. And it was so good to see you." He pulled back and smiled at her. "Good luck in Italy. We'll all be thinking about you."

"Thank you, TJ. Let us know how Jen is."

He nodded and was gone. For the rest of the evening, Alex felt a lot more at ease. Tension between Dean and her always sucked, although considering he'd practically raised her after her dad and their mother passed away when she was thirteen, they'd had their fair share of it over the years. It wasn't an easy position he was in, wanting to be the cool big brother, but also feeling the need to step up and be the only parent she had.

The tone of the event hadn't been one that encouraged

people to get wasted and hang around, so by nine thirty or so, most everyone had left. Alex saw that Dean's father, Joel, was getting up out of the chair he'd been in most of the evening, so she walked over and gave him a big hug.

"I'm sure glad I got to spend some time with you this evening," he said as he patted her back. "Make sure you send me some emails when you get a chance."

She smiled. "You know I will, but I told you, you need to get a social media account so you can see everything I'm doing. Being stationed in Italy I think I'll have more time and ability to keep up with that sort of thing."

"Oh, Alex, I'm an old man. I don't have any use for that sort of thing."

She pointed at herself. "Your use is right here. Keeping up with me."

"I'll think about it," he said with a wink. As Dean's father, Joel Troyer had become like a grandfather to Alex over the years. He'd always taken her to breakfast on her birthday, gave her ten bucks for every *A* on her report card, and even taught her how to drive a car. She adored him.

Watching Dean and Charlotte say goodbye to Joel and discuss going over to his place for lunch the following weekend, it suddenly hit her that she would be leaving in less than forty-eight hours. Alone.

A weight came over her then, her legs suddenly feeling as if they might give out. Turning, her eyes flickered around, looking for somewhere she could retreat to and find a moment of privacy. Her eyes burned, her vision beginning to blur, as she finally saw the door to the left of the bar. She took off, her heels clacking along the wood floor so loudly in her ears.

Sucking in a deep breath she opened the door, relieved to realize it was the small retiring room that vendors used to hold their gear and eat dinner, and nursing mothers used to evade the crowd. Two sofas faced each other, and Alex collapsed onto one of them, her face instantly falling into her hands.

Her chest heaved in and out with gasping breaths as she tried to get her emotions and her thoughts under control. This was the second time this week this had happened. She assumed it was a panic attack, and each time it had come out of nowhere. She pinched her eyes shut.

The sound of the door opening made her want to groan. *Why right now?*

"Alex?" a deep voice said.

She turned her head, still keeping it rested against her hands. "Hey."

Taking her word as an invitation, Jake stepped in and closed the door behind him. "You okay? I got worried when I saw you rush in here. I'm sorry I've been behind the bar for so long."

She gave him a weak smile and sat up straight, grateful the interruption had seemed to force her lungs to get control. Had he been watching her? "I'm fine, Jake. It wasn't your job to babysit me tonight."

"I didn't mean it like that," he said. She knew that and regretted saying it. The last thing she wanted was to hurt his feelings after he'd been so sweet tonight.

"I'm sorry. I just . . ." Blowing out a deep breath, she tried to hold in her tears as he sat down on the sofa across from her and leaned his elbow on his knees.

His brow furrowed as he looked at her intently.

"I can be doing really well. Feel happy and normal, but then the sadness just hits me out of nowhere. Like . . .

for a moment I'd forgotten that Nate is dead, and then I remember. I remember everything. The pain. The fact that I'll never see him again." Her voice broke on the last few words, and he got up and moved to sit beside her.

Instantly he wrapped his arms around her. Without hesitating she turned into his chest and let her arms snake around his waist. That was all it took for the tears to flow. The strength of his body made her feel safe enough to break down, her shoulders shaking with her tears. And still he held her. She'd almost forgotten what a strong man—who wasn't her brother or her dead fiancé—felt like, and just for a moment she let her eyes close and pretend that she was holding Nathan.

Two mornings later, her eyes were still puffy from tearful goodbyes as she fastened her seat belt and pushed her handbag under her plane seat. She was just about to shut her cell phone down when she received a messenger notification.

She opened it, surprised to see that it was from Jake. They didn't have each other's phone number, so this would have been his only way of contacting her—unless he'd asked Dean, which she couldn't see him doing.

> **JAKE:** Hey. You may have already left but wanted to tell you to have a great time and a safe flight.

Biting back a grin, she ignored the flight attendants speaking up front and replied.

> **ALEX:** About to take off. Thank you!! Take care of my brother. ☺
> **JAKE:** Will do. Stupid question, but can you use this app in Italy?

ALEX: Not stupid. And yes. This time I can use my cell most anytime and I splurged for an international plan.
JAKE: Cool. Let me know when you've landed safely.
ALEX: Okay. Xoxo

She waited, watching to see if he replied and wondering if he'd be weirded out by her kisses and hugs. Hopefully he knew that was just her style. She was a hugger, and she also appreciated him worrying about her. It was nice to have a trio of guys looking out for her. Finally, she figured the conversation was over, which was fine, and turned off the phone. Glancing out the window she smiled to herself. His message had made her feel a lot better. Everything was going to be okay. This year deployed in Italy would be good, and for the first time, she felt optimistic.

Two

A year later

Jake shoved his phone into his jeans pocket and glanced up at the flight status board one more time. Flight 456 from D.C. was still delayed. Not a surprise, considering it was dark and stormy outside. He let out a sigh and crossed his arms over his chest, leaning against the wall he'd been holding up for almost three hours. Thankfully he'd taken the day off so no one—specifically Dean— could question why he'd been gone so long.

He wasn't mad about waiting so long for Alex's plane to arrive. But the delay was allowing his nerves to get the better of him. When she'd messaged him a week ago asking him to pick her up, he'd happily agreed and been excited to finally see her after a year away. But now he couldn't help worrying whether their first interaction would be awkward.

It was a ridiculous thought. They were just friends. But since the last time they'd seen one another, things had changed. Over the past year, they'd gotten close. Not romantic close, nowhere near that. Just . . . *friend* close. It had been easy to confide in each other because it was all through words and a screen. And she was just so easy to talk to, especially when she opened up to him about so much. So here they were, about to see one another again for the first time since all these personal thoughts and secrets had been revealed between the two of them. Not everything, of course. Some things he just didn't share.

"Thank God," the woman sitting on the floor beside him muttered.

Jake glanced up to see that the screen now said LANDING next to Alex's flight. The poor woman waiting beside him for the past few hours had a tiny baby with her, and she'd been having a rough time of it, the baby crying for nearly the first hour of the delay. Jake had felt bad for her, but there was obviously nothing he could do, so he'd just watched with sympathy as she'd paced back and forth along the corridor, baby in her arms, or diverted his gaze when she was trying to nurse.

He glanced down at her once more. Trying to stand up without waking the now-sleeping baby, she began to wobble, so Jake instinctively stepped closer and reached down to steady her with a hand under her elbow.

"Thanks," she said quietly, giving him a slight smile.

"No problem," he said, making sure she had her footing before letting go. "You waiting on your husband?" he asked.

She gave him a surprised look that told him he should have kept his mouth shut. Why hadn't he checked her finger before assuming?

"No. My mother. She lives in Manassas."

"Ah, okay. She coming for a visit?" Why was he still talking? None of this was any of his business, and they'd waited together for almost three hours without conversation.

"She's staying for a while to help me. This will be her first time meeting Arabel." The woman glanced down at the baby girl who had begun to frantically suck on her pacifier.

"I bet she's excited," Jake said. He nodded at the baby. "She's very cute."

The woman gave him a wry smile. "That's very sweet of you to say, considering you listened to her scream for an hour."

He chuckled. "Ah well, we all wish we could scream in public sometimes. So I can hardly blame her."

She laughed quietly. "I felt so bad. I know the one guy left because of us." She angled her head to the end of the waiting area toward the older gentleman who'd gotten up and went to another section near the windows when she'd started to nurse the baby.

Jake had also noticed his dramatic departure and annoyed glances. "Yeah, that guy's a jerk. Don't let it bother you."

Just then the pacifier shot out of Arabel's mouth and Jake caught it in midair before it hit the dirty linoleum floor.

"Nice catch," the woman said.

Jake just smiled. Her arms were full, so he reached over and gently pressed the rubber nipple between the small pouty lips. It was more difficult than he expected, this little creature staring up at him with bright blue eyes and pursed mouth.

"I don't think she wants it," he said. At his voice, Arabel grinned up at him.

The woman laughed and so did Jake.

"Sorry, I'll take that." She shifted the baby in her arms and grabbed the pacifier as the baby continued to grin at Jake. He waved and said hi to her, feeling a little ridiculous, but how did you not say hi to a little face smiling at you?

"Are you waiting for your wife?" the woman asked after a moment of silence.

"Uh, no. Actually . . . I'm waiting on a friend."

There was no mistaking the glimmer of relief in her eyes. *Oh shit.*

"That's nice," she said. "Do you live here in KC?"

He hesitated. Was this a leading question? How did he politely shut down wherever this was going? Maybe he should not have said hi to the baby.

He took a step back toward his initial spot. "Sort of. I live just south of the metro. Maple Springs."

"Oh yeah? I live in Overland Park. Not too far from there."

He nodded. "Yeah, not at all." Clearing his throat, he decided to put up a gentle block. "The friend I'm picking up, uh . . . she is coming back from a yearlong deployment in Italy. I'm really excited to see her."

He felt like a bit of an ass when her eyes dimmed, and her lips parted. "That's nice. Wow, a year. But in Italy, I mean . . . that would be awesome."

"Right? Not too shabby."

There was an awkward silence between them until the baby started to get fussy again. Casually he stepped toward the gate window, hoping to see the plane, relieved when he did.

"Looks like they should be off pretty quick," he said to his waiting partner.

"Thank goodness," she said. Jake stole another glance at her. She was an attractive woman, if not a little tired-looking. But who could blame her, a single mom with a baby who appeared to be less than a year old? He felt kind of bad when he realized that until this moment, he hadn't really looked at her. Then again, he had assumed she was waiting on a man.

The exiting of passengers pulled his attention back to the gate, and his heart rate picked up as his eyes began looking for Alex's sandy blonde hair and big green eyes. He blew out a breath, his nerves firing. Still watching the line of people filing out of the tunnel, his gaze turned to the people who had flooded the waiting area, shocked when he saw her grinning at him about ten feet away.

"Holy shit," he said, laughing as he moved in her direction. She dropped her carry-on as he approached and instantly flung her arms around his neck. "I obviously missed you with that hat on."

"Sorry," she said sweetly. Jake closed his eyes as he squeezed her waist, holding her close. He consciously pulled away after just a second, not wanting it to be weird. Alex smiled up at him. "You must have been waiting forever. Our take off was delayed, we almost got rerouted to Omaha and then had to circle for like an hour before landing."

"It's fine. I didn't mind." And it was true, he'd have waited all day. He reached down to pick up her bag, but she beat him to it, swatting his hand out of the way.

"You don't need to carry my bag, silly," she said.

He put his hands up. "Okay, just trying to be a gentleman."

She just laughed and started walking toward baggage claim. "Oh my goodness, it's so nice to walk around. I was getting so claustrophobic in my seat."

He glanced over at her, trying not to notice how good she looked in her cutoffs and hoodie. It was wild to actually be with the real, in the flesh, Alex after spending an entire year talking via keyboard. He'd almost forgotten how pretty she was. With her ball cap and tennis shoes, she looked so natural and pure—not a lick of makeup on her face. So unlike the women he usually spent time with. Was that what he found so appealing about her? That she was different? Or was it that she showed no interest in him in that way, allowing him to really get to know her without the messiness of relationship or hook-up drama.

"So Dean's at work today, right?" she asked, glancing over at him.

"Yep. Till around five. He's going to be so excited, but then you know he's going to be annoyed that you pulled a fast one on him," Jake said.

She grinned. "I know, which makes it even more fun."

He laughed, shaking his head as they approached the horde of people standing around the luggage carousel. Suddenly he was thrown off-balance by her squeezing his arm.

"I'm just so happy to see you," she said, her cheek resting on his shoulder.

"Same," was all he could say.

She looked up at him. "It will be so weird getting to talk to you for real after only talking through messenger."

"I had the same thought." His lips quirked. "How are we going to explain being such good friends to your brother?"

Standing up straight, she waved a hand. "What's there to explain? We chatted a lot while I was gone. So what?" She shrugged, her attention diverted when the first bag appeared on the conveyor belt.

"So you haven't mentioned it to him, either?" Jake asked.

"No," she said, looking at him. "It's not a big deal, Jake. We're just friends, and even if it was more than that, it's really none of my brother's business."

"You're right. I agree. But this is Dean we're talking about."

"True. But don't worry. The minute I tell him about my job in Arlington he won't be thinking about anything else." The look in her eyes let him know she was still nervous.

"How was the visit?" he asked. Part of the reason she'd left early and changed her arrival was because she'd had a job interview with the CIA in Arlington.

"Good. I guess." She looked at him. "I know taking this job is the right thing, but . . . I'll be honest, I wasn't as excited as I thought I'd be once I got there. So much is in turmoil in Washington right now."

"Exactly why they need good people," he said.

"Thanks, but it's not like a geospatial engineer is a high-profile position."

"Every job plays its role in the success of a business . . . or government office." Something he kept reminding himself these days.

She nodded. "You're right. And the people I'd be working with directly are super nice. Nonpartisan positions, so they've been there a while and seen a lot. There were good and bad things, which is normal. I'm just letting doubt and fear take over, something I've been really working hard at letting go."

Jake nodded. A lot of their chats had been about her desire to move forward and not let fear control her. She'd come a long way from the woman he'd held in his arms crying a year ago, and while he was insanely proud and impressed by her, he also sometimes wondered if she was pushing herself too hard. Fear and sadness were normal.

He knew part of the reason she felt inclined to take the job with the CIA was because her plan with

Nate had been to come back, move to Maple Springs where he could work as an air-traffic controller, and start a family. She seemed to think that his death was an opportunity for her to try another path. Something exciting and adventurous. While that all sounded fine and good, Jake wasn't convinced Nate's death meant anything, except that sometimes life threw you tragic curveballs. Alex, however, was determined to make this curveball have meaning for her. She'd nearly become obsessed with it, so who was he to talk her out of it?

"I guess it's nice you have several months to think about it," he said, reminding her how the job wasn't technically available until November, when someone was being promoted.

"Actually," she said, glancing up at him hesitantly, "I did go ahead and accept the position yesterday before I left."

Jake's eyes went wide, his chest tightening. "Oh. Wow. Really? Are you sure about that?"

"Yeah, I didn't want to get home, get comfortable, and talk myself out of it."

The feeling of tightness in his gut was not sadness, it was just disappointment. That was all, and he'd get over it.

"Good for you, then," he said, putting an arm around her. "I'm proud of you, Alex."

"I'm proud of me too," she said. "And I really want to thank you, Jake." She placed a hand up on his cheek, forcing him to look down at her. "Having you to talk to this past year . . . it's meant so much to me. You have no idea."

His lips quirked. "I'm glad. I've enjoyed talking to you too. It's not like you didn't help me out also. Shit, you talked me out of a third date with Devon."

Alex's eyes went wide. "Oh my gosh, that girl. She was totally looking for a husband. No doubt about it. You're right. If you hadn't listened to me, you might be ring shopping."

He chuckled. "You think I'm that easily manipulated?"

"Actually, no. But you *are* sweet."

He was tempted to argue, tell her he wasn't normally sweet, that it was just with her and that he'd had no problem giving Devon the slip. He decided not to reveal that about himself, though. Honestly, he'd sometimes mentioned the women he was seeing to her just to get the lay of the land. See how she responded. He really couldn't explain why. Probably just to make it clear that he didn't assume their friendship was more than it was. Because he didn't assume that. Plus, he'd always tried to find something about his own life he was willing to share since she opened up so much about herself.

"There's my bag," she said, taking off toward the carousel.

A small hand settled on his arm, startling him. He looked down to find the woman from before. "It was nice talking with you earlier. And thanks for being so understanding."

"No problem." He glanced around. "Your mom make it okay?" Just as he said it his eyes landed on a middle-aged woman holding the baby just beyond the crowd.

"Yes, she did. Good luck with your friend," she said, nodding toward Alex who was leaning over trying to grab her bag. He should be helping her. And what did she mean, "good luck"?

"Thank you," he said, unsure of how to respond. "And good luck with, uh, Arabel."

She grinned at that and gave a small wave before walking off into the crowd.

"I leave you alone for one minute and you're picking up chicks."

Jake turned to find Alex smirking at him. "I was not picking anyone up, thank you very much."

"Sure. I bet the handsome and charming Jake Cooper has no trouble scoring digits at a random place like an airport baggage claim."

He chuckled. "I won't argue with that," he teased. "My skills are not to be denied. But this was not one of those times." And did she really think he was handsome?

Alex had not been prepared for how handsome Jake had looked when she'd gotten off the plane. He hadn't seen her right away, probably because of her ball cap and lack of makeup, so she'd spent a long second watching him look for her through the glass. The way he'd shifted his weight back and forth between his legs let her know he'd been nervous, his eyes darting around, hands in his pockets.

But then the minute they'd locked gazes, he'd grinned so big all her worries had fled, and the friend that she'd been messaging with all year was standing in front of her. It had felt so natural to give him a big hug. Something she normally did with friends, but something about this time felt different. Had he been okay with it? She just felt so comfortable around him, and although he appeared to feel the same way, she didn't want this to be weird.

They walked through the airport parking lot and up to his black Jeep Wrangler. "This car is so you," she said.

He chuckled. "What's that supposed to mean?"

She watched as he opened the back and loaded in her luggage. "I don't know," she said. "It's rugged, beefy, sleek."

He looked up and gave her a roguish smile. "Keep talking."

She rolled her eyes. "You know what I mean. It's a single-man vehicle. Attracts attention, and obviously well taken care of."

"I'll pretend you didn't just insinuate that I have nothing better to do than wash my car. And it's not always this shiny, but I was picking up a lady at the airport." He closed the back then kissed his fingers before pressing them to the shiny black paint with a wink. Alex just chuckled, not missing how his eyes went to her chest.

"I just noticed your necklace. That's the one, right?" he asked.

She reached up and touched the small gold bar charm that hadn't left her neck for the past six months. "Yes, this is it."

"It's pretty," he said.

"Thank you. I like it." Her fingers rubbed over it, as they often did. She'd purchased this necklace and put it on the same evening she'd finally gotten the courage to remove her engagement ring. She wasn't sure she'd have had the strength to go through with it without a replacement. The idea had come from the grief counselor she'd visited on base, and on the back of the gold bar the date she and Nate met and the date of his passing were inscribed along with a tiny heart. When she'd told Jake about the idea, he'd encouraged her but also suggested that not even her counselor had all the answers, and that she should wait until she was certain it was the right time. For some reason that sentiment had meant more than he could ever know.

"Ready to go?" he asked quietly.

She nodded. Once they were inside she dug through her purse and pulled out a credit card. "Here, use this at the parking toll."

He started up the engine and placed his hand behind her on the headrest as he looked over his shoulder and backed out. "I got it."

"Uh, no. You were in short-term parking for over three hours. It's going to cost a fortune."

As he put the vehicle in drive, he looked her in the eye. "I got this, Alex."

She sighed in mock annoyance, silently vowing to pay him back in another way. Jake was sweet and having him as a friend over the past year had been a surprisingly critical part of her healing process. Who'd have thought the playboy of the Stag group would be her new BFF. But that's sort of what he'd become. It had started the night of the uncasking party last July when he'd made sure she wasn't alone and then let her cry on his shoulder. Most guys would have been horrified by a sobbing woman grieving a dead fiancé, but he'd been there for her, even if it had been because she was Dean's little sister and it was the right thing to do.

After that, when she'd left, they'd started messaging. Slowly at first, she'd share photos of her new place, the town and the base, and then eventually her visits to other cities on the weekends. She felt free to tell him when she'd had a particularly sad day, which had been most days in the beginning. He'd listen to her talk about her feelings, about Nathan and their relationship, and all without trying to fix it or tell her she should move on. In fact, his lack of concrete advice was one of the things she loved about talking with him. He'd always encouraged her to trust herself and her own feelings.

On the flip side, he'd update her about the Stag and his dating life, and ask her opinion on marketing social media posts and such. Gradually it built into a several-times-a-week correspondence. A little broken sometimes based on the time difference or what the other one had going on, but for the most part they'd been consistent. She didn't think they'd gone more than three days or so without speaking for the past year.

"You still want to surprise your brother at work?" Jake asked as he merged onto the highway to make the forty-five-minute drive south to Maple Springs.

"Yes. I think that will be fun. He has no idea, right?"

"None at all." Jake said, staring out the windshield. "In fact, yesterday he mentioned how he wouldn't be in next Wednesday because he had to pick you up from the airport."

Alex laughed. "Perfect. That's what I told him when we Skyped last week. I hated to lie to him, but I'm just so excited for him to be surprised." She glanced out the window, watching houses and farmland go by. "It's so nice to be back here. Kind of weird though. I'm a little nervous to stay at Charlotte's."

She looked at Jake and saw his eyes narrow. "How come? Charlotte's cool."

"She is. I like her a lot. It's just . . . now that Dean has moved in with her, it just kind of feels like I'm crashing. I don't know. Before, when I'd come home to visit and stay with Dean, it was like home. But this will just be different."

"I get what you're saying. But you know Charlotte is happy to have you stay."

"I hope so. She did seem excited the last time we

talked. She kept telling me not to rush to find a place, that I could stay as long as I needed. But now I'll get to inform them that it's three months until I go back to Arlington. Too short to get my own place but a long stay as a guest."

She noticed Jake's hand grip the steering wheel harder. "When are you going to tell your brother about this job?"

Alex sighed and let her head fall back on the rest. "I haven't decided yet. I need to do it soon because it won't be fair to keep him in the dark knowingly. Plus he'll wonder why I'm not making plans or looking for work. But I know he's going to be disappointed."

"Yeah, he will. But I agree with you that sooner is better than later. He'll get over it. It's not like you guys can't visit. Right?" He smiled at her quickly before looking back at the road.

"Exactly. That's what I'm going to tell him."

Before long they were parking down the street from the Stag. The front side of the building was mostly windows, so she and Jake had agreed that it would be best to park farther away to keep out of sight. He got out of the car first and headed down the sidewalk. The plan was for him to keep Dean out of the main room until she came in and surprised him.

After waiting about five minutes, she left the Jeep and followed the same path Jake had taken. Once inside the Stag, she inhaled the yeasty scent of fermenting alcohol. Glancing over at the front desk, she saw a grinning Jen who tiptoed around the counter and gave her a hug.

"He's going to die," Jen whispered. "Such a great idea."

"I hope he agrees," Alex whispered in reply.

Jen waved a hand. "He'll love it. Even if he acts annoyed." She nodded toward the hall. "Want me to call him out here?"

Alex nodded. "Sure."

Just as Jen made her way back to her desk, Jake came down the hallway that led to their offices. He grinned at her and nodded at Jen, who opened her mouth and yelled, "Dean, I need your help."

There was no reply, and they all chuckled as Jen rolled her eyes. "Typical," she mouthed. Then yelled even louder than before. "Dean!"

"What?" He answered, clearly annoyed.

"I need your help with something."

"You'll have to wait a minute, Jen." He called down the hall, "Where's TJ? He's supposed to be at your beck and call."

TJ came down the hall just then. "This one requires *your* expertise, man. Get out here."

"Is there a reason we're all screaming like children?" Dean yelled.

The old brick building carried voices well due to the tile floor and exposed ducting, and Alex swore she could hear Dean's deep sigh and the creaking of his desk chair.

"Here he comes," Jen said, stepping back around the desk.

The minute he came out of the hallway his eyes went straight to the front desk, so Alex called out, "Surprise!"

His gaze darted to her and his mouth dropped open. "Alex?" His voice was a mix of shock and excitement. She was so happy to see him she rushed toward him, ignoring his question. "How did you get here?"

The minute they collided she wrapped her arms around his torso and he pulled her close. "Holy shit, how did this happen?" he asked.

"Teach you not to answer my calls for help," Jen said behind them.

Dean's chest shook with laughter and he squeezed Alex tighter. "Somebody tell me what's going on here."

She pulled back and looked at him. "I'm home!"

"Well, yeah. But how? I thought you were coming next week."

"I wanted to surprise you." She nodded toward the quiet man standing off to the side watching, hands in his pockets. "Jake picked me up."

Dean's eyebrows nearly hit the ceiling. "*Jake*?" He looked over his shoulder at Jake, who just shrugged. "How did you arrange that?"

Alex went for light, not ready to explain that Jake was her new bestie. "I asked him on Facebook."

Dean shook his head and hugged her again. "Okay. Well, this is a surprise. I guess I'm just glad you're home safe."

"Happy surprise?" she asked, knowing that Dean wasn't a big fan of things out of his control. But sometimes even the most type-A personalities needed a little excitement and something unexpected.

"Very happy. I've been waiting for you to finally move home a long time."

Alex smiled and met gazes with Jake, who raised an eyebrow. "Me too," she said.

She'd tell him about her job soon. But right now was a time for happiness. Something she desperately needed to feel.

The following Monday Jake overslept, something he rarely did. For some reason he'd struggled to fall asleep the night before, so he'd ended up watching television until nearly two in the morning. Also something he never did, but he'd been feeling a little off lately.

He walked in to the Stag an hour later than he normally did and gave Jen a muttered "Good morning" before heading to his office. Before he made it to the doorway, he passed TJ's office, and his best friend hollered at him.

Jake backed up and peeked in. "Hey."

"Where you been?" TJ asked. There was no accusation in his tone, just mere curiosity. As co-owners, the three of them were careful not to make the others feel like they answered to one another. That had been working, for the most part, although lately he'd noticed TJ and Dean chatting together more frequently.

"Slept in this morning."

"Up late?" TJ asked, eyebrow raised. Jake knew exactly what his friend was insinuating, probably because normally he'd be spot on. Today, however, it just pissed him off.

"No," Jake said a little too tersely as he sat down in the chair in front of TJ's desk.

TJ stared at him a moment.

"What's up? You need something?" Jake asked, not in the mood for small talk. He was still tired and had shit to do.

"Actually, I do." TJ clicked with his mouse, staring at his computer screen full of Excel files and all manner of screens that Jake wouldn't understand. As the geek-in-residence, TJ was the business-and-money brains behind the Stag. Made sure they were profitable, paid their bills, and kept track of anything that had to do with numbers. Dean was in charge of product production, knowing the ins and outs of the distilling process. He was also assisted by their newest member, John.

As for his part of the process, Jake was the marketing and publicity guy. He dealt with their website and social media and did promotional tours. Nothing that required a high IQ or a Master's degree, thank goodness. He'd lucked out with this job. At least that's what his parents liked to say. Most of his school career he'd been told he probably wouldn't go to college and would need to learn a skill to have a decent future. His high school guidance counselor had encouraged him to apply to trade schools or find an apprenticeship. There was nothing wrong with any of that, but he'd resented the fact that no one pushed him to do more. Or even thought he was capable of it.

Thanks to a solid pitching arm and an amazing senior season, he'd gone to a state college on a baseball scholarship. For a couple of years, anyway. But he knew his parents were right. If it wasn't for his friendship with TJ, and the two of them meeting Dean, he would probably be doing manual labor or working retail somewhere. So while he was grateful, he sometimes felt a little paranoid. And bitter.

"Everything okay?" He asked TJ.

"Yeah," TJ said, but the way his brows narrowed had Jake worried. "But there is something I need to talk to you about."

Jake inhaled, his pulse picking up speed. He folded his hands together. "Okay."

TJ rested his elbows on the desk, and it occurred to Jake that he really wasn't crazy about this setup. TJ in his favorite attire of dress shirt and pressed slacks, sitting behind his desk, while Jake sat on the other side like he was ready to take a tongue lashing from the principal. This exact scenario was a solid part of his youth that he hated to recall, although his well-honed charm had usually been his saving grace. These days that usually only benefited him in one arena, and this wasn't it.

"First thing is, I just took a call from the mayor of Olmstead, Tennessee."

Jake's brow furrowed. "What for?"

"I don't know if you saw it on the news back in May, but they suffered a tornado that practically leveled their tiny town."

"In Tennessee? Wow, that's awful. I don't recall hearing about it."

"They're doing a benefit concert on August seventeenth. Since it's located so near to Nashville, several local musicians are performing, and a couple of big names have agreed to headline. Anyway, the mayor wants to have a reception the night before to honor all the first responders who came from around the area. He's asking for free liquor to be shipped, but I feel like we can do better."

"You want me to add it to my trip," Jake said, catching on, and starting to feel a little relieved. Why had he been so paranoid about his place in this business lately?

"Yeah, I figured it made sense, seeing as you'll be there around that same time. You can be there to serve the people directly. I'm happy to help out, but I'm not against using this for marketing."

Jake nodded. "I agree. I'll do it then."

TJ went on. "Problem is, he said they're expecting about two hundred people. That's a lot."

"I'll make it happen. No big deal."

TJ's eyebrows raised. "You don't think you should have help?"

Jake hesitated, his thumbs rolling around each other. "I've never taken help before."

"I know. I just . . . well, we could hire someone there. To serve and help."

"I can handle it, TJ."

TJ backed down, putting a hand up. "Okay, it's just, this will be the final leg of your tour, which as you know is the biggest tour you've done so far. You're gonna be tired. It will have been a long two weeks."

"Why are you so worried about me this time? I've handled things just fine until now." This would be his fourth trip in their Stag Wagon. A fifth-wheel RV they'd purchased and renovated a couple of years ago. It had proven to be a great investment since they not only used it for these tours, but sometimes parked it around town for brand exposure, and even used it for local events around Kansas City.

So far Jake had taken it through the South, up to Chicago, around Texas, and even to Denver. His traveling had gotten them a lot of new accounts—liquor stores and restaurants and bars—and even more customers over the years. It was just a great marketing gimmick and kept their social media accounts interesting and popular. That was all his doing, and rarely did the other guys mention or notice what he'd brought to the business, both being so caught up in their own jobs.

"I know you've always handled things amazingly." TJ looked down, and Jake could tell by the way his desk was vibrating that his friend was bouncing his leg up and down. A classic TJ sign of nervousness.

"What's going on, man?" Jake asked.

Blowing out a hard breath, TJ looked up at him. "I got a call the other day from Amanda Frye of Favorite Entertainment."

"What about? I just talked to her last week about this weekend. Did she ask for you?" Jake said, completely confused. He usually dealt with all the booking agents and event contacts for his trips. Amanda was kind of a ball-buster, but he'd always gotten along okay with her, considering she did events in Memphis and Nashville.

"She asked to speak with the owner. You were gone, apparently picking up Alex, and Dean was in the distilling room. So Jen gave it to me."

He was going to try not to be offended that she didn't realize he was an owner. "What did she want? Everything is square for that event in Memphis this weekend."

"Well . . . she wanted to bring to our attention that she'd received complaints from your last two events with her."

"What?" Jake said, eyes wide. "Complaints about what?"

"What do you think, Jake?" TJ said, and his tone was so full of condemnation that Jake felt like hitting something. He could think of only one thing, but he didn't want to say it. He leaned forward and looked at the floor.

"Apparently, Chuck Ross caught wind that his daughter had been spending time with you when you came for the Boots and Beer Festival. He is the main donor for that event."

"Yeah, I follow," Jake said, feeling sick to his stomach. He put out his hands. "So I slept with his daughter. She's an adult. How did he even find this out?"

"Hell if I know," TJ said. "Maybe she told him."

"No way. Can you imagine a daughter saying something like that?"

TJ gave him a long look. "You've met the people I

grew up with, TJ. I don't put anything past anybody. People do crazy shit. But the point is, we've known this is a problem."

Jake's head jerked back. "We have? And who do you mean by we? You and Dean?"

"No, all of us. You can't deny that you've had a hell of a good time on these tours the past few years. It's obvious by the social media posts that you're drawing in a crowd of ladies."

"And that's a problem?" Jake asked. He knew he was getting defensive, but every time he went on a tour, their online following jumped by the thousands.

"We've never really sat down and discussed what we want our online branding and social media presence to look like. It's just sort of happened organically."

Jake froze. "So what you're saying is, I haven't done my job well."

"No." TJ shook his head. "That is not what I'm saying. Not at all. You're great and you know it. It's just that . . . I went over our social media accounts this morning. It's a lot of bikinis, drunk women, and good times."

Wow. So he had taken an interest—when someone complained. Interesting. "Did you happen to see that our Instagram alone has over three hundred and seventy thousand followers? And I'm not sure if you understand something." Jake was pissed now. "We sell hard *liquor*. People drink it and they often get drunk. Our business name is the *Stag* and it's run by three single guys."

"Not anymore," TJ said flatly.

"Ah, so is that what this is about?" Jake asked. He laughed bitterly, running a hand over his chin and down his neck. "I'm now the lone bachelor who is ruining the brand by fucking around and having a good time. Is that it? Are we now supposed to become the classy drink of pussy-whipped douchebags everywhere?"

"Stop it," TJ sneered. "You're not ruining anything, but when I get phone calls from event planners telling me that maybe you should hand out condoms with your samples, and that fathers are pissed off, then maybe it's time to come together and reevaluate."

Jake's jaw clenched and his arms flexed. He would never hit his friend, but damn, if he didn't feel like upending the desk sitting between them. Yes, he was being an ass. He never acted like this, but everything felt oppressive and infuriating right now. Lashing out felt like the only way to handle the anger and humiliation he was feeling.

"Before you get pissed off at me, remember, I'm on your side here," TJ said. Some nerve he had. "But this is a business and we need to act accordingly. If someone calls us on something, we need to fix it. Especially when it comes to how we appear online and act in public. This is a company run by men and a product mainly consumed by men, and we can't let it look like we promote treating women as objects. Especially when we have the wedding side to consider."

"You can't be serious. I always treat women with respect and you damn well know it."

TJ sighed. "It doesn't matter what I know, Jake. Perception is reality. So far we've gotten away with this, but it could backfire if we don't change it."

Jake stood up, nearly lost for words. He was heading for the door—ignoring TJ's request for him to sit back down—when he stopped and turned around. "You know what, fuck you, TJ. You and your pompous, rich ass. You think you're too good for everyone's bullshit. It's clear now that you think I'm just the dumbass who posts pictures on Facebook and updates the website. Any idiot could do that, right? Actually, you don't even think I've handled that correctly."

"Wrong. Stop being a defensive asshole and let's figure this out." TJ was now standing, too, hands on hips.

"Figure this out yourself. If I'm a liability, I'll step out. I won't even make you say it."

He walked out before he said something else he'd regret. Heading through the main room, his eyes glanced toward Jen, who he could tell was trying not to make eye contact. She'd probably heard most of it, and no doubt the entire thing had already served as pillow talk.

"Later, Jen," he said as he pushed the door open and headed back to his Jeep.

There was nothing he hated more than being made to look or feel stupid. As an adult he thought he'd put that feeling behind him. In school he'd had to be in the special class that got extra help. Sometimes there was even a para in his classes to assist him if needed. It was humiliating, and his brother had given him shit over it constantly.

For it to now come from his best friend was too much to handle. He and TJ had known each other since Little League, and because they'd gone to separate schools, he'd relished the fact that he'd finally been able to feel equal to a peer. They'd both been really good at sports, so they'd had a lot in common. Still did, until recently, but now TJ was obsessed with Jen. Had been for nearly the past year since they'd finally hooked up. And it wasn't that Jake wasn't happy for him—hell, he'd encouraged it since he'd known about his friend's crush for years. But now that everyone was hooking up and settling down but him, he was starting to feel like the third wheel of their business. This conversation just solidified it.

He was *jealous*.

Insecure. And tired of being seen as the playboy, which was obviously no longer even an option. Getting in his Jeep, he decided maybe he just needed to go back to bed.

Three

Day 406

I'd been doing so well before I left Italy, but lately I've felt like I regressed. Being in Dean and Charlotte's house is becoming suffocating. They're so happy. And I'm happy for them. But I wasn't prepared for how it would make me feel to constantly witness a couple like this. I know this is an acceptable feeling and this situation is temporary, but I really wish I had a place of my own for the next three months. One positive, Charlotte makes the most amazing coffee using a milk frother. Sometimes it's the little things. Today I plan to feel more content.

Alex closed her journal on the words and placed it carefully on her bedside table, the same as she'd done nearly every day since Nate died. Sometimes she wondered if she'd ever stop keeping track of how long it had been since he passed. Would it ever cease to matter?

She'd been spending a lot of time in her room for the past five days she'd been home. It wasn't as if she wanted to be unsocial, but there was only so much she could take. To add some variety to her life, she'd gone running every morning, spent some time over at Joel's watching daytime television, and even met up once with a couple of friends she hadn't seen in ages. Other than that, there wasn't much to do. She hadn't even done much chatting with Jake since she'd been home, and it made her realize how much she missed him.

She glanced at the clock. It was nearly eleven on a Tuesday morning. She wondered if he was busy at work. Deciding to just text him—now that they'd exchanged real numbers—she picked up her phone.

ALEX: Hey you.
JAKE: Hey.
ALEX: Feel like lunch today? Here we are in the same town and we've barely talked.
JAKE: True. But maybe another day. Cool?

Okay, that was weird and sort of unlike him. Not the turning her down for lunch. She had little to judge him on in that regard since they'd never even be able to make real-life plans. But just the short tone of his message was odd.

ALEX: No problem.

Sitting there on the bed, she twisted her lips, waiting to see if he'd say anything else. Finally she decided to hell with wondering.

ALEX: Everything okay?
JAKE: Yeah. Just a lot going on. You okay?
ALEX: Yes. Just tired of being at home.
JAKE: I understand. Promise we'll do something soon.

She smiled. Then wondered if she'd sounded that desperate? Oh well, it was only Jake. No need to worry if she'd seemed weird or needy.

ALEX: Sounds good. Whenever.

Putting her phone in her pocket, she left her room and headed to the kitchen to find something to eat for lunch. On her way, Charlotte called out from her desk, which she'd temporarily moved to her and Dean's bedroom so Alex could have her own room until she figured out what she was doing.

"Hungry?" Charlotte asked.

Alex stopped in the hallway and peeked into the bedroom. Charlotte's desk was impressive, with two big monitors for editing photos. "Yeah, I am. I was just going to make something. Can I bring you anything?"

"I was just texting with Jen and we were going to go to Sylvia's for lunch. Want to come? They have the most insanely delicious sandwiches. I swear we're in there like once a week."

Alex considered it. "Sure. That sounds good."

"Perfect," Charlotte said. "I'm going to save these files I have open and we'll go."

Alex smiled and went to wait in the living room with their little dog Fernando, whom she had quickly grown to adore. She glanced around the room, taking in the photos of Charlotte and Dean, the pillow with HELLO stitched onto it, and the bouquet of peonies on the coffee table. The home of someone happy and creative. And it was so Charlotte.

It was impossible for Alex not to love her brother's fiancée. She was beautiful, kind, and loved Dean, which made her likable on that merit alone. She'd also helped him plan Alex and Nate's wedding that never happened. An undertaking most women would not have considered. Sure, it probably had a lot to do with having a crush on her coplanner, but still, it was a kind gesture Alex would never forget.

Last year she and Nate had surprised everyone by announcing their intention to reenlist and spend a year in Italy. The catch was that they'd wanted to go as a married couple, so they could live in the village. Alex had gone out on a limb and asked her brother to plan their wedding so they could come home on leave, get hitched, and then fly off to Italy for a yearlong deployment honeymoon.

Like the saint he was, Dean had accepted, and done an amazing job with Charlotte's help. Being a wedding photographer, she'd been an amazing resource, and the two of them had done everything. Made the décor, ordered the cake and flowers, booked a DJ. The works.

Sadly, Nathan had been killed in a helicopter accident just a couple weeks before the big day. She'd only known how hard Charlotte and Dean had worked on their behalf because when she'd come home a grieving fiancée, Charlotte had gifted her a little photo album of the planning process. Dean had worried it would upset her, but it had been exactly what she'd needed at that time. An acknowledgment of how big and important their love had been, because not only had she felt robbed of him, she'd also felt robbed of being his wife. That photo album was still one of her most prized possessions.

Charlotte came out of her office. "Ready?" she asked, smiling when Fernando reached up to lick Alex's face. "Fernie loves you."

Alex laughed, the tiny tongue tickling her chin. "I like him too."

After putting Fernando in his kennel, they were off. Maple Springs was not a big town, so it wasn't ten minutes before they were being seated by the window in Sylvia's Café on the square.

"Jen should be here in a minute. She just walks down since it's so close," Charlotte said, pointing at the menu. "I highly recommend the chicken avocado club, which is amazing, or the French dip, which has been my recent fav."

Alex nodded, glancing over the menu, just as Jen came bustling over to their table. As soon as she sat down, Charlotte gave her a look.

"So, did he show up?"

"Nope," Jen said. "I told TJ that if he doesn't go over there today and check on him, I will. They're all acting like toddlers."

Charlotte rolled her eyes. "Dean seems to think he should let the two of them work this out on their own. I told him that was crap. He totally let TJ take the hit for this."

"Not completely his fault. TJ had wanted to be the one to discuss it, thinking that since they'd always been such close friends he could soften the blow. That's not what happened though. I felt so awful when he stormed out of there yesterday, and you know, I'm not one for feeling bad," Jen said, pursing her lips.

Charlotte gave Jen an eyebrow raise. "Please. You act tough, but you hate to see people hurting."

Alex had just about had enough of being out of the loop. "Hold on, what is happening here?" And she was almost afraid to find out.

Charlotte and Jen looked at her.

"Sorry, we should have filled you in." Charlotte hunkered down and whispered as if they were discussing government secrets. "TJ had to confront Jake yesterday about some work things and it didn't go well."

A pit opened in Alex's stomach. The feeling was a mixture of sadness and, strangely, defensiveness. Whatever they were about to say, she suddenly felt prepared to tell anyone off who had anything negative to say about Jake. "What was it about?"

The two other women exchanged glances before Charlotte spoke up. "So, Jake's main role—besides being a co-owner, which they all are equally—is the marketing and publicity."

"Right, I know that," Alex said.

"Well, part of that involves him doing these festival tours. He travels in the Stag Wagon and gives out samples at concerts and events, and also hits up the local bar scene and such."

"Okay, so what's wrong with that?" Alex asked.

They were interrupted by the server, so they took the time to place their order. Alex went with the grilled chicken salad, suddenly feeling obstinate.

"So, go on," Alex said when the server left, needing the full story even though she was suddenly tempted to just leave and head over to Jake's house. Even if she wasn't sure where he lived. Funny to be such good friends with a person and not know so many normal things about them. And why hadn't he told her any of this had transpired?

"Okay, so like I said, Jake goes on these tours. And . . ." Charlotte hesitated, laughing a little. "You know how Jake is."

Alex shook her head. "No . . . what?"

"He's a player," Jen filled in, not one to mince words. "He gets a lot of action on these trips. It's kind of been a running joke. And nobody really cared."

"Well, nobody thought much of it, until someone called and complained." Charlotte's eyes went wide as she said it.

Alex suddenly felt a little lightheaded. "So . . . he sleeps around a lot? Is that what you mean?" She'd heard the jokes over the years about Jake being the playboy of the group, but she hadn't realized there was literal truth to it. Or maybe she'd just never cared. Did she care now? Probably just because he seemed so sweet. It didn't match the idea of him she'd developed in her head over the past year. That was all.

"He seems pretty normal to me," Jen said with a shrug. "What do you expect from a thirty-two-year-old man who doesn't do relationships? He doesn't lead women on. He just has a good time."

"You're right. But, apparently someone's father caught wind," Charlotte said.

Alex's lips parted. "What? Was this woman an adult?"

"Oh yeah, of course. But they met at an event where her father's company is a premium supporter."

"Huh." Alex really wasn't sure what to say. Luckily the other two continued to converse.

"So, long story short," Jen said after taking a sip of the lemonade that had just been delivered, "yesterday TJ said something to him about it and it didn't go well."

"What do you mean?" Alex asked.

"Jake got super defensive. Walked out pissed. I heard most of it and they both got upset, which sucks because they've been friends since they were like nine years old."

"They don't want him out of the business, do they?" The thought wrecked Alex.

"No!" Charlotte interjected. "Of course not. He's a critical part of this company. They just need to come together and figure out how to move forward since this complaint was made."

"It was just one complaint. What business changes things based on one complaint?" Alex countered.

"Well, yeah, just one, but they've known that it's probably not ideal for Jake to be hooking up with women while he's out promoting the brand." Jen said, nodding at Charlotte. "We've talked about it. We adore Jake, and shit, I get it. He's hot. And single. But in this day and age, you have to be careful about your social media presence. Plus, we're really expanding the wedding side of things."

Charlotte nodded. "Jen's going to become the official wedding contact and planner diva. And don't forget, now that you're doing the Little Stag Community Theater, we really need to make sure the brand is clean and classy. Even on the road."

Alex couldn't help noticing the "we." Yeah, Charlotte was Dean's fiancée, so she had a vested interest in the company, but she was not an owner. Jake was, and she suddenly felt disloyal talking about this behind his back.

Pushing that thought aside, Alex smiled at Jen. "I forgot to congratulate you on the theater thing. That's so exciting. Dean had sent me a clip of your *Grease* performance." Which was only a tiny lie. Jake had shown her and told her all about it.

"Thanks. It's been great. Even better than I'd hoped."

Jen had a theater background and was also an amazing singer. When Alex had first met her several years ago, bartending at the Stag for weddings was her side gig in addition to working at Maple Springs Community Theater. About a year and a half ago, that had sadly been closed due to government funding cuts. Being the creative soul that she was, Jen had eventually presented the idea to the guys to have performances in the upstairs of the Stag. According to conversations with Jake, they'd all agreed that it was an interesting way to utilize the space that sat vacant unless there was a wedding on the weekend.

It also probably hadn't hurt that she was dating one of the owners. But Jake had told her that it was helping them connect with a demographic of the community that they may not otherwise have connected with.

"They're even getting ready to move Jen upstairs into her own office," Charlotte said.

"Wow," Alex said. "That's exciting."

"It is. A year ago I would have never dreamed this would be what I was doing, but it's pretty awesome. With my own office I can easily run the wedding side of things and deal with theater stuff. Which means"— Jen waggled her eyebrows at Alex—"they're going to need to hire a new front-desk person."

Alex's eyes went wide. "Oh no, don't look at me. I don't want the job."

"No worries. I figured you wouldn't," Charlotte said, chuckling. "But I promised Dean I'd throw the idea out there even though I told him you were way over-qualified to work as a receptionist." She glanced at Jen. "No offense, girl."

"None taken," Jen said, shrugging.

Charlotte looked back at Alex, who was stunned. "Consider the case closed."

"Thanks," she said. Had her brother really thought she'd want to become the Stag's receptionist?

"Do you know what you want to do?" Jen asked.

Crap. She glanced over Charlotte's head, praying to

see the server approaching with their food. But no dice. She'd have to answer. "Yeah, actually I do."

"What was your job in the Army?" Charlotte asked. "Dean's told me, but I can never remember what it's called."

"Geospatial analyst. Or engineer. Basically, I spent a lot of time looking at maps and satellite images."

"Can you get a normal job doing that?" Jen asked.

"Sure. Lots of places employ geospatial teams. Cable, oil, private firms. But . . ." she hesitated, meeting each of their eyes briefly. "Can you two keep a secret?"

Charlotte squirmed in her seat, so Alex clarified. "Just until tonight. I won't ask you to lie to Dean."

"Okay," Charlotte said, nodding.

"I was contacted a month ago by someone in Alexandria and was offered a position with the CIA."

"Shut the hell up," Jen whispered, eyes wide.

"Oh my God," Charlotte said at the same time. "That's amazing."

"That is so badass." Jen's expression was one of pure admiration.

Alex laughed. "It *sounds* badass. But remember, I look at maps."

"Yeah, badass top-secret maps."

Charlotte gave Jen a silly look.

"What?" Jen asked. "Am I right?"

"You're sort of right. It does require a security clearance."

"See?" Jen pointed at Charlotte. "I watch *Homeland*. I know about this stuff."

They all stopped chatting while their food was delivered, but as soon as the server walked away, Charlotte was back on the case. "So, are you interested in this job?" she asked.

"I've already accepted. That's the secret," Alex said.

Charlotte's eyes went wide. "Oh. Wow."

"I know Dean is going to freak, but . . . sometimes—although losing Nate was the worst thing that's ever happened to me, even worse than losing my parents in a lot of ways—I kind of feel like I have gotten a second chance. You know?" She looked up at the other two women who'd gone quiet. "Before, we'd had to discuss everything. Compromise. Even fight sometimes. We'd wanted to have a family, and that meant a normal life. And I'd wanted that, don't get me wrong. But now . . . it's like, I can do anything. Be anything. I know that sounds selfish." Alex shook her head, suddenly feeling frustrated and confused.

Charlotte put up a hand. "Stop right there. It doesn't sound selfish at all. You're right. This is a chance to take another path. And as for Dean, this is your life, Alexis. It will take him a minute. You're right. But he'll be fine. Besides, how awesome to have a sister-in-law in the CIA."

They all laughed at that, and at Charlotte's prodding, Alex began to fill them in on the details, telling them about her interview and the timeframe. It felt good to get it out there. Share it with some friends.

"Okay, so you leave for Virginia in early November. Correct?" Jen asked when they were wrapping up lunch.

Alex nodded. "I'll probably need to go sometime in September to find an apartment."

"It's not even August yet. You should just work the front desk for a couple of months," Jen said. "Make some extra cash. It would give you something to do while they look for my replacement."

Alex considered that. It wasn't a horrible idea, but she'd kind of wanted to relax. Maybe do a little traveling.

Then again, her entire mode of survival for the past year had been to keep busy. Maybe her lack of activity had been why she'd felt a little depressed this past week. She'd thought of Nate much more than she had in a while. It had felt like a bit of a backslide. "Yeah, maybe. When do you move your office?" she asked Jen.

"Not for a few weeks. TJ and I are going to start working on it this weekend."

"I'll think about it," she said, before giving Charlotte a pointed glance. "Remember, not a word. I'll tell Dean about my new job tonight."

Jake took the towel he'd been using to dry the Stag Wagon and tossed it into his yard. All morning he'd been busy working. First cleaning out the inside of the RV and then driving it over to the extra-large car-wash bay on the edge of town. He was exhausted, hot, and starving. And according to his overly worried geriatric neighbor who'd brought him out a glass of tea a half hour ago, he was sunburned from working shirtless for the past two hours.

Next up, he needed to wax the giant diesel pickup that the fifth wheel was hitched to. Not his favorite thing to do, but hell, none of this was his favorite. Especially when he was feeling so pissed off.

So far over the past twenty-four hours he'd ignored eight phone calls, a dozen texts, and even an email from his fellow co-owners—and supposed friends. He'd get back to them when he was good and ready. And not so damn hurt. And ashamed. And pissed off.

The conversation had come at exactly the wrong time, because his insecurities with his role at the Stag had been at an all-time high. Also, the fact that he knew that TJ was sort of right had made it even worse to hear.

But at the same time, screw that Amanda woman for thinking she had the right to call him out. She'd flirted with him the first time they met. Wasn't even subtle about it, and he hadn't taken the bait, so this felt a little like revenge. She was probably smug as hell when she'd made the phone call to TJ to tell on him.

But it didn't change the fact that deep down, he'd known it wasn't the best idea to sleep with women he met while on tour. That shit always got out. But hell, he was always alone, at events where people were having a good time, and surrounded by available ladies. Only a monk could have resisted, and even he'd have struggled.

Jake put his hands on his hips and stared at the front of the pickup. Jerking his head to the right, he gazed at his neighbor's window. Were the curtains moving? He turned away and grinned. Mrs. Curtis was a dirty old lady.

He sighed, recalling what a shitty day he was having. Although he'd threatened to leave the Stag the day before, TJ and Dean would have to buy his ass out before that happened. He'd been trying to prove his worth to them for the past six years. He wasn't about to stop now. Thursday, he'd leave on the late summer festival tour and he would be damned if he didn't kill it with sales and new contracts. There was no doubt that these trips had contributed to their success. Purchasing the RV and the truck and doing these tours had been his idea. The guys had been on board and had never questioned him since, but TJ had also never bothered to crunch the numbers and announce how effective they'd been, even though Jake was certain that the data would prove his worth.

"If you set out a tip jar, you'd be rich by the end of

the day." A sweet feminine voice called out behind him. Jake turned to find Alex getting out of Charlotte's car at the edge of the cul-de-sac his duplex was on.

"Didn't even hear you pull up. What are you doing here?" he asked, feeling a smile creep up on his face.

"Came to check on you," she said, walking toward him.

He forced his eye on her sunglasses, far away from her legs, which were on full display in those shorts she had on. "Were you sent as the sacrifice, or maybe pulled the short straw?"

"None of those things, considering no one knows I'm here." She stepped up to him, and even behind dark lenses he could tell her eyes had gone sympathetic. "But I did hear what happened. I'm sorry."

He shrugged. "No big deal. Obviously, I had it coming."

Her head tilted to the side and she mirrored his crossed arms. "Don't say that."

She was wearing a tank top, revealing firm and shapely little biceps. He reached out and squeezed one. "Damn, girl. You in the Army or something?"

Laughing, she swatted his hand away. "Don't change the subject." Her face tilted, eyes running down his body. "Besides, you're the one standing out here showing off your six-pack for the neighborhood."

He put a hand on his stomach and nodded slightly toward the duplex. "Charity. I do it for little old Mrs. Curtis. In fact, don't look now, but I betcha she's watching."

Alex bit back a laugh, her bottom lip tucked under her teeth. She hesitated a second and then nonchalantly glanced over and then jerked her head back grinning. "Oh my God. She is."

"Told ya." He flexed his arms. "A purely selfless act."

She shook her head. "Show me this Stag Wagon."

"All right but be careful. Word on the street is that women are not safe in here," he said, turning and heading for the door.

"Whatever," she said behind him. "I'm always safe with you."

Her words surprised—and pleased—him. He wanted her to feel that way, because he cared about Alex a lot. Probably more than he had any woman outside his own family. A shock, considering it was a purely platonic relationship.

They stepped up into the RV and he held out his arms. "This is the main room."

She walked in and took her sunglasses off, eyes darting over the light tiled floors, blonde cabinetry, and ivory vinyl seating. Jake knew it was slightly dated, but it was clean and well maintained.

"It's nice," she said, walking into the galley kitchen area. "Roomier than I thought."

"Yeah, it's not bad. I've even been known to cook in here."

"I'm impressed." She opened a cabinet that contained a big canister of protein powder. She turned and gave him an eyebrow raise.

"Can't let myself go just because I'm on the road." He nodded in the direction of the house. "Mrs. Curtis is counting on me."

She laughed. "Of course." The next cabinet she opened contained the three packages of cookies and two bags of chips he'd bought for the trip. When she looked over her shoulder again, he just grinned.

"What can I say? I believe in living a balanced life."

"Makes sense."

He lifted his chin toward the back of the RV. "Don't forget the master suite."

"Of course not." She took the very few steps to the far end and peeked into the pocket door that led into the bedroom.

"Wow," she said, walking in. Jake followed her in just in time to see her flop onto the bed. "This is better than I expected."

"Not too shabby, huh?"

Dipping her chin, she looked at him. "Maybe *I* should buy an RV. This is great." Rolling over, she looked the back wall up and down where there were cabinets across the top of the bed and then down each side. "Who'd have thought there'd be so much storage?"

"Yeah and most of those are empty or just holding Stag stuff."

She rolled back over and sat up, crossing her legs. Her perfectly toned, sexy legs. *Look. Away.*

"What do you do in here when you're not working?" She asked. Before he answered, she put up a hand. "Except for . . . you know."

He laughed. "Honestly, I read."

"That doesn't surprise me," she said. And it shouldn't. They'd messaged before about the books they liked and both of them were fans of suspense.

She glanced around again, then back at him. "When are you leaving?"

"Thursday."

Her eyes widened. "This Thursday? Like, in two days?"

He nodded, crossing his arms and leaning against the doorframe.

"I'm kind of jealous."

"Don't be. I work hard and obviously now I'm not

allowed to have any fun." He hoped that hadn't come out sounding too bitter.

"Let me come with you," she said, shocking him.

He chuckled. "Uh huh. Sure."

"I mean it."

He widened his eyes. "Alex, are you serious?"

She shrugged. "I have nothing else to do and I told you once how much I wanted to travel during my off time. Besides, I'm sick of being at Dean and Charlotte's. He may even kick me out tonight after I tell him I'm moving to Virginia."

"Not a chance," Jake said.

"Okay, you're right. He would never do that. But still, let me come, because I've been depressed since I came back. The past few days I've felt almost like I was regressing through the stages of grief. I need a distraction." She let her shoulders slump and tilted her head to the side.

He matched her head tilt and raised an eyebrow. "Are you using my concern for your emotional well-being to manipulate me?"

She gave an exaggerated grimace. "Is it working?"

He sighed and sat down on the foot of the bed, halfway facing her. "Alex, I'll be gone for nearly two weeks."

"So what? I was just gone for a year. I can certainly handle a couple of weeks."

How was he going to talk her out of this idea? A better question was whether he wanted to? Maybe this was what he needed. A friend to keep him company while he traveled. Someone to help with the work. That actually didn't sound too bad. Things could get crazy, hauling boxes of product, setting up and taking down.

Never mind the lonely drives. Podcasts and audiobooks got old fast. And yet, Dean would have a fit.

Right now, though, Jake was struggling to care about Dean's feelings on the matter. Alex was his friend. She wanted to come. And if he was honest, he liked the idea. Maybe a little too much, but after what had just gone down yesterday with TJ, he'd be damned if he laid a finger on any woman on the Stag's dime. Not now, and definitely not Dean's little sister. Besides, he knew better than anyone that she still wasn't fully over Nate. As hard as she tried to project otherwise.

Over the past year he'd come to realize that Alexis Parker was one of the strongest people he'd ever known. Her determination to overcome, to keep moving forward, and at the same time to look out for those around her was incredibly admirable. And appealing. He liked talking to her. Liked that she didn't push but was always willing to listen.

Today was a perfect example of her compassion. His friends had blown up his phone in every way possible. Alex had gotten in her car and driven over to check on him. And although her concern got him right in the chest—among other places—he knew that he needed to keep this on the up-and-up. That being said . . .

"Okay. If you want to come . . . I think you should."

Her mouth dropped open and then slid into a grin. "Really?"

"Really. But you better be ready to work your little army ass off. This is no senior road trip."

She sat up straight and gave him a salute, which was just about the hottest thing he'd ever seen because it was obvious she'd done it a million times. "You're pretty good at that. Looks like you almost got it down."

Rolling her eyes, she leaned over and slapped at his bare arm, except he jumped off the bed and dodged her. They were both laughing as they stepped out of the RV and as he walked her to the car.

"So we leave Thursday," she said, turning to look at him as she opened the car door.

"Yeah. Early. Are you really sure you want to do this, Alex?"

"Yes, really. In fact, the more I think about it, the more excited I get. It'll be fun." She gave him a serious look. "Now, when are you going to go talk with the other guys?"

He sighed, shoving his hands in his pockets. "Not sure. I'll text TJ today just to let him know I still plan on going Thursday."

"Okay. Good. Should I bring anything specific?"

He shook his head. "Nah. I'll grab you some Stag shirts to wear when needed. But other than that, just some comfortable clothes. Maybe a couple of nicer things. I do some restaurant and bar visits, and one day is a liquor convention."

"Huh. Okay." She bit at her lip, looking concerned. "I should probably go shopping."

"Don't stress about it. I can always do those things alone if needed."

"No, no. If I'm going to come I'm going to be an asset. It's fine. I needed some things anyway."

"Okay," he said.

She put one foot in the car to go and then hesitated, looking up at him. "Listen, I don't know everything that TJ said, but don't let it get you down. I think he and Dean both can be a little uptight. Still, none of it's worth you guys arguing, and for what it's worth, according to Jen he's pretty upset about how it went down."

Jake sighed. That made two of them. "Thanks," he said.

She smiled, put her sunglasses on, and then nodded toward the duplex. "Also, you should probably flex. Your number-one fan is watching."

With a big grin, she got in and he watched her drive away.

Four

Alex squared her shoulders and repeated herself. "I've accepted a position in Alexandria, Virginia. With the CIA."

She wished she could read the look on Dean's face, but it was one she'd never seen before. There was definitely shock, possibly mixed with disbelief.

He leaned forward on the sofa, hands together and elbows resting on his knees. "How long have you known about this?"

"I was approached about the possibility a few months ago. I visited and interviewed last week before I came home."

Dean's eyes shot open. "You've already been there?"

"Just for a day. One night. Then I flew home and Jake picked me up."

"Did Jake know about you accepting this job?"

Alex sighed and gave Dean a long look. "He did, but I obviously wanted to be the one to tell you."

Dean's brow furrowed. "What's up with you and Jake talking so much lately?"

"We've become friends. No big deal. We've been messaging for the past year."

"What?" Dean asked, sitting up.

Charlotte—who'd been sitting beside him the entire time—gave his thigh a gentle squeeze. "Don't get loud. Alex is a grown woman. And Jake is your friend."

Dean scowled over at her. "I know that. I'm just . . . surprised." He looked back at Alex. "Why didn't you tell me that?"

She shrugged. Good question. "I don't know. It happened slowly. He was so kind to me the night of the uncasking. Listened to me when I talked. That's why I like him—he's a good listener, and he doesn't try and tell me what to do."

Dean's expression made it clear that comment had hurt.

"And this." She held a hand out toward her brother. "I didn't want to hurt your feelings. You and I are super close, Dean. But you're still my brother. You want to fix things and you hate for me to be sad. Jake was a connection home, but also someone who just let me feel how I needed to feel."

"I always let you feel how you need to feel," he said defensively. Charlotte touched his leg again but this time in support, which made Alex feel bad. "I've done everything I can for you, Alex. Your entire life."

"I know! And that's part of the problem. I'm an adult and yet you still feel responsible for me. Especially now that I've lost Nate. I know you do. I've always had you or him. But it's been good for me to figure out how to find my own way. Not only as an adult, but as a woman who is now on her own in the world."

"By talking to one of my best friends? And you're never going to be alone in the world."

She sighed. "I don't mean it literally. And Jake and I are just friends, Dean. But as for this job and this move, these are things that I need to do. For me. I've worked really hard to heal and get to a place where I feel confident in my own abilities. I've also worked really hard in my career. Because of that I was offered a job with the CIA. It's a big deal. I have to take it."

He didn't look convinced. "Nobody is prouder or more impressed with you than I am, Buzz. But it's so far away."

"We can visit her, babe. I love D.C.," Charlotte said quietly, looking at him. "And she can visit us."

Alex nodded, silently thanking Charlotte for her support.

He blew out a breath. "You're right. It just feels like you've been gone for so long and I was just looking forward to having you back."

Alex's smile faltered. "I know you were. But like Charlotte said, we can visit all the time. And who knows how long it will last. Maybe I'll hate it."

His eyebrow went up. "You working on national security? That's right up your alley."

She laughed. "True, but what do you think I've been doing all these years?"

"When do you have to leave?" he asked.

"Not until November, so you've still got me for a while."

"Well, that's good. Maybe I'll be sick of you by then." He smirked, and she knew then that he would be fine. Except there was one little thing left.

"Also, I want to tell you something else." She paused for a minute, and then decided to just say it. "I'm going with Jake on his festival tour Thursday."

She bit her lip, watching, as both Charlotte and Dean's eyes went round.

"What the hell for?" Dean asked.

Alex shrugged. "Because I can. And because I want to. Also, honestly, it sounds like it would be good to have a woman along keeping him in check."

"Has he been hitting on you?" Dean asked, his voice turning angry.

"No! What the heck? Why would you even ask that? Did you not hear me a few minutes ago? He's been a complete gentleman. He knows there's no way I'm interested. I just lost my fiancé, Dean."

"A year ago. And shit, we all know he has no trouble putting his di—"

"Stop right there before you say something you'll regret," Charlotte said, turning to her fiancé and shutting him up. "Don't you dare imply that Jake has to coerce anyone to sleep with him. There are plenty of women out there that are looking to get laid. You need to give him a break. And you wouldn't be friends with him if you didn't trust him."

Now it was Alex's turn to be shocked, and she was ready for Dean to be upset at Charlotte. But seeing as she was proving to be the Dean-whisperer, he wasn't.

Sucking in a deep breath, Dean looked at her. "He's okay with this, I assume?"

"Yeah, but you should know it was my idea. I'd wanted to do some traveling between now and November. This seems like a perfect way to do it."

"You know he's going through Atlanta, right?" Dean asked, and Alex knew exactly what he was implying.

"Yes. I know that." Nate had been from Atlanta, and his family was obviously all there. She'd kept in touch with them over the past year, but not as much as she should have. "I'd planned to visit them this year, but honestly, I don't think I'm quite ready."

Dean nodded. "Well, if you're going to go, I'm assuming you're going to work. So we're going to pay you."

"I won't argue with that," she said. She looked at Charlotte. "And I've been thinking, I don't mind helping out at the Stag a few hours a day when I'm back. Until you find someone," she said to Dean.

He looked visibly relieved. "That's really helpful. Thanks, Alex."

"What are amazing sisters for?"

"I could go for a pretzel. You?" Alex looked over at Charlotte as they walked through the mall.

"Yeah, that sounds good. I'm also dying for a drink," Charlotte said as they made their way to the Auntie Anne's kiosk. They set down their bags at a table. "You watch these. My treat."

"No way, you've already—"

Charlotte stuck a hand out. "Don't. I got this. Consider it a going-away celebration."

Alex just smiled and relaxed into the chair. Charlotte had been way too generous with her today, buying her lunch and a pair of shoes she'd waffled on. Alex knew the other woman was incredibly successful in her business as a wedding photographer, but still, she didn't owe Alex anything.

With a sigh, she stretched her feet out, popping her ankles. They'd been shopping since the mall opened. And who knew trying on clothes was so exhausting? She hadn't shopped like this since high school. But she had to admit that it had been a lot of fun finding clothes to take on her trip. She'd purchased clothing in Europe, but not a lot of everyday items sufficient for work and travel. Now she was stocked up on shorts, tops, a few pairs of pants, a couple of nice dresses, and even bras and underwear. The only stop they had left was the makeup store. It had been ages since she'd wanted or needed to wear makeup every day.

After a little while Charlotte returned with two sodas, a large cup of pretzel bites, and a tub of cheese.

"I got the spicy kind," Charlotte said, pointing to the tub. "Hope you don't mind."

"Of course not." Alex didn't hesitate, picking up a pretzel bite and dunking it. She put it in her mouth. It was divine, fake cheese with a kick.

They both ate for a few moments in silence. "I had some really good food in Italy, but nobody does crap snacks like the U.S."

Charlotte laughed. "Right? And the health statistics to match."

"Seriously," Alexis said before taking a drink of her soda. They continued to eat, and after a few moments she glanced over to find Charlotte wistfully staring at an incredibly pregnant woman shopping near the front of a toddler- and baby-clothing store nearby.

Last year when she'd been home after Nate's accident, she'd learned that her brother was unable to have children, and that it had been a key factor in the demise of his first marriage. His divorce from Amy, his ex, had been hard on Alex because they had taken her in when her parents—her father and Dean's mother—had died in an accident. The news of her brother's sterility had made her sad, but also explained a lot about her brother and his ex.

When Alex realized he was about to let it ruin another relationship—this time with Charlotte—she'd given him a piece of her mind. Thankfully he'd gotten his shit together. Well, actually, the credit all went to Charlotte, who was basically amazing for telling him that he didn't get to decide what she did and didn't want or need. But Alex knew that although Charlotte loved Dean enough to deal with his inability to get her pregnant, it didn't mean it wasn't a harsh and painful reality for her. She was still a young woman.

"She seems ready to pop any minute," Alex said teasingly.

Charlotte's head jerked toward her. "She does, doesn't she? I was thinking the same thing."

"Looks miserable," Alex said, reaching for her drink. She quickly realized that may have been the wrong thing to say.

"Worth the short-term pain, I'm sure," Charlotte said.

"Oh I'm sure it is, I didn't mean to imply it wasn't." Alex cleared her throat, knowing that this could backfire, but this woman was going to be her family soon, and she wanted them to be close. "Have you and Dean . . . well, have you talked about . . . alternatives?"

Charlotte's eyebrows went up and she swallowed, hesitating. "Some. Nothing too serious, as we're not married yet."

Alex nodded. "True, but Dean's not getting any younger."

Charlotte laughed. "That's for sure. Neither am I. We realize that, and well, between you and me . . ." Charlotte scooted in her chair, so instinctively Alex did the same. "I've been doing a little research on adoption. Just finding out what our first steps would be. Asking questions. The sooner we start the process the better, because it could take years."

"Good for you," Alex said. "And, when *are* you guys going to get married?"

Charlotte smiled. "Well, funny you should ask, because we did finally agree on a date."

"Oh my goodness. When?"

"April twenty-fifth. It's a Thursday evening."

"Thursday, really?" Alex said, confused.

"Well, it's going to be a small wedding. Everyone at the Stag and our families. Only the important people. And, well, we had to be sure it didn't conflict with events at the Stag."

Alex nodded. "That makes sense. I'm excited. Congratulations."

"Thank you," Charlotte said, smiling. "I was also hoping you would agree to be my maid-of-honor."

Alex froze, her eyes wide. "Seriously?"

"Seriously," Charlotte said, biting her lip nervously.

The back of Alex's eyes suddenly burned. "I would love that, Charlotte. Oh my God, yes." She leaned over and awkwardly wrapped her arm around her. "Does this mean now I get to help plan *your* wedding?"

Charlotte sat up straight. "You're welcome to, and I'd absolutely love that. But please don't feel obligated. I know that might be . . . difficult."

Alex considered that as she tried to brush a wayward tear from her eye nonchalantly. She hated that she'd felt inclined to cry so often lately. "Maybe, but that doesn't mean I shouldn't try." Forcing a smile, she looked at Charlotte who had sympathy in her eyes.

"I admire you so much, Alexis," Charlotte said.

"Oh gosh, what for?" She laughed awkwardly. "I'm good at keeping it together on the outside, but I have some ways to go on the inside."

"And that's what's so amazing about you. What you went through—are going through still. Well, I just think the fact that you pulled yourself together, deployed and got back to work, it's just sort of amazing. I don't know what I would have done."

"You probably would have done the same, honestly. I'm no superhero. You just go on because there is nothing else to do. You put one foot in front of the other every day and then cry yourself to sleep at night." She let out a hard breath, internally cursing the next few tears that escaped. "Sorry," she said, grabbing a napkin and wiping her eyes. She was usually so damn strong.

Charlotte reached out and touched Alex's hand on the table. "Don't apologize. Please. I want you to share whatever you need to share. I know it's not quite the same, but before my failed engagement to John, we suffered a very traumatic miscarriage. I'd carried that baby for an entire trimester. Losing it was the most horrible thing I'd ever gone through and I kept it all bottled inside. Didn't share it with anyone except John. I had a support system that I refused to reach out to because I didn't want to burden them. Instead I just laid all my pain on one person—even worse, I kept most of it inside."

"I'm so sorry to hear that, Charlotte."

Charlotte gave her a sad smile. "Thank you, but it's been a long time now. And I'm obviously not sorry that things with John didn't work out."

Alex laughed through her tears at the cringe on Charlotte's face. "Well, yeah, thank goodness it didn't, or we wouldn't be here now," she said. Many years ago, Charlotte's first fiancé—and high school sweetheart—had stood her up on the day of their wedding. Funny thing, he was now a distiller at the Stag and everyone seemed to get along okay. Some things were just too crazy to be explained.

"Agreed. But isn't it a little twisted that I'm secretly looking forward to John watching me walk down the aisle to marry someone else?"

They chuckled together. "Not at all. I think you deserve that feeling. And I'd be happy to help you choose an amazing dress for that occasion. I bet we can get a lot of planning done before I leave in November."

"I agree. Especially with all my contacts. And now I'm super excited." Charlotte leaned back and tossed their empty pretzel cup into a nearby trash can. "But for now, let's get some makeup and then get home so we can get these new clothes washed and packed for your trip."

Alex nodded and stood up, taking a final sip of her drink, and then followed Charlotte toward the makeup store. "You know where else I'd like to go? The bookstore. I could use a few things to read on the road."

"Think you'll have time for reading?" Charlotte asked.

"Why wouldn't I?" Alex replied. "Two weeks of on and off driving."

Charlotte just shrugged, an odd smile on her face. "I don't know. I just figured you two will be having too much fun for reading."

Alex's head jerked back. "What does that mean? This is Jake we're talking about here."

Charlotte grinned. "Exactly. Jake knows how to have fun."

"Yeah, too much apparently."

"I know, I know," Charlotte said. "But that doesn't mean you guys can't have a good time."

"You don't mean what I think you mean, do you?" Alex asked in shock. "Because my answer to that is 'no way no how.'"

"No, I didn't mean anything like *that*. But it can still be fun. Two young people, road trip, concerts, and lots of people." Charlotte glanced over at her. "Just make the most of this time. That's all I'm saying."

Five

Thursday morning, bright and early, Jake pulled the truck—and the Stag Wagon—up to the curb outside the Stag. He could see Alex waiting behind the front door and as soon as he got out of the truck, she was bending down to pick up her things. Before he could get to her, he saw Dean step outside with a bag.

Great.

"Hey," Dean said. He shoved a thumb over his shoulder. "Alex will be out in a minute. Decided she needed to use the restroom before you got on the road."

"No problem." Jake held a hand out for her bag and Dean handed it to him. Turning around, he opened the back-seat door of the truck and placed it on the seat.

Dean was still standing there when he turned back around.

"It's good to see you, man. We missed you the last couple of days. I feel like I owe you an apology."

The sincerity of Dean's words didn't entirely shock Jake, considering Dean was for the most part a pretty levelheaded guy. There were a couple of things that riled him up. Anything that threatened the safety of someone he loved, and a grain mash going bad in his distilling room. But Jake had kind of assumed that after Alex had told him of her plan Tuesday evening, he'd be hearing from Dean. Jake was almost impressed with his friend for not showing up at his door to give him a set-down. So yeah, maybe this cool, calm, and collected interaction was surprising him a bit.

And if Dean was capable of handling this like a man, Jake figured he ought to follow suit. "I appreciate that. I just needed a couple of days to process some things. I think I owe you guys an apology also."

Just as he finished speaking, the front door opened. Jake turned, but instead of only Alex, TJ was stepping outside with her. It was early. Earlier than TJ usually got there, so Jake knew his best friend had shown up just to have this conversation.

"Morning," TJ said. "I'm glad I caught you."

"Yeah, well, I was just telling Dean I owed you both an apology."

TJ's eyebrows went up. "What for?"

"For screwing around."

"Jake—" TJ started, but Jake wasn't finished.

"It was stupid of me. I should have known better, and it won't be happening anymore."

TJ and Dean exchanged a look. Finally TJ looked at Jake. "Listen, none of us have been saints for the past five years. That Frye woman was very smug and self-righteous when she called. I apologize for not handling our conversation better on Monday. We're all in this to-gether, and I hate that you felt ostracized."

Jake nodded, unsure of what else to say. He wasn't completely over what had happened, mostly because his feelings of insecurity had been brewing for a while. But he appreciated the apologies.

He glanced over at Alex, standing off to the side by the pickup. "You ready?"

She pushed off the door and gave him a small smile. "Yep."

"I know it doesn't need to be said," Dean started, "but please take care of my sister."

"You're right, it definitely didn't need to be said." Jake picked up Alex's other bag.

Dean put up his hands in surrender, then headed over to Alex, wrapping her in a hug.

Jake turned to walk around to the driver's side of the truck but was stopped by TJ. "Hey, man, we good?" he asked.

"We're good." Jake's jaw tensed as he put his sunglasses on. "I'll see you in a few weeks."

TJ nodded. "Have fun. But . . . be careful. You let anything happen to Alex and you may as well not come back. Know what I'm sayin'?"

"I hear ya," Jake said, heading for his door. "We'll be fine."

Alex hadn't said much since they'd left the Stag twenty minutes earlier. She'd been too busy thinking about the man sitting beside her. It was a relief that he'd finally spoken with the other guys, but it hadn't gone how she'd expected. When it came to her and Jake, she'd basically been the needy one in the relationship. He'd seen her through some dark thoughts over the past year. Let her message long, overwrought monologues where she went on and on about her dreams, her fears, her emotions. And he'd always responded and either gave his own thoughtful insight or often just agreed with her.

He'd shared plenty, but nowhere near what she had, which made sense to a point. He hadn't been the one grieving a loved one, she had. But it suddenly occurred to her that their closeness was a little one-sided. Maybe more than a little. Was it because he had no desire to share his deep or painful emotions, or because he didn't feel welcome to? The thought made her feel incredibly guilty. Only one way to find out.

"Do you feel better after talking to them?" she asked.

He didn't respond right away, but she could tell by the way his fingers tightened on the steering wheel that he was considering her question. Finally, he sighed. "I don't know. I guess."

Okay. That wasn't much of an answer. But he also hadn't given her a reason not to prod for more. Yet, anyway. "I was surprised you apologized first."

He huffed out a quiet laugh. "Yeah, well, it's usually for the best. They wouldn't have understood if I tried to explain how I feel about it all."

"How do you know?"

He shrugged. "It's fine, Alex. I just wanted it to be over."

"It's not really over if you're not heard, or your needs aren't met."

The look he gave her was pure confusion. "Business isn't always about getting your needs met."

"Uh, when you own the company, it most certainly is. Especially when you work with your two best friends."

His lips quirked, and he glanced over at her quickly. "Thanks for looking out for me, but I'm fine. Really."

She wasn't convinced, but she also knew that frustrating him within the first hour of their two-week trip might not be the best tactic. "If you say so. But remember, undealt-with emotions fester. And I don't want to see you festering."

His throaty laugh, and the handsome wink he sent her way, had a chill running down her arms. The sensation was so unexpected and alarming she had to look away. Closing her eyes, she tried to imagine Nate winking at her.

She couldn't.

Jake caught himself glancing at Alex's legs across the seat of the truck. Again.

He had to stop it, but damn, she was wearing little denim shorts and a striped top that accentuated her breasts in a way he hadn't been prepared for when he'd seen her this morning. Her quads were probably stronger than his, and it had been distracting him for nearly two hours.

"Okay," she said, scooting forward in her seat and bringing his focus back to the task at hand, which was getting where they needed to go. "In about a mile you're going to take a left on Ohio Street."

"Got it." A little way down the road he put on his blinker and made the turn. Driving this rig required a lot more thought than a normal vehicle. You couldn't just swerve into your lane at the last second.

"Now we stay on this road for a bit."

"You're a better navigator than my satellite or my phone," he said.

"I should hope so. I get paid to analyze maps."

"True," he said, then grinned over at her. "But you also have that pretty voice in your favor."

She looked away, but he caught her smile.

"Should I try an accent?" she teased. "Maybe one from the deep South. Wouldn't that be awesome?" She sat up straight and put a hand on her chest. "Bless your heart, y'all missed your exit. Let me recalculate 'cha.

Now keep right for the next mile." Except "mile" came out sounding more like "mall," and she laughed at herself, which he loved.

One thing he hadn't anticipated was how funny she would be. Of course, she'd joked around some over their messages, but it wasn't as easy to work out a person's tone in that format. Plus, the first four months or so, she hadn't been in the best place emotionally, and a lot of their conversations weren't happy. She would share with him that she'd almost cried at work that day, or how she'd had a dream about Nate. Those dreams had come frequently for a while.

When he thought about it, he was still surprised that he hadn't kindly shut their communication down. He certainly could have, and it wasn't as if he hadn't considered it. As a rule, emotional women were not usually his thing. Any man's thing. But whether it was because she was the sister of a best friend, or he just felt compelled to be a good guy, he'd always looked forward to talking with her. He'd wanted to see her get better, and slowly, he had. Secretly, he liked to think it was partly due to their friendship.

He glanced at the clock. It was almost noon. "Our timing today is perfect. We'll have plenty of time to prep for this afternoon's boat trip."

"Tell me more about this boat situation," she said. "You'd never mentioned boats before we left."

"You nervous?"

"No, not really."

He nodded. "Good. I've got a solid connection with a guy down here who owns Lazy Days, a boating company. They do—I guess what you'd call party boat rides. Short cruises on large pontoon boats."

"Nice. So what do *we* do on the party boat?"

"Well, we're serving drinks on this afternoon's boat ride, and on one tomorrow at eleven."

He saw her head jerk in his direction in his periphery.

"People take drinking boat rides at eleven o'clock."

He chuckled. "This is the lake of the Ozarks. People drink all day."

"Oh my. I can see I clearly missed out on a lot of the important developmental years being in the Army."

"I'm sure you're better off for it. Although, it's not all young people. I did one of these last summer and it was full of women over fifty. They had a heck of a time."

The sound of her laughter made him smile. "That sounds amazing. I hope today's group is like that."

Several hours later, after getting the RV situated at the campground and making their way to the marina, they began to carry boxes of product, cups, and swag down to the pontoon boat. It wasn't long until the parking lot started to fill, and they found out exactly what kind of group they were dealing with. It wasn't ladies over fifty, that was for sure.

"Holy shit," Alex said under her breath. "I may have gotten in over my head."

Her reaction surprised him a bit. It was just a noisy bunch of young women, but there was no mistaking the anxiety in her demeanor. "It will be fun. Don't worry," he said, nodding at the walkway that led down from the boathouse. "Here comes the captain, Ted. You'll like him."

That seemed to help her a bit. Ted was probably in his seventies, short, with a sizeable belly. He whistled as he made his way along the dock wearing a colorful button-up shirt and a white sea captain hat that had probably come from a costume shop.

"Jake my boy, how's it going?"

Jake stepped forward and put his hand out as Ted stepped onto the platform. "Good to see you, Ted." He turned to Alex. "I brought a partner this time. This is Alex."

Ted nodded and took Alex's hand. "Nice to meet ya young lady."

"Likewise," she said quietly. "This is a lovely boat."

"Thank you. I enjoy her. And you let me know if I can be of service in any way," he said to them, sliding glasses onto his round face. He nodded up to the parking lot where the first group of women had finally begun making their way to the trail that led down to the dock. "See that group? Woo wee, they're gonna be a handful," Ted said with a chuckle that made his chin vibrate.

"We can handle it," Jake said.

"If anyone can handle a boat full of women, it's this guy," Ted said with a wink and a hearty chuckle that nearly had Jake groaning. His eyes darted warily to Alex, but she seemed to find Ted amusing. "But if you two are about ready, I think I'll go up and lay the rules down. Make sure you use the restroom. Our stop won't be for an hour. And Jake, I've got ice up in the kitchen."

"Thanks, Ted," he said.

Alex looked up at him as Ted walked away. "First stop?"

"This is kind of like a bar hop," he explained. "They get on here, hang out on the boat as it cruises around the lake and then he pulls up at a bar on the other side. Everybody hangs out there for like thirty minutes and then we end up back here."

"So this is for serious drinkers."

"It's just for fun. People come to the lake to leave their responsibilities at home."

"Huh. Okay," she said.

They took Ted's advice and headed for the boathouse. Once they were ready to board again, the pontoon boat was full of people. The original group of young women, and now a group of middle-aged ladies. There were also now about eight men.

"This is weird, but I feel nervous," Alex said as they made their way toward the dock.

"What for?" Jake asked, hefting the bag of ice he'd picked up in the boathouse onto his shoulder. He looked down at her, still in those denim shorts, but sporting a white Stag T-shirt. His was identical.

She sighed. "I don't know."

"You're not afraid of water or boats, are you?" He hadn't even considered asking her about that.

"No, not at all. Just . . . I don't know. Ever since last year . . . sometimes situations with a lot of people—strangers—give me anxiety. It's stupid, I know—"

He grabbed her hand and gave it a squeeze. "Hey, no. It's not stupid at all." She glanced up at him, her pretty blue eyes shielded behind her sunglasses. "Don't worry, okay? I'll handle the socializing if you want. You focus on making the drinks. We do this however makes you comfortable."

She nodded. "Okay. Thank you." She paused and took a deep breath. "Sea Breeze. Two ounces of cranberry, half ounce of grapefruit, and three-quarter ounces of vodka."

"Perfect." They'd gone over it several times on the drive down. "What about a highball?"

"Ounce of whiskey, ginger ale filled to two thirds of the cup."

"You got this, babe." He grinned, giving her hand a final squeeze. "Now let's set sail with good ol' Ted."

The look of relief on her face sent a flood of happiness through his chest. That was, until a shriek call rang through the air. "Get on this boat, Mr. Stag! We booked this tour just to see you!"

Alex's eyebrows rose over her glasses. "Wow, the legends are true. You really *do* have groupies."

Jake held back a groan. He thought maybe he'd recognized a couple of the women from last year. Not because he'd slept with them though, like everyone seemed to think, but just from previous visits, probably from passing out drinks at the marina and the campground where the RV was. He'd probably flirted with them, but that was all.

He gave a quick wave to the ladies on the boat. They whistled. Glancing down at Alex, he sighed. "It's not what you're thinking."

She put her hands up and grinned. "Hey, no judgment here."

They made their way down the dock and got on the boat as catcalls rang out around him. The deck was narrow wood planks, and there was a bench down the center and one on each side with a large red awning covering about two thirds of the vessel. Toward the back, Ted steered and manned his speaker with a fist microphone held up to his mouth. "I promised, and I delivered, the one and only Jake the Stag whiskey guy . . . oh, and his sidekick Alex."

Somewhat embarrassed about the fanfare, Jake gave a quick bow and headed over to the small bar area they'd set up near the back. Several women waved and said hello as he and Alex passed by. He couldn't help noticing how they eyed her. Not with malice, more like curiosity.

"Sidekick, huh?" Alex whispered as they began to

get situated at their station, which was basically a small folding table with a cooler shoved beneath.

"Sorry about that," he said, as the boat's engine roared to life. He placed a hand around Alex's waist. "And hold on. The boat's a little rough when it first takes off."

Her body jerked a bit in response, so he immediately let go.

"Sorry, I just didn't want you to lose your balance," he said. He should have known better than to assume she wanted him to help her. Or touch her so closely.

She glanced up at him, a nervous quirk of her lips. "I know. It's fine."

Just then the boat gave a lurch and she reached out and gripped his shirt with her hands. He lifted an eyebrow. "See?"

"Is it like this the entire time?"

"No. Once he gets going and maintains his speed—which isn't very fast—it will be fairly smooth. In fact, we'll basically be stopped a lot of the time."

She nodded. "Okay, sorry." Her brows narrowed as she swiped at his chest trying to get out the wrinkles in his T-shirt from her grasp.

"It's fine, Alex," he said, smiling at her.

Music came over the speakers, and it wasn't long before a few of the passengers started to dance and sing along. As always, it was clear that for some of them, the drinks about to be served would not be their first of the afternoon.

They got to work, creating a bit of an assembly line. He lined up the cups and filled them with ice, while Alex poured the ingredients.

"Let's just start with ten of each and see where we are from there."

"How many drinks do you usually serve on these cruises?"

"Around sixty or seventy."

She glanced up, eyes wide. "Really?"

"Really. They're not that big, and we don't add a ton of alcohol."

As they were working, it suddenly occurred to him that although the women had made a big deal at the beginning, not one of them had yet come over to talk to him as they usually did. Was that really because of Alex's presence? He often had someone offer to be his "helper" by now. But clearly, he didn't need it because she was there.

"Okay, here's ten highballs. Should I start passing them out?" she asked.

"If you're comfortable. If not, I can do it."

"No, I think I'm good," she said, picking up the tray. "I don't know why I got panicked back there on the dock."

He nodded. "Okay, here." He placed a handful of napkins on her tray.

Continuing to finish up the remaining drinks, he tried to keep an ear out for what was happening on the boat. He glanced up a few times to see where Alex was, watched her smile at a few of the passengers. She was using the only tray, so he picked up two drinks to hand out just as he caught sight of her making her way to the group of men. They were all about his age, late twenties to early thirties, and leaning against the railing. She handed them each a drink, making her way down the row until her tray was empty. One of them began to speak to her, and then as she began to walk away, he caught her empty hand, holding her in place.

Jake froze, not letting his eyes off the asshole's

fingers clasped on her skin. Protective anger washed over him, and in his head, he began to count down quickly, and if he got to three it was on.

Two. . . . Three. . . . Jake stepped forward just as the guy let go. Alex moved on as the men laughed among themselves. She turned around, and he watched as she walked back toward him. Her sunglasses hid any sign of what was in her head, but Jake wasn't going to let this go unquestioned. He refused to allow her to be mistreated on his watch.

"What the hell was he saying?" he asked when she made her way over.

Alex began to place more drinks on her tray. "He asked if all the cruises came with a pretty waitress. What a dick."

"What the hell?" Jake's heart raced as his body's fight reaction tried to simmer down. Damn, had he ever said something so douchebaggy? Shit, probably. Why did it piss him the hell off to watch another man do it to someone he cared about? He'd process those thoughts later. Right now, he had one mission. "He grabs you again and I'll be forced to give him a swimming lesson."

Her shoulders sagged as her eyes met his. "You're sweet, but seriously? I've lived on military bases for almost seven years. If there's one thing I can handle, it's a man with a big ego."

He knew she was right, but that didn't mean he had to like it. They continued to pass out drinks, and as soon as he made his way to the group of women he'd recognized, one of them jumped up and wrapped her arm around his neck. A bit of liquid sloshed from one of the plastic cups he had balanced in his palms.

"Finally!" she said. "We've been waiting for you."

"Nice to see you ladies again," he said, gently pulling away. He held out a hand so she could take a drink, which she did with a flirty wink. "One for you. One for you, and one for you."

When his hands were empty, he turned to walk away.

"Come back and sit with us," the first woman called after him, a clear pout in her voice.

He turned and put his hands out. "I'm working," he teased. As he headed toward the back he heard one of them whisper, "Bet that's his girlfriend." He was stunned when another followed with, "No way. Guys like that don't have girlfriends."

Wow. Really? Was that how they saw him? How he came off? The kind of man who didn't . . . what . . . settle down? Value women? Deserve a partner? Or maybe they just assumed he didn't want one. Maybe that was the vibe he emitted. He had to admit, a year or two ago he'd have been happy to hear that's how he came off, but now? He wasn't so sure. Being the lone single guy out of his friends had started to suck, and he hadn't helped noticing that Dean and TJ seemed to be happier than they'd ever been now that they'd given in to the ball and chain.

Part of him wondered if this was just what happened when a man aged—he started to feel the pull of settling down. But then he'd think of the guys he knew who were well into their forties and were still living bachelor life to the fullest. Maybe he was starting to feel the tiniest desire due to osmosis, from being around happy couples at the Stag.

"You okay?" Alex asked, her brow furrowed.

"Yeah, fine."

"Sure? You looked deep in thought." She pushed her

glasses up and angled her head to meet his eyes. "Did you get harassed too? I mean, I know you did, but I wasn't prepared for it to upset you."

She was teasing. He forced a smile and shook it off. "Nah, I'm good, but thanks. Let's make some more drinks."

Alex tried to avoid the group of men for the next hour, which was easy because ever since the guy had grabbed her, Jake had beat her over to them to pass out fresh drinks. By now, all the passengers seemed to be having a good time getting to know one another. She leaned against the railing and watched them dance to some eighties hip-hop song.

"This is the point where we can sit back and be thankful that they're all drunk and we're not," Jake said.

She laughed, pointing at a woman who was probably in her sixties but trying to pull off forty-five. "Did you see the lady in yellow? She's managed to do the electric slide to every song that's come on."

"An undervalued talent these days. If only she hadn't almost knocked several people overboard in the process."

She giggled quietly, and then even harder when Jake looked at her with a huge grin on his face. "What?" she asked.

"That was a cute laugh, that's all," he said. "Never heard you do it before."

"Oh," she said, a little embarrassed. She instinctually grabbed at her necklace, heat warming her cheeks. Here she was, smiling and laughing with him *again*. More than she had in . . . forever. It felt nice, and the time on the boat had gone really quickly since she'd been enjoying herself. Too quickly, because she felt like she could cruise over the lake forever. On its last stretch of the trip, the pontoon had dropped anchor in a quiet lagoon not far from where they'd started. The sun was warm, but they were mostly shielded from the blaze by the boat's cover. And the slight breeze coming off the lake was exquisite. Even with loud music blasting through the speakers, she found it relaxing.

Shoving her hands in her pockets, she stared out at the passengers. Some dancing, some talking. One couple seemed to have met that afternoon and were already snuggled into a corner on the far bench, having an intimate whispered conversation. Alex watched as the man slyly touched the woman's thigh. And then a bit higher. Was that how fast things moved with couples these days? Would they go home with each other? And how had she become so out of touch with what modern couples did? Yes, she'd been with Nate for nearly her entire adult life, and yes she'd been a bit sheltered having been living a military life for so long. But she suddenly felt twice her age, even though she was probably the same age or younger than many of these people.

Shaking off her sullen thoughts, she saw several people finding partners as a slow song came on. The first one of the day. She and Jake continued to lean against the railing, taking in the entertainment of other people having a good time.

"This is what it's like working a wedding at the Stag," he said, leaning down toward her. "Kind of voyeuristic. Stone sober, watching intoxicated strangers enjoy themselves."

"I bet. Seems kind of fun though, and hearing Dean and Charlotte talk, there are a lot of interesting things that happen."

"Sometimes, yes. Most don't get too crazy, but one

time a mother of the groom got so wasted she ended up on the dance floor with her skirt hiked up over her underwear trying to do the splits."

Alex's jaw dropped. "What?"

"The funniest part was that the groom's new step-mother was the one who ended up helping her up and getting her out of there. She ended up passed out on one of our lobby couches."

"Wow. That's a true act of decency. Wonder if they were friendly before that," Alex said, shaking her head. "How often do you have to work weddings?"

"These days it averages about one a month since Dean, TJ, John, and I rotate. Occasionally Jen does it, but only if necessary."

"It still blows my mind that you guys do weddings."

"Yeah, crazy, right? But it's turned out to be insanely profitable. We may not have stayed in business long enough to see our first barrels uncasked without that extra income. A lot of distilleries struggle these days, and plenty fold before the three-year mark."

"I'm proud of you all."

"Thank you," he said. His hands were angled back, resting on the metal behind him, and she couldn't help noticing how muscular they were. Jake was handsome. The kind of man she might have noticed before. She noticed him now, but things were different. She was different, and as good looking as he was, she also noticed all the ways he was different from Nate.

Her brother had always joked that Nate looked like Jamie Foxx, and while she'd seen that a little, in her mind he'd just looked like himself. Muscular, but tall and lean. She could still remember meeting him for the first time, his smile lighting up the room. But his personality had been her favorite part because he was funny and sweet in a more reserved way. He didn't draw attention to himself and he wasn't a flirt. In fact, she'd had to ask him out first because he was a gentleman almost to a fault. But once they'd gotten closer and she'd seen the private side of him, he'd made her laugh constantly with his wit and intelligent sarcasm. He'd also made her swoon with how much he loved her and how he was never afraid to show it, in front of anyone or at any time. It was not uncommon for him to hold her hand or place kisses on her temple, no matter who was around or what they were doing.

She looked away, unsure of why she was even processing thoughts of this nature. It seemed like she wouldn't think of these things for a few days, and then bam, they'd hit her like a lead weight out of nowhere, sometimes knocking the breath from her lungs.

This was why keeping busy was critical.

Another slow song came on. One of her favorites from Adele. She heard herself saying as much out loud, and Jake angled himself toward her.

"Then we should dance."

Her head jerked up. "No way."

He shrugged. "Okay, no big deal. Just an idea since we're just standing here like party poopers."

"We're not party poopers," she teased. "We're tired from working."

He raised an eyebrow. "We passed out drinks and Stag koozies. You *can't* be worn out."

She considered his idea. Maybe dancing *would* be nice. How long had it been since she had? Years. Pushing off the railing, she held out a hand. "Fine."

With a quiet chuckle, he pushed off also and took

hold of her fingers gently. His skin was warm and his grip firm as he led her out to the sunlit section of the boat deck. About five other couples were slow dancing.

Turning to her, Jake slid a hand around her waist, was careful not to pull her too close. Their right hands remained clasped as he smiled down at her and then slowly began to sway.

"Okay?" he asked.

She could only nod, because it *was* okay. Nice even.

It was much warmer in the sun, which was now hanging lower in the sky, just above the treetops so that its warmth was directly on her face. She closed her eyes, listening to the water slapping against the boat, the birds chirping as they flew overhead, and the music coming out of the speaker above them. A soft breeze pushed her hair off her face and caressed her skin. She inhaled a bit as they swayed back and forth, and her lips quirked as she realized how nice it was to feel so relaxed and happy. This was the feeling she was constantly striving for and often falling short of.

When she opened her eyes and looked up, Jake was staring down at her. She flushed. "Sorry, I was just . . . enjoying the weather."

"I see that. You looked far away."

Funny he would say that, because for once she'd felt very present in her surroundings. So often over the past year she'd wished to be anywhere else. Go back in time to a specific moment with Nate or even her parents. A day where she'd felt nothing but love and happiness. A time where loss and pain weren't a constant in her life. Or maybe into the future, or even an alternate reality, where everyone she loved was still whole and living.

She shook her head. "No, I was right here. This is good."

His eyes darkened, brow narrowing. "I want you to be good, Alex."

Their eyes met and held. "I know you do. Thank you."

She had the sudden urge to stroke her necklace, but her hands were busy holding Jake. "This feels kind of like a middle-school dance, doesn't it?" she asked.

When he grinned, she was reminded how ridiculously handsome he was, his teeth perfectly straight, and the creases that bracketed his mouth showing off how often he showed them. "Kind of, although you are much prettier than the girls I went to school with. And it's probably been that long since I danced like this."

"Me too," she said, trying not to think about his compliment. "Except . . ." She unclasped their hands and reached up to wrap both of hers around his neck. "It would have been more like this, wouldn't it? Super awkward."

"Yes, I remember that." Both of his arms went around her waist, and this time he *did* pull her a little tighter against his body. "And us guys would try to slowly get closer and closer."

"Don't underestimate us girls, we wanted to be close too. Well, we did if we liked you."

"Yeah, I know I got a few pity dances."

"Oh, I can't imagine that." She smiled up at him, noting how close their faces were, her nose inches from his chin. "I bet you were as handsome in seventh grade as you are now."

His lips quirked, and she was suddenly embarrassed. It wasn't as if she'd never complimented his attractiveness before, just never while they were holding onto each other. Thankfully he didn't respond, just pulled her closer. Dipping her chin, she wasn't sure where to put her face without it being awkward, so finally she just leaned in and rested her cheek on the front of his shoulder.

That left her nose nestled near his collar. He smelled good, like a spicy aftershave and sundrenched skin. She watched his neck bob as he swallowed and then let her eyes close once more, just enjoying the embrace of another person. His arms were big and strong, bracketed on each side of her ribs, hands locked on her lower back.

His head brushed against hers, turning. Had he just pressed his lips into her forehead? Her eyes flew open, but she didn't move. Could he feel her heart pounding against his chest? When her gaze landed on a few of the women standing off to the side watching them with interest, she stood up straight and slowly pulled out of his arms. Thankfully the song ended at the same time, immediately leading into another pop song.

"Thank you for that," she said.

"It was my pleasure," he said, giving her a wink.

And that was when she understood the full extent of Jake Cooper's potency. He was a charmer, and it made sense that he had groupies from past tours. He was dangerous, so maybe it was a good idea she was here to keep him from breaking hearts. Other women's hearts, not hers obviously, because hers had already been broken.

Six

The next afternoon they left right after the second cruise. Jake was tired, having been up half the night trying to get comfortable on the pull-out bed in the main area of the Stag Wagon. He didn't regret having Alex come along, but damn, he was now lamenting the fact that he didn't get to sleep in the bedroom. But there was no way he'd have asked her to take the pull-out.

Now they were headed toward Memphis to attend the Boots and Beers country music festival. The drive had been quiet, Alex scribbling in some red book, giving him time to imagine how he'd act or what he'd say when Amanda Frye came by their booth. If he was lucky, she'd stay away.

About an hour and a half outside of town, Jake glanced across the truck cabin for the fiftieth time. Alex was still writing. She hadn't been at it continually—sometimes she'd gaze out her window, but then eventually her pen would scratch again.

"You must not get motion sickness," he said, breaking the long stretch of silence. He liked hearing her voice. He'd never realized how boring the drives had been before.

She stopped and looked up. "Not really. Why?"

He lifted a shoulder. "I can't have my head down like that in a moving vehicle. Definitely can't read or write."

"Guess I'm used to it by now, being in the Army, there's a lot of moving around in bumpy vehicles. I probably wasn't always this unaffected."

"Makes sense." He focused on the road for a minute, watching for the exit she'd briefly made sure to tell him to take ten minutes earlier. The woman could multitask, that was for sure. "You writing a book or something?"

Her head came up again. "No. It's just a journal."

He nodded, glancing out the rearview at the RV. "Like, a diary? To talk about what you do every day?" Yes he was being nosy, but he wanted to talk.

"I guess."

He could tell she was amused with his question.

"I don't write everything I do. More like . . . I try to keep track of my feelings."

"Ah, okay. Sounds like an interesting idea." And also seemed like something she'd do. It did sort of surprise him though that she'd never told him about it.

"Remember when I read a bunch of books last fall about grief?"

He nodded. "Yeah."

"Well, several of them mentioned writing in a journal. One in particular talked a lot about how you shouldn't suppress any emotion that came up, but just really feel them and let them come through fully. No matter what they are. Sadness, anger . . . guilt."

"That makes sense." He'd learned over the past year that even if he didn't completely understand or relate to what she was saying, it was best to just agree or say it made sense. Probably not the best way to handle it, but it seemed to appease her every time, and his main goal had always been to make her feel better even if he'd been coming through a screen half a world away.

"It helps me to write my feelings down," she went on. "Sometimes I don't know why I feel certain feelings on any given day. It's frustrating when I have like . . . three good days and then wake up furious or sad. If I start writing, it just kind of helps my thoughts sort themselves out. And then I try and set an intention for each day."

"I see." He realized now that as deep as their conversations had gotten over messaging, they could have gotten deeper had they been face-to-face. He chanced another personal question. "I'm curious. What would make you feel guilty?"

Her gaze cut quickly to his, but she didn't look upset or shocked by his question.

"You can tell me to mind my own business if you want."

"Why would I do that? You probably know more about what I've been going through than most people."

Was that true? He still felt like there were parts of her he knew nothing about, which meant she'd been holding a lot inside. This guilt was something she'd never touched on before.

"I feel guilty . . ." She hesitated to go on.

Gripping the wheel, he waited to see if she'd continue. He hadn't necessarily been asking her to bare her soul, but hell, if that's what she felt like doing, whatever. He'd listen if that's what she needed.

"It's complicated. There are different things I feel guilty about. Happiness. Making future plans that he wouldn't have wanted. Like taking the job in Virginia for example. I'd have never done that if Nate was alive. Speaking of which, just being alive makes me feel guilty."

He could see that last one, although it was unrealistic. That helicopter accident was obviously no one's fault.

"For a long time, smiling or laughing made me feel guilty," she said. Jake glanced over quickly to find her staring out her passenger window. "I can vividly recall lying in bed one night last August and realizing I'd gone the entire day without crying. It was the first time since Nate's death. The guilt in that moment was so intense, I ended up crying so hard I could barely breathe."

A quiet moment passed between them, and Jake regretted bringing it up. Obviously since she hadn't mentioned it when it happened, she hadn't wanted to share it with him. He heard her shift in her seat. "I'm just so terrified of forgetting him. That every sign of moving forward is letting too much of him go. Even though I know it's necessary for me to heal and be happy."

Her voice quivered on the last word, and he found himself rearranging his grip on the wheel and using his right hand to reach over and gently squeeze hers where it rested on the center console. Surprisingly, she flipped it over palm up and grabbed him back.

She'd seemed to be doing so well the past few months, and certainly since she'd been home the past week. Maybe that's just what she wanted everyone to believe. He could easily imagine her not wanting to come back home and be a downer for anyone.

"I don't think you'll ever forget him, Alex. You'll always have a piece of him with you," he said quietly, trying to keep his eyes on the road and hoping he was saying the right thing. Before getting to know Alex, he'd had absolutely zero experience with grief on this level. He'd lost several grandparents, and a teammate on his high school baseball team had committed suicide their junior year. But for this, losing the love of your life, he had no point of reference. Absolutely no pain to compare it to because he'd never even been in love with a woman.

"I hope so," she whispered, still holding his hand. "It's a balance though. Wanting to think of him constantly, and hold on . . . but also wishing he would just go away." She glanced over at him. "There's more of that guilt. Because how awful is that?"

"Not awful at all, Alex. I don't know, but I think your feelings are probably pretty normal. Besides, everyone knows you loved Nate, so it's no one's place to judge how you handle this."

"Thank you," she said, squeezing his hand again.

He passed a sign that signaled a rest stop a mile ahead, so he made the decision to give them a moment to get out and get some fresh air. They were still touching when he came upon the exit. There was no way he could maneuver this beast of a vehicle and hitched fifth-wheel with one hand, but just pulling away from her without warning didn't feel right. He lifted their joined hands, quickly leaned down to give her knuckle a quick kiss, and then placed her hand down on the console so he could manage the steering wheel.

Her head turned back to the front when he did it, but she didn't look at him. Hopefully she took that for what it was, a kind gesture. He wasn't trying to come on to her. Far from it.

"We stopping?"

"Yeah. Thought we could stretch our legs and maybe hit the restroom before we navigate the city. That okay?"

"Of course."

After he parked in the RV area, she grabbed her purse, and before he could say anything she took off. He sat there a moment, watching her walk across the parking lot in her denim cutoffs and tank top. Her hair in a low ponytail. Damn, she had amazing legs.

Stop, asshole. He let his head fall back to the headrest and closed his eyes. During those hours of discomfort on the pull-out bed, he'd thought about their dance on the boat deck. She'd smelled so good, like spicy oranges, and she'd absolutely shocked him when she laid her head on his chest. He'd seen the way the women on the boat had watched them, and he knew what they must have been thinking. At least two of the ladies had asked him why he wasn't hanging out with them this time. Hell if he knew. It was partly because Alex was there. But if he was honest, it hadn't appealed to him this time like it had in the past.

But that dance . . . that had been a highlight.

He sat up and moved to open his door when he caught sight of her journal sitting in the passenger seat. Wide open. Instantly his eyes caught sight of his name and he jerked his gaze back to the windshield. She was nowhere to be seen, obviously in the restroom.

Get out of the truck. Do not intrude on her privacy.

Getting out as fast as he could, he locked up the truck and strode across the parking lot to the men's restroom. It was relatively clean for a rest stop, but he still tried not to touch what he could help before washing his hands and stepping back out into the sunlight. It was a beautiful day, and there were plenty of people on the road vacationing. A family at the front of the lot was loading back up into their minivan.

Jake stood outside the building a few minutes to wait for Alex. When she finally exited, she smiled up at him, although it did nothing to hide the fact that she'd been crying. Her eyes were reddened, and her makeup had obviously been touched up a little. God, he wanted to hug her, but he only returned her smile.

"Hey, would you mind if I walked a bit?" she asked. "I just need a couple of minutes. Maybe all that writing in the truck *did* get to me."

"You feel bad?" he asked, brow furrowing.

"Not too bad. I just need a few minutes. By myself."

His eyes widened. "Okay. Sure. I'll just wait in the truck."

She nodded quickly. "Thanks, Jake."

He watched her turn and head down a little path toward a play area with two swings and a slide. With a sigh he made his way through the parking lot and got back into the truck. He tracked the grassy area and located Alex. She'd sat down on one of the swings and was using her feet to gently push herself back and forth.

Picking up his phone he scrolled through the Stag twitter account, replied to a few tweets, and then put together one of his own about how the Stag couldn't wait to be at the Boots and Beer Festival that evening. He'd been in charge of the marketing for the business from the beginning, but he hadn't been prepared for how much it would require him to learn about social media. Turns out it was now a critical part of owning a business, and while he didn't mind too much, sometimes it was a drag staying on top of it. He often wondered if TJ and Dean were aware of how much work he put in on those things.

Glancing sideways, he eyed the journal again. Then Alexis, still sitting on the swing, facing the tree line that ran along the back of the property. Was she okay? He was about to spend nearly two more weeks with this woman who was clearly still struggling with her pain.

More so than he'd first assumed. He wanted to know how to help her, or at least how to be there for her.

He cursed under his breath and leaned to the right to quickly scan the page, because he was a total piece of shit. The top read: *Day 408 Day 2 on tour*

Without touching the book, he ran his gaze down the page until he found his name again. That's all he wanted to see.

I danced with a man yesterday. Jake Cooper. I'm trying so hard not to think about it but I keep remembering how good he smelled and felt. I can't recall the last time we danced, Nate. I tried to dream about dancing with you last night and I couldn't. I woke so angry because I couldn't even see your face in my dreams. Today I intend to feel forgiveness toward myself.

Without thinking, Jake reached over and flipped the book closed, his breath suddenly rapid. He glanced up to see Alex making her way toward the truck. Shit, had she seen him through the windshield? Picking up his phone he opened an app just as her door opened.

"Hey, feel better?" he asked. How had he become so breathless?

"Yeah. Sorry, I just wasn't ready to get back in the truck."

"It's no problem."

After picking up her journal and placing it in her bag on the floor, she pulled herself up into the truck and sat down. As she buckled her seat belt, he decided she must not have thought anything about the journal being closed. She picked up her phone and opened her map.

"We're almost there," she said. "I'm excited. I've never been to Memphis."

"No? It's nice. Too bad we won't have time to go out and see the sights. Today we will be getting checked in and finding our location." He started the truck, the diesel engine roaring to life.

"That's okay. Just being in another city is good with me. And I looked up the Boots and Beer lineup. Do we get a chance to see any of the shows?"

"Sure. There's some downtime, and free entrance is one of the perks of the tour."

She grinned at him. "Nice. I'm excited."

Driving through the rest stop parking lot, he made his way toward the ramp to get back on the highway. He couldn't help noticing that her time alone seemed to lighten her mood. Maybe he needed to be sure to give her plenty of space.

They were about a mile down the road when she shifted in her seat. "Listen, I know I've said it a million times, but I want to thank you for being such a good friend."

He chanced a quick glance in her direction. "You're welcome."

"I hadn't realized how much I'd needed someone who just listened, and you've totally been that for me. Ever since the uncasking last year. You just . . . are present, and I appreciate it. You always make me feel okay with whatever I'm feeling."

"I'm glad. I want you to feel comfortable, Alex."

"I believe you, and it shows. I sometimes feel like I'm still trying to figure out who I am after Nate's death, and I appreciate that I don't feel obligated to be fake around you. I feel like I can be me and not worry about you trying to dig into my head. Like my brother." Her quiet chuckle had him glancing her way. She pulled her ponytail around to the front and held on to it. It was such an innocent gesture.

"Dean loves you like crazy, Alex," he said.

"I know he does, and he's done so much for me, I'll never be able to repay him. But sometimes he can be overbearing, and it's exhausting because he wants to be a fixer, and sometimes I just need to feel what I'm feeling."

"I get it. And I'll try to keep being cool—and if I'm not, you just tell me what you need."

"Thank you." She turned back in her seat to face the front.

He worked his bottom lip with his top teeth, his eyes focusing on the lines that ran down the highway. Damn, right now he felt like such an ass. She trusted him, and he'd sort of betrayed that by peeking at her journal. What had he been hoping to find? That she was crushing on him? Shit, maybe. Was *he* crushing on *her*?

His eyes darted to the right as she slid one of her legs to the side. Her hand settled on her thigh. She didn't paint her nails. Or maybe she just hadn't lately. They were bare and perfectly filed. Neat and perfect. Just like so many things about her.

Yeah, he might have a tiny crush. She was sweet, beautiful, and incredibly smart.

Also vulnerable, hurting, and trying to figure herself out. All good reasons to keep his distance. He needed to get his head on straight and get through the next week and a half as a perfect gentleman. If he needed a reminder, all he had to do was picture Dean's face.

Shit. Yep, that did it.

So no more thinking about touching her. Or that dance. Or how he'd leaned down and kissed her hair. Had she noticed? She hadn't written about it in her journal. Damn, he shouldn't even know that.

Guilt. She was right, it was a horrible feeling.

* * *

The next morning Alex dragged another box of Forkhorn White Whiskey from the bed of the pickup and carried it over to the table they'd set up under the awning that hung off the side of the Stag Wagon. "Is this enough, you think?"

Jake glanced down at the boxes. "Yeah, should be. For today at least." He glanced at his watch. "Gates open in thirty."

"Tell me what to do," she said.

"Maybe grab the window cleaner from below the sink and wipe the outside of the windows down. They get a little dirty on the road."

"On it," she said, making her way toward the RV door.

"There's a step stool in the closet near the fridge," he called.

Stepping inside, she found the cleaner and paper towels, and then retrieved the step stool. Before she went back outside she glanced at the interior of the windows. She knew he'd cleaned everything earlier in the week, but they seemed a little spotty, and another quick wipe couldn't hurt. The RV was an important part of the brand on this tour and the guys had done a good job with its design. It was covered in a full-wrap decal that made it look like it was all wood paneled—like a ski lodge or, even more appropriate, the side of a whiskey barrel. On each side was the logo, a white silhouette of a stag head and of course the name STAG DISTILLING. It also included the standard info like their web address and phone number. She'd noticed it got a lot of glances as they drove down the highway.

With the white awning rolled out of the side above their long tabletop that rested on a row of whiskey barrels, it made an impressive, eye-catching display at events like this one. And Jake definitely had the setup down to a science, but he seemed to be thankful for her help since today was a lot more involved than the cruise yesterday.

She leaned over the bench sofa and gave the window a squirt. As she wiped it clean, she glanced out the window to see Jake chatting with the overly friendly guy they'd met when they pulled into the vendor area of the lot. He was running the Ford dealership booth next to theirs and had come right over and talked to Alex as soon as they began setting up. Even trying to offer her a squishy truck toy, which she'd politely declined. She'd also declined the beer bottle key chain, the pen, and the "test drive." She could only imagine how often he'd used that creepy line on women.

Outside, Jake nodded politely and began to rearrange the perfect row of Stag liquor bottles on display. Alex laughed. He was obviously trying to shake their neighbor. She should go out and save him. Pushing up off the sofa, she made her way to the door just in time to see a long-legged brunette walk up in the tiniest shorts Alex had ever seen and a fancy pair of turquoise cowboy boots. They looked . . . bedazzled.

She froze, her hand on the door handle, as the woman wrapped her arms around Jake's neck and pressed her perky—completely on display—breasts into his chest before laying a kiss on his cheek.

Alex stepped back enough to try and stay out of sight but still watch, her stomach clinching. Even inside she could easily hear their conversation through the screen on the door.

"I wasn't sure if you'd be here, this year," she crooned.

"Yeah, well, here I am," he said. "I thought *you* gave

up this gig. Didn't you transfer to Texas A&M for this year."

Alex could tell by the sound of his voice that he wasn't thrilled to see the woman, but obviously they had a history.

"I did," she said grinning up at him. "But Daddy bought me a ticket to fly in this morning, so I wouldn't miss it. I fly back tomorrow."

"Nice," he said, glancing over his shoulder quickly. Alex dipped farther back into the shadow of the RV. So Boots was in college. This had to be one of his past conquests, considering how comfortable she was touching him. And Alex could hardly blame him, as young and gorgeous as this woman was. "Speaking of your dad, maybe it's best if you're not hanging around here with me."

Alex's ears perked up at that. Was this woman part of the reason he'd argued with TJ and Dean?

"Oh gosh, don't worry about him. He's not going to do anything."

Jake let out a bitter laugh. "Well, according to someone, he's not real happy with me. Which makes me wonder how he may have found anything out about us."

"I didn't know they were going to talk to you about it." The defensiveness in her tone pissed Alex off. "And it's not my fault. The woman in charge of this told him she'd seen me leave here that morning."

Alex let out a quiet gasp. She wished she could see the look on Jake's face, but Boots wasn't finished.

"She's just been jealous of me ever since last year when my father threatened to pull sponsorship if she didn't agree to include backstage passes for me and my friends."

Alex rolled her eyes. *Really?*

"Well, whatever the reason. You should probably go."

"Because of my father? You can't be serious," she said, letting out a bitter laugh. "I'm twenty-five years old. What do you think he's going to do? Have you arrested?"

"Listen, Whitney, let's not make this something it doesn't need to be. Okay? He was pissed, my company got an angry phone call, and so I think we need to heed the warning."

Alex could tell that Jake was trying to keep the conversation private. But he had to know she could hear him, and hadn't she tagged along partly to save him from this kind of drama?

"But we're both here, I'm free tonight, and we had so much fun last year. We'll just be careful, and he won't find out."

That was it. Boots was not taking the hint. Steeling her shoulders, Alex grabbed her step stool and pushed open the RV door. Instantly Jake turned in her direction, an uncomfortable look on his face.

The first thing Alex noticed was that Ford guy had walked back to his own booth, but his eyes were all over the massive amount of skin and turquoise leather on display. At least now maybe he'd start offering his swag to someone else.

"Alex," Jake said, stepping away from Boots. "This is Whitney Ross. She works over at the Ross Boots booth." He nodded at the massive booth at the end of the vendor area. It sat under a giant banner that read BOOTS AND BEER FESTIVAL, and off to the side was a big inflatable cowboy boot. Alex noticed that Whitney wasn't the only scantily clad lady working there. Nice.

"Of course." Alex stepped forward and put out her hand to Whitney. "That explains your boots. Cute."

Whitney's lips were slightly parted in shock at Alex's arrival, but like a pro, she pulled herself together and pasted on a smile before taking Alex's hand. "It's so nice to meet you."

Now that Alex could take in all of the young woman, she noticed she wore a tight-as-hell navy tank top that stretched the words Ross, and then below it, Boots, across her chest. In fact, at first glance at the stretched and distorted letters, it looked like her boobs were labeled "boobs." Great marketing.

"Good idea to bring a helper," Whitney said to Jake with a smile. "We are always so exhausted by the end of this weekend. Of course . . . I guess it's not all because of work."

Even after eight years in the United States Army, multiple deployments, and several combat situations, Alex did not consider herself a violent person. Not even a little. But the smug look on Whitney's face suddenly made her want to knock her in the head with one of those ridiculous boots. Especially since Jake had just mentioned his concern with them interacting. It was like she didn't even care, probably because she was used to flitting her way through life by batting her eyelashes.

"Aw, I bet you two usually have fun," Alex heard herself saying. "It's too bad we have plans with your . . . mother tonight." She smiled at Jake. *What was she doing?* She wasn't even good at this, and the smirk on his face said he was thinking the same thing. But to her surprise, he went all in with her, turning to a confused-looking Whitney.

"Yeah, Alex's right, tonight we have plans. My mom happens to also be in town for a purse convention." The words slid easily from his tongue. Wow. Alex bit her lip, desperately trying to conceal her amusement.

"A purse convention," Whitney repeated dryly. Nothing got by this one.

Jake shrugged. "Lot going on in Memphis this weekend. We've got late dinner reservations and I have no idea when we'll be back. But, sure was good to see you again."

Her furrowed brow had "fuck off" written all over it, and suddenly Alex felt bad. It was none of her business if these two wanted to hook up again, and it wasn't right of her to encourage him to blatantly blow off a woman he'd clearly given his time—and other things—to the last time he was here.

What was wrong with her?

"Actually, if you want, uh, I can just have dinner with your mother alone," she said, backtracking. Jake's eyes went wide. Shit, she was making a mess of this.

Whitney looked back and forth between the two of them and then put up a hand. "You know what, I'm out. You two have fun tonight." She walked away, her ass looking too good to be true in those panty-sized denim shorts.

"Oh my God, I'm so sorry," Alex said immediately as Jake stepped toward her, his eyes narrowed. He kept coming closer. Was he that pissed? "I should have kept my mouth shut. I don't know why—"

He reached up, palmed the back of her head, pulled her toward him and pressed a quick kiss on her forehead. "You're fine, Alex. Don't apologize."

"I couldn't help overhearing what she said about that Amanda woman. I could kind of understand her wanting to piss off Spoiled Boots, but doesn't make sense why she'd want to call *you* out."

He shrugged. "I have some ideas, but it doesn't matter. Thanks for the save, by the way."

She grinned. "That's what I came for, isn't it?"

Seven

"Well, it's eight," Jake asked as he carried the last box back into the RV. They'd stopped passing out samples at seven when the main act took the stage and were now completely broken down until they had to set it all back up for day two in the morning. "What time did you and my mom make our dinner reservations for?"

Standing at the fridge, Alex glared at him playfully. "She was just going to give us a call when she left the purse convention."

He laughed. It was fun teasing her, although they'd been so busy today he hadn't had much time to give her shit for what had happened earlier. But there was no denying it, she'd been a tiny bit jealous. If there was one thing he'd been witness to in his life, it was jealous women. It was still hard to believe that was what he'd seen in Alex's eyes, but the minute she'd come out of the RV and taken in Whitney—and he understood, there was a lot to take in—he saw it come over her face. Maybe it was just a woman jealous of another, in general. Whitney was bold, and she put off a bit of an arrogant vibe, so it was possible her presence had just rubbed Alex the wrong way and it had absolutely nothing to do with him. But he kind of liked the idea that it might have.

One thing that had been bothering him all afternoon, though, was the idea that she must think he screwed every woman he came in contact with. It was far from true. Yes, he'd been a bachelor his entire adult life, and sure he took advantage of that. More than the average man? It was hard to say. He didn't feel like he did. And he also wasn't an asshole. He always treated every woman with the utmost respect. Never left their bed in the middle of the night or asked them to leave his. Plus, he'd really cooled it over the past year or so. Meaningless flings didn't hold the same appeal they did in the past.

He watched Alex walk back toward the bedroom with a bottle of water in her hand. They hadn't really discussed what they'd do this evening, so he followed her back and knocked on the wall as he stood in the doorway.

She had sat down on the side of the mattress, but now looked at him. "Hey," she said in response to his presence.

"Hey. I was just thinking, just because my mom's not really here doesn't mean we can't go out to dinner. I'm starving, and I'm sure you are too. Or we could go see part of the show."

She considered that. "I'd considered going to watch, but honestly I'm not a big country music fan. But dinner would be good. What are you in the mood for?"

"I'm easy. You pick."

"Okay," she said before giving him a mischievous grin. "How about Pho?"

He cringed. "Pick again."

She laughed. "How about Italian?"

Tilting his head, he narrowed his eyes. "You just spent a year in Italy. I don't think there's anything here that will compare."

"Of course not. But as crazy as it sounds, I've been craving an Olive Garden salad. Right now I could probably eat one all by myself." She motioned toward him. "Unless it's not Italian enough for you?"

"SpaghettiOs are Italian in my world. Want to find the nearest one on your phone?" he asked, leaning on the doorframe. He watched as she pulled out her device and began to type. She twisted her lips to the side, something he noticed she did when she was concentrating.

It had been really nice having her there with him today, and surprisingly, he'd noticed that more women seemed to come up to try samples with Alex there. Maybe it was more comfortable for some women to approach another woman, or maybe having two of them made things run more smoothly, which made the booth appear less crowded so more people were likely to approach. Who knew, but it had been a good day.

At one point in the afternoon he'd caught sight of Amanda Frye driving by their booth in her golf cart. He'd almost pretended not to notice her, but then decided to lift his hand in a wave. She'd turned away, pretending not to see him.

Her sly drive by, and the fact that he now knew that her phone call had most likely been prompted by jealousy, made him feel only slightly better. But the fact of the matter was, her call could have been legitimate, and he knew it. And wasn't proud of it. Whitney's visit in front of Alex was a harsh reminder that maybe his carousing had gotten a little out of hand in the past.

"Listen, I just want you to know," he started. Alex's fingers paused and she glanced up at him. "What happened today, that's not going to be how it is on every stop."

"You mean there aren't Whitneys in every town?"

"Absolutely not. In fact, I haven't even been with a woman in months."

Her eyes went wide before she let out an awkward chuckle. "You don't owe me any explanations, Jake. I hope I didn't make you feel that way."

"No, I'm sorry, I . . ." What the hell was he doing? Why had he offered up that bit of information, acting like she was concerned about his sex life? "Forget I said that. I guess I'm just feeling a little defensive after what's happened this past week."

She let her hands drop down to the bed. "Don't. Please. You're a good guy, I know that, and I shouldn't have butted in today. I'm not even sure why I did. I saw her out the window and . . . you . . ."

Alex swallowed. She wasn't looking at him anymore, rather gazing out the small bedroom window at the sun setting over the trees.

"Were you a little jealous?" he asked quietly.

She let out a hard breath, as if his words had pulled the air from her lungs. Her eyes met his and held for a long silent moment until she finally spoke quietly. "Yes."

The instant look of shame as she dropped her head down in embarrassment made him regret being so forward. He wasn't even sure why he'd asked. Maybe because he wanted them both to feel like they could be honest with each other.

"That sounds so stupid," she said, her eyes getting a little glassy. "I kept telling myself it wasn't jealousy though. But it was a little bit. You're right. I mean, when she made that blatant innuendo, not even knowing who I was, I guess it irked me a little. That's all."

"I get that," he said, surprised about how worked up she'd gotten there for a second. "For all she knew, we were a couple."

"Right? She had no idea. I just thought it was kind of rude. That was it. I mean, yeah. That was all it was. Like, what . . . there was no way you would be here with *me?* Anyway . . ."

She shook her head and let out a forced laugh as she went back to her phone. She was pulling back on her admission, but he wasn't going to challenge her. He'd already pushed too much and didn't feel great about the outcome. He never wanted her to feel uncomfortable around him.

"Well, I just wanted you to know that it won't happen again. You won't have to deal with my past every damn stop we make."

"You are two for two, you know," she said with a half smile.

He pointed at her playfully. "Hey, I did not hook up with anyone from that boat. Swear. Now let's go get you a giant salad."

"And breadsticks," she called out.

The rest of the evening they were thankfully back to normal, discussing how the day went, talking about the next stop. Alex had a lot of ideas for marketing and the booth setup, and he liked discussing all of it with her. Of course both of them steered clear of any more conversation about what had happened or the jealousy discussion.

But that night when he settled onto the pull-out bed and grabbed the book he'd been reading, he could have sworn he heard her sniffling. *Damn.* It was sort of difficult to hear, considering the concert had just gotten over and the sound of people walking to their cars was like a high school full of drunk people at the end of a school day. Laughing, yelling, singing, and even horns honking. But soon they'd all be gone and it would get fairly quiet again.

He tried to listen again, hating the thought that something he'd done or said may have caused her to be upset. She'd seemed fine at dinner, but one thing he'd learned about Alex was that she could hold her emotions in when she wanted to. Especially if it would protect the feelings of another person. He laid there, debating if he should check on her. They'd discussed a lot of personal things over the past year, but doing so like this might not be as easy for her. Especially if it was because of him, but he couldn't stand the thought of her in there upset.

Reaching up on the window ledge, he grabbed his cell phone and opened the text app. He lay there for a minute debating how he should word this. He didn't want to embarrass her by implying he could hear her, but then again, why else would he bother texting if he couldn't? Taking a risk, he typed out a quick message.

JAKE: You okay?

He didn't hear her phone get a notification, so either she had turned it off or it was on silent. When she didn't reply after a moment, he laid the phone down. As he adjusted himself on the pull-out bed, he heard feet shuffling and looked up to see her standing in the kitchen.

"Hi," she said quietly.

"Hi. I didn't wake you up did I?"

She just shook her head, her eyes a little puffy. Every instinct in his body wanted to get up and hold her, beg her to tell him what was wrong and what he could do to make it better.

"Want to hang out?" he asked, nodding to his bed, praying it didn't come across as creepy or anything inappropriate.

Thankfully she came over and sat down, legs crossed. He rolled over onto his side and rested his head on his hand. She slept in tiny little shorts and a tank top, and for the love of all that was holy, she had no bra on. He forced his eyes on hers. "Talk to me."

She pulled all her hair around to one side of her neck and held onto it. "I've been thinking a lot the past couple of days."

"What about?"

Dropping both of her hands, she sighed and began to pick at the blanket. "Do you think I made the decision to accept the CIA job too quickly?"

His eyebrows went up. This was not at all about what he'd thought. "I don't know, Alex. I don't think that's something anyone but you can answer. Are you having second thoughts?"

"No. Well, maybe, but not because I don't want the job. Because I do."

"Then what's going on?" It was difficult not to touch her as he spoke. Her knee was right there near him, her skin looking soft.

"The last few months in Italy I felt like I'd really turned a corner. I'd been happy. I was reading all these motivational self-help books. I just really thought I finally knew what I was supposed to do."

He nodded. "Yes. You seemed the happiest you'd been all year."

"I was. And I thought coming home would make me even happier."

"It hasn't?"

She let her head fall back and stared at the ceiling,

the long line of her neck creating a direct line down to her chest. With her eyes averted, he took her in, the soft angle of her jaw and throat, the swell of her breast.

"Not entirely," she said.

Her voice brought his eyes back to her face. Finally she looked back down at him. "I sort of feel like I'm having to deal with some of my grief emotions all over again. I thought I'd gotten past imagining doing daily things with Nate, feeling sad, angry. But it's back. My guilt . . . it's worse than ever. And that is what makes me question every decision I'm making."

"Don't you think maybe that's normal? You're back in a comfortable element. Maybe it was easier in Italy because it was all new."

She nodded. "I thought about that. But thoughts of him keep making me doubt myself. The me that was marrying Nate was happy with the idea of coming home and starting a family. Getting normal jobs close to home. But the me that's now on my own wants none of that. I want to explore and be independent, work in a new town, and do an important job. And that makes me feel . . . like I'm being disloyal to his memory. I mean, had I deep down not wanted him all along?"

Jake shook his head and couldn't help himself, he reached out and palmed her knee. "Don't do that to yourself, Alex. The truth is, you're no longer the same person that you were when Nate was alive. And yeah, maybe part of you, deep down, wanted to do something exciting and amazing, most people do. But we know that when we love someone we often have to make sacrifices. That's normal."

She nodded, a tear escaping her eye that she quickly wiped away.

"I think . . ." He carefully considered his words

because he honestly had no idea what he thought or what he was saying. But he wanted to help. "I think you can want more than one thing at any given time. But one thing is just more important in that moment. When Nate was alive, you wanted him more than anything and that was more important. I'm sure there were things he secretly wanted that he couldn't accomplish if he wanted to be your husband."

She laughed out loud at that, wiping at her tears. "God, you're right. He did always talk about being a commercial airline pilot. I never took it that seriously because he'd follow it up with a comment about how that would mean too much time away. But, damn, I bet he would have done it in a heartbeat if he hadn't met me."

"Without a doubt," Jake said. "But he wanted you more."

Her lips quivered. "I'd let him be any kind of pilot he wanted if I could have him back. We'd make it work."

"That's the thing about hindsight," he said, squeezing her knee. She laid her hand on his, her thumb looping around his. Had she even noticed she'd done it? "I bet if he could come back, he'd fly right to Virginia for you. But now you have to do what's best for you, and just make him proud."

Another tear slid down her cheek and she sniffled. Jake got up off the bed, grabbed the closest thing he could see—a paper towel—and handed it to her. After she blew her nose, he lifted up the blanket on his bed. He didn't say anything, but she climbed in immediately and snuggled up beside him, her back to his front.

Holy hell.

She angled back and looked at him over her shoulder. "Sorry you had to trade in a hot night with Boots for listening to a crying widow."

He rubbed her shoulder. "Aw, Alex, I'd rather be here for you than get laid anytime."

She laughed, which was what he'd hoped for, but at the same time, he realized that he absolutely meant it. At least right now in this moment. "Get some sleep," he said.

Nodding, she positioned herself onto the pillow a little better and he reached for the other one and turned out the light before getting comfortable himself at a reasonable distance.

They lay there a moment in silence before she finally spoke quietly. "I really am grateful for you, Jake. You've been the best friend to me. Thank you for listening."

"Always," he said.

Eight

Day 413 Day 6 on tour
Yesterday was a long day of driving but it was nice to relax after working hard all weekend. We stopped in Jackson, Mississippi, for lunch and had the most amazing burgers. Pretty sure Jake managed to get a new account with the manager. I swear that man could charm a nun. He's so sweet and I'm really lucky to have him as a friend.

It's nice to see and do things that have no memories attached to anyone I've lost. Although Nate had never been to Italy, every sight there had his face on it because I'd cried for him at nearly every turn. I was so ready to be away from the base because it represented so much of our life. Mine and Nate's together. It was our everything. Now, everything is new, and belongs only to me, which is both good and makes me sad sometimes. It's fun to do this with Jake, though. I love that I can share my thoughts with him and not worry about hurting his feelings. I couldn't do that with Nate. In some ways, Jake knows more about my dreams than Nate ever did. Is that weird?

Anyway, this trip was a good idea. Even the drive is relaxing. Listening to music, talking about any random subject that comes up. Jake doesn't even mind when I play folk music.

Today we're in New Orleans and I'm so excited. I've never been. I don't know if Nate had ever been there, but considering he was from Atlanta, there's a good chance he had. We never discussed it. I'm glad. I don't want to see him there. I need New Orleans to be mine. Today I plan on feeling carefree. Beignets . . . I'm coming for you!

Alex shoved her journal into her bag and glanced around the room, waiting. They'd arrived in New Orleans late the evening before and came straight to the hotel where they'd be attending a liquor convention on Wednesday. As a vendor, they were given a room for two nights at a deep discount, so Jake had allowed her to stay there while he stayed in the RV at a park nearby. She'd offered to share the room with him, but he'd said no. It had been weird and a little lonely after sleeping in the RV for several nights.

A knock came at the hotel room door. They'd agreed that he'd come up this morning and use the shower, which had been great after the tiny RV shower they'd been using. She'd already been up, gone for a gorgeous run through Woldenberg Park, all the way to Jackson Square and back, and was now showered and ready.

She opened the door to find him standing there, hair mussed adorably, holding a backpack over his shoulder.

"Good morning," she said.

"Morning," he answered in a raspy voice as he looked her up and down. "You ever sleep in?"

"Can't. I'm just so used to getting up early. Army problems. Plus, once I'm awake my mind starts working and there's no drifting back to sleep." She stepped out of the way so he could come in.

"Let me guess. You've already run through every street in town."

She rolled her eyes playfully. "Only half."

"You sleep okay in here?" he asked, looking around.

"Honestly? I like the RV bed better."

"I'm not surprised. It's a pretty good bed. I love it."

She frowned. "I'm sorry. We should switch it up from now on. It's not fair that you've been sleeping on the pull-out." She didn't mention that they'd slept there together the other night.

"I didn't last night," he said with a wink.

"Well, still. I had it four nights." She quickly tried to think about what she'd left in that bedroom. Hadn't her bra been strewn over the little closet door? She said a silent prayer that nothing more embarrassing than that had been left out.

"You're good, Alex. Promise. I don't mind sleeping on the pull-out." She watched him head for the bathroom. "I'll try to hurry, but I'll admit, I've been dreaming about a long hot shower." The grin he sent her over his shoulder made her stomach clench.

"Take your time," she said.

Standing in the middle of the room, she looked around. What now. Slowly she walked toward the bathroom and spoke through the door. "Hey, uh, want me to go find some breakfast nearby?"

"I was thinking maybe we could find those beignets you mentioned yesterday. If you want to."

She sucked in a breath as she heard clothing hit the floor with a *whoosh*. Was he completely naked? "Okay. Sure. Yeah, that sounds good. I'm excited."

I'm excited?

His chuckle filtered through the door. "I'm excited, too." *Oh jeez.*

She quickly rushed back to the bed, her heart pounding. Here she was, a grown woman, freaking out about a naked man on the other side of the wall. She'd seen men in many states of dress throughout her years in the Army. But now she was here. With Jake. Single.

And attracted to him. Yes, it was official. She found him incredibly attractive. There was no more ignoring that fact that had been niggling at her mind. He was insanely handsome. Sweet. Charming. A good listener. Sexy.

Shit. He was so, so sexy. With that little swoop in his hair, the crinkles near his eyes. Even the large masculine bones in his wrists had caught her eye more than once.

She closed her eyes and blew out a breath as the shower came on in the bathroom. "It's okay. It's okay. It's going to be okay," she whispered.

Picking up her phone she glanced at the time. Nine. Were they in a different time zone? She thought about it for a minute. No. She opened her calling app and found Charlotte's number.

"Good morning," Charlotte answered.

"Hey, how are you?"

"I'm good."

"Just good? You having fun?"

"Yeah, actually it's been more fun than I expected." She gave Charlotte a very quick overview of the past five days.

"I'm so glad you went. Sounds way better than editing photos. By the way, Fernie says hi."

"Oh, I miss him."

"He misses you, don't you Fernando?" Charlotte crooned, obviously nuzzling her dog. "So what are you doing right now? Where's Jake?"

"He's, uh, in the shower."

"Oooh," Charlotte said and then laughed. "So besides the fun stuff you've been doing, how has it been hanging out with him?"

"It's been good. After talking so much over the past year through messages, it's fun to hang out. And surprisingly, he's just as good of a listener in person. We've had a lot of fun together."

Alex's comments were met with a long silence. Finally Charlotte spoke. "Alexis?" she said quietly.

"Yeah?"

"Is it possible that you could be into Jake?"

She considered the question a moment, because wasn't that what she'd just been thinking about?

"You are, aren't you?" Charlotte whispered. "You were thinking about it."

"Oh my God, I don't know," Alex whispered back. "I'm definitely not into him in a relationship sort of way. Not a chance I'm interested in anything like that."

"That's fair. But that's obviously not the only option."

The thought terrified Alex.

"Has anything happened?"

"No! Certainly not," Alex said. Then again, there had been the dance, and the sleeping in the same bed. And that kiss on the head. But all of that could be considered innocent. Right? Friend stuff. Maybe.

"Do you want it to?" Charlotte asked.

"I'm not sure," Alex said, going for honest.

Charlotte let out a little squeal on the other line. "I'm sorry. Ignore me, I just find this a little exciting."

Alex laughed. "Why?"

"Because you deserve it. And let's be honest, Jake is kind of hot. Right?"

Alex squeezed her eyes shut. For the past year, his

looks had been a nonissue. He'd been the caring ear on the other end of a screen. But now, in person, watching his eyes as he listened, and feeling the warmth of his body as he held her . . . "Yes. He is," she said. "But admitting that out loud sort of makes me want to throw up."

"Oh sweetie," Charlotte said. "Don't feel that way. Listen. There was no way in hell you were going to go the rest of your life not being attracted to another man. It's normal, and it has nothing to do with how you felt about Nate. You understand that, right?"

Alex nodded, realizing how much she'd needed someone to remind her of that. "You're right. Of course, I'd have to be attracted to a total playboy."

Charlotte laughed. "True, but maybe that's for the best. You know?"

"How so?"

"Well, it can just be for fun. Maybe you need a fling to ease yourself back in. What better way than to do it with someone safe."

"What if he's not into me?"

"Only one way to find out, but I don't think it will be a problem."

"Do not repeat this conversation to my brother," Alex said, listening to make sure the shower was still going. It was.

"Alex, trust me. As long as you're not in any harm, it is never my place to share your business—especially in regards to your sex life—with your brother. You have my word."

"Thank you. This conversation makes me feel better and worse at the same time."

"Oh no, don't feel that way. Don't stress it. But if the

moment presents itself, you know, let it happen. Follow your instincts."

"My instincts are out of practice."

Charlotte laughed. "They'll come back. I promise. And no matter what, remember—Jake is a good guy."

"He is. You're right."

"So right now, focus on what makes you feel good. You deserve it, Alex."

"I agree somewhat, but then it feels selfish, to even consider it."

"Sometimes selfishness is necessary. Especially when it doesn't affect anyone else. That's called self-*care*."

Alexis smiled, picking at the bedsheet. "I'll think about it. Thanks for listening."

"Hey." Charlotte stopped her. "One thing, though. I adore Jake, but don't do this if you're going to fall for him. I don't want him to hurt you. Even by accident."

"I know better than that. I've got too many plans to think about that," Alex said. "Love you, Charlotte."

She wasn't sure what Charlotte would say to that because they'd never spoken those words to each other. But it was true.

"Love you too, Alex. Call me again if you need to talk."

When they got off the phone, she heard the shower turn off. Alex flopped back on the bed. What would it be like to touch Jake? To have him touch her? God, she wanted to know. Was she crazy for even considering it? What if he didn't see her that way. Yeah, they'd had a few tense moments. Occasionally she'd look up and find him watching her, but maybe she was imagining it. He may very well laugh at the idea.

Just then the bathroom door opened, letting out a furl

of steam. Through the mist came a half-naked man, only a towel around his waist to cover his body. She'd seen his chest before, but damn. The only difference was this time it was beet red.

"Shit," he said, grinning. "I think that's the hottest shower I've ever taken. I might have overdone it."

"You know a shower that hot is actually not good for you."

He shrugged. "If it makes you feel good, how bad can it be?"

Funny, she'd just been thinking the same thought.

There was no better way to spend an evening on Bourbon Street than in an open-air jazz bar, enjoying the carefree vibe and the buzz of people as they walked past on the street. Jake had the added bonus of watching Alex dance with an elderly black man on the dance floor. Five minutes earlier, he'd been killing it on the piano, and then he'd come over and asked her to dance in the smoothest southern drawl Jake had ever heard.

Alex's head flew back with laughter as she and her partner moved around the dance floor and Jake couldn't help grinning as he took in the sight. Today she'd worn a gray tank top with a black skirt. The kind that had a tight band around her waist but then flared out with lots of pleats. Every time she spun around in her black sandals, it showed off her thighs. Almost indecently, and yeah, he'd looked.

Her dance partner, who called himself Mr. Stan, had weather-worn skin and a puff of white hair haloing his head. It was comical to watch him trying to teach her the steps—what dance it was, Jake had no idea. Something that seemed too fast for a little old man in suspenders to be able to do, but hell if he wasn't pulling it off with the grace of someone half his age.

Alex, not so much, but it was amazing watching her try. Jake guessed the two-foot-tall hurricane daiquiri she'd been sipping for the past hour probably hadn't helped, but the happiness on her face was worth it. And she was safe here with him watching over her. Yeah, he'd sent a couple of leering guys warning looks, and so far that seemed to do the trick.

The jazz band ended the song with a dramatic flourish, and Alex clapped and cheered before making her way back to the table.

"That was impressive," Jake said.

"Oh my God, I can barely breathe!" She held a hand to her chest. "And I thought I was in shape. Did you see that guy?"

"I almost couldn't see his feet moving he was so fast."

"No kidding, I think he could have gone all night. And I had no idea what I was doing."

"Looked like you were having fun, though."

"I was." She smiled right up at him, and that was when he realized how close she'd sat next to him. "And to think, when he asked me, I almost said no."

"Oh yeah? Could have fooled me. You jumped right up."

She took another sip of her daiquiri, then turned back to him. "I'm trying to force myself to do things that will make me feel good. Even if they're scary or . . . embarrassing."

He nodded. The band had picked back up, the trumpet carrying the tune rather loudly, so he leaned down closer so she could hear him. "Sounds like a good plan."

"I hope so."

That was an odd thing for her to say, he thought. They sat a while longer, listening to the music and watching couples dance. The bar was busy enough to be entertaining but not so much that it was annoying, considering it was only a Tuesday. Either way, relaxing here was nice since they'd both complained that their feet had hurt after walking through town visiting bars and offering free sample bottles of Stag Signature Bourbon.

But it had been worth it. Jake felt pretty solid about three contacts he'd made today, and one place had served them a free dinner, so that had been a bonus. He'd even let Alex lead on a couple of the stops, and not surprisingly, she was a natural. Tomorrow they had a booth at a liquor convention back at the hotel, and then after that they'd head down the Gulf and stop in bars along the way to Panama City.

He glanced over at her, their chairs side by side, their arms touching. "You want to hang here for a while, or walk around?"

"Let's walk," she said, taking the last sip of her giant drink. "And can you believe I finally finished that?"

He chuckled. "Honestly, no."

When they stepped outside it was full night, although the street was well lit from the bars, shops, and street lamps. The crowd had also thickened. It was a gorgeous August evening, obviously warm because it was Louisiana, but there was the slightest breeze in the air.

"This really makes me miss Europe. This might be as close as I'll get here in the U.S."

"You think?" He asked, looking around. The most interesting place he'd been to was London in high school with his family, but honestly, he hadn't appreciated it as much as he should have.

"Yeah, the buildings, the art, the people walking around. The amazing music. There's so much culture here. You have to admit, this isn't like other cities in the country."

"I'll definitely give you that. It's special."

"Very special," she said, smiling up at him.

As they headed down another street, they came upon what appeared to be a folk band. Three male musicians and a young woman playing a banjo. He glanced over to Alex, and sure enough she was into it, if the smile on her face was any indication. After listening to her music all day yesterday, he knew this was right up her alley.

Apparently, it was a lot of people's jam, because they'd attracted quite a crowd, which had congested the roadway. Plenty of people were still trying to funnel through, though, creating a tight fit.

As they moved closer and bodies crushed into them, Alex reached out and grabbed his hand, grasping his fingers. He held on back, pulling her hand in front of him to keep them close.

"Let's stop a minute, they're so good," she said, leaning up toward him. He nodded, moving in behind her when she positioned herself to get a better view of the singer. She was right, they were talented. Not something he'd play at home or anything, but live, with the fiddle, ukulele, washboard, and banjo, it was really something.

The woman switched to a guitar, and they started another song. This one he recognized as an Indigo Girls song—because he wasn't completely without culture. Alex began to sway gently back and forth in front of him, her ass brushing against his dick.

Great.

Before he could step back, she leaned into him, her shoulder blades pressing into his chest. He took a deep breath. She'd been drinking. Wasn't thinking. He could be cool about this. Had to be. When she began to sway again, he cursed silently. Their left hands were still joined down at their sides, and she obviously had no intention of letting go.

Her backside pressed against him harder, and he wrapped his right arm around her waist to keep them in sync. If she was going to sway, he needed to sway also to lessen the friction on his nether regions. If not, he'd be stiff as hell in no time.

She didn't miss a beat when he pulled her in with his hand, wrapping their clasped hands around the front also. Her swaying intensified, obviously thinking he was getting into it.

Goddamn.

There were worse ways to avoid an erection than dancing with a beautiful woman. Suddenly she pulled away and lifted their hands, spinning in a circle to face him. She was beaming, her eyes lit up by the lights of Royal Street. Wrapping her hands around his neck, she continued to move her body to and fro.

"This is the best song!" she yelled over the music.

There was no fighting the grin that spread across his face. She was absolutely stunning right now, so full of life and absolute contentment, it was contagious.

"Closer I am to fine," she sang dramatically, dropping her head back, because she knew he wouldn't let her go. And he didn't.

Nine

Alex felt like she was floating, leaning back, Jake holding her tight. She knew she could lean back like this forever, just letting the perfection of the moment carry her away. One of her favorite songs, a beautiful city, lovely people, and a strong, handsome man pressed against her.

She lifted her head and stood upright, once again letting the melody carry her, her body swaying. Every word of this song was as if it was dragged out of her soul. She leaned into Jake and rested her head against his chest, just how she did that evening on the boat. It felt warm and safe, his scent enveloping her. This city, with its sights, sounds, tastes, and diverse and interesting people, was like magic, and she never wanted the moment to end.

They continued to move their bodies against each other until the band ended the song with a dramatic guitar strum and the crowd around them clapped loudly, a few whistles filling the air.

Looking up, Alex found Jake staring down at her, his lips quirked. That was all she needed to see to know exactly what would make this moment better. Her hand slipped up the back of his neck until her fingers touched his hair. She pulled gently on his head at the same time she went up on her toes, until her lips were barely pressed into his.

She froze, their lips touching. He didn't move. Not a breath. Lowering her feet slowly, she met his eyes, which were wide and wary. He swallowed.

"Alex," he said. Although she could barely hear his words with the noise surrounding them, she'd felt the rumble of his speech in his chest, which was pressed against her breasts.

Oh God, she'd made a horrible mistake. Misread this entire situation, because obviously he hadn't wanted that at all.

She parted her lips the slightest bit, trying to think of how to apologize, her face on fire. But before she could take a breath, his lips were back on hers, but for real this time, kissing her firmly. Her entire body sighed with relief as she pressed her lips onto his. Her arms tightened around his neck as he angled his head and took her mouth again.

He continued with gentle nips and soft presses, and not once did he try and take it too deep, only small swipes of his tongue against her bottom lip as he tugged at it ever so gently.

She could die from the pleasure of it. The gentleness of his touch and the ecstasy of having his hands travel up her back, lock onto each side of her face, and tilt her to his preference as he tasted every inch of her mouth.

When his tongue finally dipped past her lips, she tasted strawberry daiquiri all over again, mixed with bourbon and vanilla. It was the sweetest thing she'd ever tasted. Right here in the middle of the street, surrounded by people and serenaded by beautiful music.

When they finally each took a breath and locked

eyes, she giggled, suddenly shocked with what had just happened. Pulling an arm from around his neck, she touched her lips lightly.

Jake didn't take his gaze off her, but he didn't look nearly as enraptured as she felt. More . . . nervous.

Before she could figure out the right thing to say to make this less awkward, he took her hand and led her off the street and onto the sidewalk. When a car drove by she realized why.

The folk band had stopped with that last song, and although plenty of people still mingled and passed by, there was an eerie silence compared to the joyful melody that had filled her heart with lightness a few moments ago. The fruity drink filling her gut began to turn on her.

"Thank you for that," she said, tucking her hair behind her ear.

His eyes went wide. "*Thank you*?"

"For that kiss."

He let out a surprised chuckle. "You're welcome, although I can assure you I got something out of that too." A quick shake of his head, and his expression went serious. "Was that a mistake? Please . . . I don't want that to be a mistake."

"No, it wasn't a mistake. And if it was, it's my fault. I did it. You were just gentleman enough to make me feel wanted in return."

"Alex, there was nothing gentlemanly about me kissing you. I wanted it. I want it again. The only thing that has me pumping the breaks on this is . . . that it's *you*. And you've been through—"

Her hand shot out and shook rapidly. "Stop! Stop, stop, stop, stop. Don't even go there right now." The last thing she wanted was thoughts of Nate floating around this moment. Then he would be latched on to this memory. A memory where she didn't want him.

"Shit," she said, turning around. *Too late.* She started to walk.

"Alex, wait," he said, following her.

"I'd really like to go back to the room." She kept walking, picking up her pace.

"Okay, fine, but can you just look at me for a minute?" He grabbed her arm and she turned. Jake's shoulders slumped. "I'm sorry, okay?"

"What are you sorry for?"

His hands went out in frustration. "Kissing you."

Her head tilted to the side. "I don't want you to be sorry. *I'm* not sorry. I just don't know how to do this."

"I don't either."

That wasn't true. It was no secret that Jake was well versed in the art of sexual encounters, so the real truth was that he just didn't know how to do this with her. Maybe that's what he'd meant, and she was just being overly sensitive. Silly of her considering she'd started this.

They stared at each other for a moment. The area of the street they were on was not as well lit, which she preferred right now because she could feel the tears threatening. Why, she wasn't even sure. She didn't feel sad, necessarily. Maybe overwhelmed. Frustrated.

"Let's just go back, okay? I'm tired. It's been a long day."

He sighed. "Okay."

The five-minute walk back to the convention hotel was made in near silence between the two of them, which was thankfully made less awkward by the ruckus of the French Quarter buzzing around them.

When they arrived at the front doors, she turned and

faced him. "So, tradeshow tomorrow? What time do we start?"

His face couldn't hide the fact that he was frustrated by her back-to-business demeanor. Too bad—it was what she needed, and thankfully he obliged her. "They're doing breakfast for the attendees from seven to nine, and we're included. Want to eat about eight thirty?"

"Sure. You still plan to come up and shower?"

"Actually, I'll just shower real quick in the RV. No big deal. I'll meet you in the lobby about twenty after."

"Okay. That's fine." He was avoiding being in the room with her, she knew that, because showering in the RV wasn't great.

"Good night, Jake."

"Good night, Alex."

She could feel him standing there watching her as she entered the hotel, and she rushed through the lobby to catch the closing elevator door, wanting to be alone as soon as possible. The moment she was inside, and the doors sealed, she pushed the button for floor eighteen, leaned against the mirrored wall, and let her head fall back.

What had she done?

I kissed Jake Cooper.

She wasn't going to let the past ten minutes of awkwardness ruin what had been an amazing kiss. She didn't feel bad or guilty. Despite her confusion over it all, she felt . . . alive. Excited. Aroused. The slight smile on her lips at that thought began to quiver. It was just adrenaline coming down to a simmer, that was all. She wasn't sad. Wasn't guilty. She'd done nothing wrong.

In fact, she wished she'd done more. Why had she shut him out so quickly?

When the elevator opened on her floor, she rushed to her room and opened the door. The air-conditioning was on full blast, sending goose bumps across her skin. She walked into the bathroom, flipped on the light, and took in her appearance. Turning side to side, she realized she looked exactly the same. She touched her lips, staring at them. Pressing on them. Same lips. Her hair was weary of the day, hanging limply around her face. But it was the same hair. Everything about her was the same.

But somehow, she felt like a new woman.

Jake began the walk to the RV park. It was only four blocks away, and right now he appreciated the time to clear his head.

Six days ago, outside the Stag after Alex had gotten inside the truck and buckled up, Jake had looked his friend and business partner in the eye and told him he would take care of his little sister. "Don't you dare put a finger on my sister" had never been spoken, but there was no doubt that Dean had been thinking the words. If he had said them aloud, Jake would have been offended, because at the time, it would have been ridiculous to imagine. Not because he didn't find Alexis attractive. She was insanely beautiful. But more because he'd known that she was fresh off a painful loss. They were friends—that was all.

So what the hell had he been doing kissing her?

Enjoying it, that was for damn sure. But more than that, it had felt natural. The past six days with her had been some of the most pleasant he'd had in a long time. Her presence, her voice, and their conversations had made him laugh, think, and feel happy. She was a good listener, was incredibly honest and intelligent. All of that, added to her beautiful smile and killer legs, and yeah . . . kissing her had come easily. Especially since she'd done it first. Damn, it had been one of the most amazing shocks of his life.

It was still probably best that they'd gone their separate ways now. He was suddenly grateful that she was staying in the hotel, otherwise, who the hell knows what would have happened. Because there was no denying that he wanted to kiss her again. And more. But he had a feeling that she'd gotten caught up in the moment with that band. She'd been drinking, she was feeling free and happy. It probably had nothing to do with him. Alex was a woman learning to be happy all over again, and as much as he would love to help her with that, he just couldn't.

It would kill him to do anything that might lead to them ending their friendship. Or to her regret. Then again, the thought of her finding another man to get back on the horse with, so to speak, made him livid. If she could wait until she got to Virginia to do that so he didn't have to witness it, he would appreciate it.

Entering the RV park, he was thankful they'd gotten a spot near the entrance. Before going inside, he checked the pickup to make sure everything was still locked up tight, since they still had thousands of dollars in product in the bed. Once he was satisfied, he took out his keys and went inside, locking up behind him.

He flipped on the lights and sighed. Another night alone.

A stupid thought, considering this was his fourth RV trip for the Stag. Kicking off his shoes, he used his foot to push them against the far wall, next to her hot pink flip-flops. He'd never really been lonely before. But in less than a week, he'd become used to having her around. The smell of her lotion, the sound of her laugh as she watched her favorite Instagram stories, her bag of sour watermelon gummies out on the counter. Even just sitting across from her reading—something they'd done almost every evening on the trip—had been nice.

Walking back into the bedroom, he stripped off his shirt, then tossed it into a corner. The small room was dotted with the belongings she hadn't taken into the hotel with her. Hanging on the back of the door was a white cotton bra.

Was he the biggest creep on earth for wanting to touch it? He'd seen plenty of bras in his life, but this one was the ugliest, most utilitarian bra he'd ever seen. His lips quirked at the thought of her wearing it. No nonsense. That was this woman. But in the best way.

Did she own a sexy bra? Something soft like silk or see-through like lace? He inhaled, imagining her in something small and sheer enough that he could see her nipples through it.

A soft knock sounded on the door, and he dropped his hand. "Shit," he muttered, realizing he'd been touching the bra.

Heading back through the RV, he unlocked the door and opened it. "Alex, what the hell?" he asked, his thoughts racing. "Are you okay?"

"Yes, I'm fine." But she didn't walk up the steps. Instead just stood outside on the concrete.

"I can't believe you walked over here. It's late." He realized his words may have come out wrong, too terse, but the thought of her walking the streets of New Orleans alone at night made him crazy.

He knew his reaction had upset her when her eyes went wide and she turned around and began to walk away.

"Alex, stop. I'm sorry."

Catching up to her, she finally turned. "You don't need to apologize. This was stupid."

"No, I was a dick just now. But I was just worried about you. Tell me why you're here."

Her eyes were sparkling from the lamps that lit the entrance of the park. She glanced down at his bare chest, and then his socks, before gazing back at his face.

Finally, she answered. "I don't want to be alone," she said quietly.

His heart nearly gave out. It was hard to know exactly what she meant, but he was pretty sure he had an idea. But she was going to have to make it explicitly clear. And even then, he should say no. He'd just spent the walk back convincing himself that nothing should happen between them. So he should definitely, without hesitation, say no. He'd consider that. Probably.

"What do you mean, Alex?" he asked. "Tell me what you need."

She swallowed, but her gaze never wavered. Jake knew without a doubt he was not the smartest guy. He'd barely passed high school and never ended up getting a degree. Things didn't come easy for him when it came to learning. But for some reason, everything about Alex made sense to him. She was a tough-as-nails woman who had suffered deeply and was trying like hell to gain her confidence back.

"I decided," she said quietly, "that I'd rather sleep in that more comfortable bed."

Stunned a little, his mouth slid into a smirk. But it still wasn't clear enough for him to make a move that he shouldn't be making. "Okay. And so you want me to move back to the pull-out?" He cleared his throat, waiting.

Her chin lifted the slightest bit before she shook her head. "No. I don't want you to do that. I want you . . . with me."

The words had been spoken, and like a boulder crashing from the sky, reality set in. Damn, he wanted this woman. Maybe more than he'd ever wanted anything, and definitely more than he should. But . . . "Your brother will dismember me, Alex. Slowly. With a dull knife."

Her brow furrowed, shoulders stiffening. "My brother has nothing to do with this, and I have no intention of him ever finding out." The look on her face changed a bit. "Is that a no?"

Reaching out, he grabbed her hand. "It should be. But I want you too bad."

She stepped into him, instantly wrapping her small but strong body around his, their lips meeting in a kiss much more forceful than the one earlier and quickly turning much dirtier.

Once he had her mouth good and loose, he pulled back. "Come in."

Following him back to the RV, she kept a hold of his hand. They went inside and as soon as he locked them inside, she was back in his arms, the sound of their wet mouths filling the air. As they kissed, he gently maneuvered her backward, angling her through the kitchen and into the bedroom.

When her calves hit the mattress, she stopped and looked up at him, her breath coming fast. The light in the room was dim, but still bright enough to see her well.

"How do you want this, Alex?" he asked. There was no way of knowing for sure, but he'd be willing to bet money she hadn't slept with anyone since Nate, and he had no idea how she wanted her first time to go. "Fast? Slow? I want to give you what you need."

"Not fast," she said. "But I don't need you to be soft or gentle. What I need is for it to be good. Make it good. Please."

His lips quirked up. "I can do that."

With the sexiest smile he'd ever seen lighting up her face, she got a hold of her tank top and pulled it over her head. The sight he was presented with took his breath away and had him cursing obscenities under his breath as he lifted his hands to the black mesh bra.

"I was trying to imagine what your nipples looked like when you knocked on the door."

The look of shock—and lust—on her face made the words worth it. "You were?"

"Yes I was, and they are even more perfect than I'd imagined."

Her hands came up and covered his, forcing him to cup each breast tighter. The smallest moan came from her lips as he leaned down and kissed right below her temple. "Lay down, Alex."

She did, her gaze never leaving his as she scooted to the top of the bed. He followed, knees dipping into the mattress as he crawled over her. Her chest rose and fell with each breath, and he could see the excitement in her eyes. With a hand on each side of her body holding him up, he watched her. "You stop me at any time this isn't okay."

Nodding, she reached up and ran a hand down his chest and stomach, making him shiver. Her fingers stopped when they hit the top of his jeans.

"Not yet," he said. "Right now, I'm only interested in fulfilling your wish, which was to make this good."

"Good will include you ditching these pants," she said, tugging once more.

With a laugh, he pushed up and made quick work of removing the denim before resuming his position.

"You forgot something." She pointed to his boxer-briefs.

"We'll get there, babe, just let me touch you for a little while."

Ten

Alex sucked in a breath and let her eyelids flutter closed as Jake began to kiss her neck. He was so gentle and so good at this, just like she knew he would be. It felt safe to just tilt her head back and let him have her. As soon as her back bowed, he slipped a hand underneath and had her bra unclasped with a few quick flicks of his fingers.

Yes, he knew what he was doing. His experience was undeniable, but right now, it was what she wanted. A man who knew exactly what her body needed. Because that was what this was, the next step in her letting go, being free. She wanted to feel. And be felt.

"Oh," she gasped as his hot mouth closed over her nipple. Her hands touched each side of his head, holding on as he licked and sucked at her.

"Tell me it feels good," he said as he moved to the other breast.

"It feels *so* good."

He let out a groan as he pulled the other one into his mouth and sucked harder than she was expecting. The noise she made had him lifting his head.

"Too much?" he said with a sly grin.

"No. Don't stop."

It wasn't long before he'd worked her into a near frenzy from her nipples alone. As if he could sense her need to go further, he began to slowly make his way down her ribs and stomach, stopping to kiss every swell and valley until he got to her skirt band.

As she reached to push it down, he grabbed her hand and held it at her side. "Let me," he said. He met her eyes once more. "If that's okay."

She nodded, her chin tucked into her chest so she could watch him. His free hand hooked under her left thigh and then he slid it up behind her knee, gently pushing and parting her legs. Naturally she lifted the other one, shushing her inner voice telling her that she should be self-conscious. Nathan had taught her to love her body by loving it so well. She wouldn't let that lesson go now.

Oh, Nate. Don't hate me.

For a moment she could hear his voice. *"Baby I could never hate you."* She let herself feel him for one painful second and then pushed it away. This was not the time. She wouldn't feel shame or sadness. She was only going to feel good so thoughts of him had to go.

Her skirt slid down, pooling around her waist, and she was grateful she'd taken a moment to freshen up in the hotel room before she headed over here. Because he was right there, his eyes taking her in.

"These are pretty," he said, running a finger along the trim of her lace underwear and back down. On the next pass he let it slip under the elastic, the back of his finger tickling her sensitive skin. She shivered as he slowly pulled the material aside, exposing her just a bit. "This is pretty, too."

She smiled up at the ceiling, trying not to be

embarrassed. How long had it been since someone had explored her so thoroughly? So closely? Maybe never.

"Is it okay if I put my mouth on you, Alexis?" he asked, his finger petting her softly.

"Yes."

He pulled her panties down, dragging them off her and tossing them aside before positioning her exactly how she'd been before. Legs bent back and spread open. She closed her eyes in anticipation, breath bated, legs tense to the point of shaking. The minute a puff of warm air hit her skin, followed quickly by the heat of his mouth, she was lost. After several soft kisses she began to relax, her legs falling open farther, her hands sliding into his hair. She could tell he liked that because his tongue took a long swipe at her in response. When she bucked against his mouth, he groaned, and the firmer she held onto his head the more frantic his ministrations became.

"Show me where you want it, Alex," he said breathlessly, without raising his head. "Here?" His tongue speared into her. "Or here?" Followed by a firm stroke to her clit.

Her hands slid to the back of his head, holding him right where he was as her body undulated, searching for the perfect rhythm. "Yes, there. Both. Just don't stop."

He chuckled quietly and did as she asked, moving from one place to the other fluidly, taking her close and then pulling her back. Finally, he focused on one spot and it wasn't long before she was coming with such intensity she felt tears prickling her eyes. "Holy shit," she whispered. "Oh God." Her head fell back to the mattress as the waves crested and then ebbed.

Taking a deep yet shaky breath, she looked down to find him watching her face. She couldn't quite read his expression, but it didn't recall the look of a man about to get laid.

"Come here," she said.

He did, crawling up her body. When she could tell he was about to lie to the side of her, she stilled him with a hand on his firm chest.

"What are you doing?" she asked. "Stay here."

Sliding her hands around to his butt, she tugged him down on top of her. He allowed it, holding much of his weight off of her by resting on his elbows.

He swiped her hair off her face. "Was that good?" he asked. She realized he meant it as a legit question, and she let out an awkward laugh.

"Weren't you here?" Suddenly it occurred to her. She frowned. "Wait, was that . . . a pity orgasm?"

His eyes narrowed. "Of course not. Why would you say that?"

"Well, because I thought we came in here with the same end goal in mind. Screwing. But I get this weird feeling that you were planning to leave it at that."

His lips pursed, and her heart sank. He ran a thumb over her lip. "Alex, I don't want to rush this. Or have you do anything you regret."

She considered that. Obviously, he was trying to be caring, and at his own peril, because she could feel an amazingly hard erection pressing against her. "Jake, I'm fully capable of deciding when I want to have sex with someone. I chose you. I thought you wanted me too."

"I do," he said intently. "Like crazy. The past day or two it's been on my mind constantly, but I also spent a lot of time telling myself to stay back. Not only are you—and I know you don't like this—but you *are* one of my best friends' sister. A sister who's been through some shit, and I know more than most about what you've been feeling because we've become close. I don't want anything to go wrong with that."

"Then don't let it go wrong. We're just making each other feel good. That's all this is. I'm leaving in a few months, so I'm not looking for a boyfriend, Jake. I don't know if I'll ever be able to do that again. But we can have fun on this trip. I need to remember what pleasure feels like. And I don't just mean my own. I want to give *you* pleasure."

Her heart soared when she felt him press his pelvis into hers in a gentle grind. She definitely wasn't letting him get away with playing the role of upstanding gentleman now.

"When we're back home, everything will be just as it was. Please." At this point she wasn't above begging. She wanted him inside of her so much, it was a physical ache.

"Alex." His whisper was part groan, his eyes settling on her mouth.

She stroked his face, cupping his jaw. "What?"

"Do you have any idea how sexy you are? How hard it is to tell you no?"

"Then tell me yes."

His eyes pinched shut for a moment and then he was on her, his chest smashing her breasts, his mouth devouring her.

"Get these off," she muttered against his mouth, shoving at his underwear.

Doing as she requested, he reached down and fumbled around. When he laid back down on her, she let out a moan at the contact of his length pressing into her. Her hands on his butt, she felt the muscles clench as he rocked against her.

"You're so wet," he whispered, grinding against her folds.

"If you keep that up, I could go again."

His deep chuckle filled her ear as he kissed along her jaw. She reached down to slip her hand in her skirt pocket, grateful he'd asked her to keep it on and making this easy.

"Here," she held the condom she'd purchased in the hotel gift shop near his face.

He grabbed it and pushed up to rest on his knees. Taking his fully nude form in for the first time, she bit at her lower lip. Right now was not the time to compare him to anyone else. She couldn't go there, and she didn't need to. He was perfect, and her body began to hum in anticipation as she watched him roll the condom down, taking note that next time she needed to size up. And there would be a next time if she had anything to say about it.

When he was finished, he gave himself one stroke and then held on, looking at her. "You sure, Alex?"

Inspired, she took the opportunity to scoot up and over. "Very sure. Lay down."

He lifted an eyebrow and then did as she instructed, lying down on his back. "Afraid I was going to try to get away?" he asked. His smile had her doing the same as she lifted a leg and straddled him.

"Maybe. I also just like it like this." Her body was positioned just above him as she took his penis into her hand.

He blew out a hard breath, an intense look of pleasure on his face. "I like it like this too."

Alex pushed every thought floating through her mind out of reach as she slowly lowered her body onto him. She watched his lips part, pecs clench, and then felt his body lift, filling her up. His hands went to her skirt.

"Hold this up," he said, lifting his head.

She filled her arms with her skirt, holding it around her waist. Jake reached back and slapped the pillow harder beneath his neck, propping his head up so his eyes could stay on that spot where they were joined.

"Can you see this?" he asked, as she rose up and then went back down. She couldn't, which wasn't fair. She grabbed hold of her skirt and drew it up over her head before tossing it to the floor.

This left them both naked and joined in the most primal way. After taking a long look at his body entering hers, she let her head lull as she rocked back and forth, hoping for a second release, something she hadn't always been able to find, especially from penetration. But she wanted it right now, more than anything.

The feel of Jake's hands on her waist, guiding her movements, urging her to move faster, harder, had the pleasure building. Dropping forward, she rested her palms on his chest, her body slapping against his. The sound of his muttered encouragement, using the most explicit and naughty language she'd ever heard, should've offended her. Instead it had her insides humming and her pelvis thrusting harder against his.

When it finally broke over her, the release she'd been working toward, she barely registered his deep, "I'm coming, Alex. Keep going, babe."

She rocked her body in a steady rhythm, loving the sound of his deep groan filling the room. When she finally slowed and looked down at him, he was grinning up at her. She let out a shaky sigh and smiled right back.

"Damn, girl," he said. "That was amazing."

"It's been a while," she said, making them both laugh. "Hope I didn't hurt you."

His hands rubbed her thighs slowly as he stared up at her. "Hell no. It was amazing."

"Yeah, it was." Almost too amazing.

Eleven

Two mornings later, Alex woke up to bright sunlight coming in the RV bedroom window. Picking up her phone, she glanced at the time. Nine. *Damn*. So much for running today.

She set the device back down and rolled over to find a naked Jake next to her. They'd had sex for the second night in a row after an exhausting day at the liquor convention. And again, she had absolutely zero regret. In fact, thoughts of all they'd done last night had her blushing, but also wanting to do it all again.

He was adorable in sleep, his mouth parted, quiet puffs of breath escaping his lips. She reached out and traced a fingernail around his nipple, watching his face. His eyes fluttered without opening, but his mouth slid into a lazy smile. Grinning, she made another circle, forcing him to let out a huffy laugh.

"Stop." His hand came up and grabbed hers before yanking her closer. Snuggled against him, her hands tucked in between their bodies and his head resting on hers, she inhaled his scent.

"You running this morning?" he asked. She smiled at the way his chin bumped into her head as he spoke.

"No."

"No? What's gotten into you? Two days in a row," he teased.

"I don't want to move from this spot. Plus, we've been getting a lot of exercise walking and lifting things. I'll get back on schedule when this trip is over."

"Mmm hmm, you're on full vacation mode. Just slumming it, huh?" He gave her butt a playful squeeze.

She loved the sound of his husky morning voice. "Guess so."

An hour later they were up, and Alexis headed to the RV park clubhouse to do her laundry before hitting the road. After getting her load started, she sat down at a table and pulled her journal from her bag.

Day 415 Day 8 on tour
Just realized I skipped yesterday. Reason is because . . .
I slept with someone. I'm sorry Nate. It makes me feel sad because it won't ever be you again, but I don't feel bad for doing it. I know you want me to be normal. And this is normal. So normal.
    I feel

She hesitated, looking around at the brightly lit laundry room. How *did* she feel today?

happy. One more week on the road and then I'll spend a few months in Maple Springs. I don't think I can go back to staying with Dean and Charlotte. I can't continue to be independent living under their roof. It's too much like staying with parents. I think I'll ask Joel if I can hang at his place for a couple of months. He's cool and laid back. In fact, the more I think about it the more it feels like the right thing.
    Today my intention is to feel optimistic.

* * *

Late Friday morning, Jake pulled the truck and RV into a giant field in Atlanta that would soon be home to the 98.9 The Hits Summer Music Fest. He hadn't been to this event before; they'd reached out to the Stag, which had been nice, and he hoped it would go well.

He and Alex had spent the previous day driving along the Gulf Coast and hitting beach bars to promote Stag products. It had been a successful day, and they'd spent an amazing night at an RV park in Tallahassee.

He smiled to himself, thinking about last night. Their third time sleeping together. It was still hard to believe that's what they were doing, but hell if he was going to complain now. These tours had always been enjoyable for him, but this trip with Alex had turned out to be better than he could have imagined. They'd had more fun over the past week than he'd had in who knew how long. And not just because they were now having sex, although that certainly had been good.

As she'd been doing for a week now, Alex jumped out of the truck and helped him maneuver their rig into a good spot alongside two other vendors. When he hopped down from the truck, he saw that one appeared to be a craft brewery from Atlanta, and the other something odd. He'd noticed it when they pulled up, a giant white spaceship-looking thing on the top of an oversized semi flatbed behind the tent they were setting up.

"What do you think that's about?" He nodded toward their neighbor who'd yet to put up a sign revealing who they were and what they were about.

Alex looked over. "Well, I know that's a blade from a wind turbine."

His eyes went wide. "Huh. I can see that now. Shit, it's huge. Wonder what they're doing here."

She shrugged. "I'm sure we'll find out, but I'd assume

promoting wind energy." Her snarky tone caught his attention.

"All right smart ass," he said, making her grin, although he was always a little defensive when it came to things that implied he wasn't as intelligent. When it came to brains, they were probably far from an even match, which didn't bother him too much, but the last thing he wanted was for her to think that he was incapable or . . . stupid.

"Anyway"—he turned away from the turbine and back to her—"we've got three hours until they open the gates. Should be a piece of cake."

She nodded, looking nervous. He frowned. "What's wrong?"

"I uh . . . what time do we start tomorrow?"

He thought about it. Tomorrow was Saturday. "I think the gates open about noon, so we should be set up by eleven thirty for sure. Why?"

"Well. We're in Atlanta. I just . . . I'd like to go visit Nate's grave."

His stomach clenched, mouth pinching shut. How had he not seen this coming? "Of course. God, yeah, why didn't you say something? We'd have left earlier this morning. Or last night."

"I don't need long. Just a little bit of time."

"We'll get you there. I promise. Is it far?"

She shook her head. "About twenty minutes I'd bet. Especially on a Saturday morning with no traffic."

His eyes narrowed as he realized something. "Do you want to go alone?"

"I can. I don't expect you to come."

"How about I drive you—but then I can wait in the car if you'd prefer."

She nodded, smiling. "Okay. I would like you to

drive. I'm not even sure I could handle that big-ass beast of a truck." Stepping forward, she reached up and kissed his cheek. "Thank you."

Suddenly feeling protective and—what else, he couldn't say—just weird, he grabbed her hand and pulled her into his chest. She wrapped her arms around his waist and sighed.

"What's this for?" She asked, her voice muffled against his T-shirt.

Hell, he had no idea. The thought of Nate's grave made him feel odd. Sad and maybe a little jealous. He didn't want to think that could be it, but he was usually pretty honest with himself. He decided to be honest with her. "I just needed to feel you for a minute."

She chuckled and angled her head up to look at him. "You're sweet, Jake."

After a quick kiss, she pulled away and headed to the RV. When he didn't follow, she turned around, hand up to her eye to shield the sun. "You coming?"

Shaking off his wayward thoughts, he smiled. "Yeah. I'm coming. Let's get to work."

Nearly seven hours later, Jake's feelings had gone from confused to all-out jealousy, but it wasn't about her dead fiancé, which had been selfish of him. No, this was about the young dude working the AnderCol Clean Energy Company next to them. He'd now been shooting the breeze with Alex for nearly an hour. Ever since things had slowed down and she'd gone over to ask about the wind turbine.

Jake had been able to tell that the blade interested her, which wasn't that much of a surprise. She was into science and maps and land formations. She'd been worried about him being alone to deal with their stuff, but he'd assured her that he'd done this a million times by himself and that he'd start loading the truck up without her. But hell, if he'd have known it would lead to her chatting with the dude for an hour, he might not have been so convincing.

Normally, he might assert himself, but every time he considered joining them he heard them using words like "cadastral," "hydrography," and "feasibility study." Things he not only didn't understand but, quite honestly, didn't care to. Not that he wanted *her* to know that.

It was the laughing they were doing on and off that was killing him. The way she'd get so excited about what she was saying that she nearly reached out and touched the guy. Jake believed in eliminating fossil fuels as much as the next person, but was clean energy that damn exciting? Or was there more going on here? The guy was good looking, Jake supposed. In a nerdy kind of way. In shape, but kind of thin, with sunglasses and super-short hair. Maybe she was into that.

From the corner of his eye, he saw her shake the man's hand and then glance down at a piece of paper in hers. Jake shut the tailgate of the pickup with a little too much force.

"Thanks so much, Garrett," Alex said before heading toward him. Jake turned, giving her his best this-has-not-bothered-me-at-all smile.

"Look at this," she whispered, holding out a business card. "That guy is the son of Nolan Anderson. One of the owners of this company."

"Sounds like he's rich," Jake said, hating how cold it had come out.

Her eyes narrowed, and she let out an awkward laugh, as if she didn't connect his point with what she was discussing. Yeah, he didn't know his point either, so he headed toward the RV, Alex on his heels.

"Anyway, he wants me to apply for a job."

Jake stopped in his tracks outside the door and turned. "*What*? You already have a job lined up."

"I know, and I told him that. But he still urged me to take this and consider it. If things didn't work out with the CIA."

Jake let out a bitter laugh. "Who quits the CIA to work on a wind farm?"

Her head jerked back. "Wow, really?"

"I'm sorry," he said, shaking his head. "Tell me about the job."

She hesitated, and he hated himself for how he'd just reacted.

"I'm being a dick, Alex. I'm just tired. Please, tell me about it."

"Well, they specialize in wind and solar. Clean energy is a field I'd never really considered getting into, but talking to him, I realized it could be something that really lined up with my values. Way more than oil or coal—and I've been contacted by people in both of those fields."

He hadn't known that. She must really be something in her line of work to be courted not only by private companies but by the government.

She followed him toward the RV, still talking, and he could tell this idea excited her. "What if I end up hating working for the government? All the ridiculousness going on in D.C. right now, and really any politics. Plus, all the bullshit red tape."

"Pretty sure there's going to be plenty of red tape and politics in clean energy," he said. That much he was certain of.

"Well, of course. But you'd be fighting *against* the Man, not for him. Whether politics and old money like it or not, wind and solar are the future."

"You don't have to convince me, Alex. Where's this company located?" he asked, fearful he knew the answer.

"Here. In Atlanta."

He sucked in a breath, lips pursing. "How serious about this are you? You've already accepted the job in Virginia."

"I know." She looked down at the ground. "It's silly, considering it. But it's something to consider for the future."

Jake sighed. "Yes, you're right. And it's true, you might start the job and realize it's not for you. Maybe you'll only do it for a little while, and like you said, wind and solar aren't going anywhere. So put his card in a safe place."

She nodded. "I will." Leaning up, she kissed his cheek. "Thank you. You always encourage me to do what makes me happy. I appreciate it, Jake."

He gave her a small smile. "That's what I want, Alex. For you to be happy."

Twelve

Alex held her breath as Jake drove into the cemetery. She'd been here before, over a year ago, riding in a black limo and holding hands with Nathan's mother, Regina. Numb, still in shock.

Today was different than any other day so far on the trip. Knowing they were visiting, she'd woken up feeling depressed, but it wasn't the same emotion she'd felt a year ago. It had become less about devastation and anger, and more about the loss of what would never be. The sadness of moving on to things that had nothing to do with Nate or the life they'd been planning. The life she'd be living right now if he hadn't been taken from this earth. From her.

"Take a right here, I think," she said to Jake, clutching the red rose she'd picked up at a grocery store nearby. "I remember that big magnolia tree. It's on this side."

She watched out the window as he pulled slowly through the tree-lined road that winded through the cemetery.

"Stop," she said quickly.

He did so, pulling over to the side. They sat there in

silence for a moment, the truck idling. Alex let her eyes scan the rows of gravestones until she thought she saw a few that might be his. It was hard to tell, considering things had looked so different at Nate's service when there'd been so many people. Or maybe it was because she'd been in such a fog that day.

"I can remember the day of his funeral like it just happened," she said.

Jake didn't reply but reached over and squeezed her hand. There was really nothing he could say. She knew this must be somewhat odd for him, but she was glad he was here with her. A strong, calm person. A friend, who let her feel what she needed and, even better, share when it made her feel better.

She looked over at him. "I changed my mind. Will you come with me?"

The look on his face let her know that he hadn't expected the request. "Of course."

Alex watched him get out and round the front of the truck. He made his way up to her door and opened it, something he'd never done before, but hadn't hesitated, as if he knew she needed help every step of the way to get through this.

Grieving a loved one was a funny thing. One moment you felt like the progress you'd made was so significant you might be a new person inside, ready to take on the world. Only to take a fresh breath and once again feel the weight of your pain like it was brand new.

The minute her nose inhaled the scent of that magnolia, she went back to that day, when she'd sat beside a grieving mother crying with so much anguish that she'd almost felt guilty for not doing the same. Was a man's fiancée supposed to be crying like that, she'd wondered. She hadn't wanted to, but the sound of

Regina Williams' pain had made her feel like she was drowning in the kind of sorrow that literally killed someone. It had taken her breath away.

"Give me your hand," Jake said quietly.

Alex looked up and realized she'd just been sitting in the truck in a daze. Jake had his hand out, so she took it and let him help her down. After shutting the door, he allowed her to lead them through the grass, past the blooming magnolia, and down a row that seemed somewhat familiar to her.

Then she saw it. Her breath hitching as she stepped up to the stone and read.

NATHAN OMAR WILLIAMS, BELOVED SON, BROTHER, FIANCÉ, AND STAFF SERGEANT IN THE UNITED STATES AIR FORCE. Below was the Air Force insignia.

Next to her, Jake remained quiet, his hand still loosely intertwined with hers. She let go and kneeled. For a moment she just placed her palm over Nate's name, then carefully slid the rose into the metal vase next to a bouquet of silk red, white, and blue carnations and an American flag that his family had probably put there for the Fourth of July.

When she stood back up, she grabbed Jake's hand once again. They stayed like that for a long time, nearly five minutes. She imagined Nate lying beneath her feet. Could he feel her here? Could she feel him? And why was she thinking such crazy things? Except, no, they weren't crazy.

Over a year had passed. She wasn't the same person anymore. Not better or worse. Different. In fact, she'd been many different versions of Alex over the past thirteen months. Like a Barbie doll. She'd left for Italy as Broken Alex. Traveled through Europe as Looking for Meaning in the Universe Alex. Now she was the most recent version. Trying to Move On Alex. She hoped this version of her was the strongest yet, although she knew there was still a ways to go.

One day at a time.

"Thank you for bringing me here," she said, finally looking up at Jake. His face was solemn, but he nodded, before trying to give her a warm look.

"You want a minute alone?"

She considered it, staring back down at the beautiful gray stone with her Nate's name etched into it. The birthday she always looked forward to and the day of pain so acute that her heart felt as if it was literally going to break into pieces remembering it. She could still recall the phone call she'd made to her brother. For some reason she'd kept herself together until then, but the minute she'd heard Dean's voice from across the ocean—her only person left in the world—it had knocked her right off her feet with the weight of her new reality. She'd sobbed like she'd never sobbed before.

The sound of a car door closing caught both of their attention, and Alex turned to look back at the road. Her heart stopped.

"Oh God," she whispered, dropping Jake's hand. A middle-aged black woman was heading in their direction, giant tortoiseshell sunglasses on her face. Alex bit at her lip as she watched the woman who was always dressed to the nines every time she'd seen her. Today was no different with her pink slacks and white ruffled top. "Regina!"

Walking quickly toward the woman who would have ended up being her mother-in-law in a different life, she put her hands out, a smile on her face.

"What are *you* doing here, Alexis?" Regina asked, tears flooding her words. The moment they were close enough, they embraced. "I couldn't believe my eyes when I saw you."

They gently swayed back and forth. "I should have called you."

"Yes, you should have. What's wrong with you?" Regina said accusingly, but there was no anger in her tone.

Closing her eyes, Alex breathed in deep. Regina smelled like Nate. The lotion he used, which his mother used to send him in care packages because you couldn't find it anywhere but the States. The scent brought tears to her eyes. She hadn't smelled it since.

When they finally pulled back, Alex wiped at her eyes as Regina held onto her arms and looked her up and down. "Don't you look lovely after a year in a beautiful place." Regina glanced over at Jake. "What are you doing in Atlanta, young lady?"

Alex looked over her shoulder. Jake had his head down, eyes up, and hands in his pockets, just waiting quietly. He'd moved a little way down from Nate's grave.

"I'm here for work." Alex took Regina's hand and led her over to where Jake stood. "Regina Williams, this is Jake Cooper. He's one of the owners of my brother's distillery. We're on a promotional tour and we came through Atlanta for the music festival up north."

"It's nice to meet you, Mrs. Williams," Jake put his hand out. She took it. "And I'm so sorry for your loss."

"I appreciate that, Jake, and it's nice to meet you," Regina said in the beautiful, rich, Southern accent that Alex loved so much. Letting go of his hand, she turned to Alex. "You know, I hadn't been here in a couple of weeks. But I woke up this mornin' and the sun was so bright, I went for a drive and something in my soul just told me I needed to visit my baby. I must have felt his happiness from seein' you here."

At her words, Alex's lips began to tremble, and Regina wrapped her arm around her.

"I uh," Jake started. "I'll give you ladies a few minutes." He walked away, heading for the truck.

Alex walked up to the gravestone with Nate's mother. "I'm so glad I saw you here," she said. And she meant it. It had occurred to her all week that she could have contacted Regina earlier, but something had stopped her. This feeling, probably. The feeling of connection to a woman who she'd wanted as a mother and who would now never be that to her. They'd kept up through emails while she was in Italy, but over the year they'd become more and more spaced out. The last one two weeks ago had been brief, just letting her know that she'd returned to the States.

"I'm glad too, although I'm still trying to figure out why you didn't call me. But I'll forgive you," she said, leaning over and placing a kiss on Alex's temple. "So you've decided to work for your brother, have you?"

"This is just temporary. I liked the idea of the travel."

Regina nodded. "You bring that beautiful rose?" she asked.

"I did."

"I know Nate loves it." The older woman looked over at her, but Alex couldn't meet her eyes. Instead she continued to stare at Nathan's name, willing her tears to hold back. "He loved you something fierce. But I know you know that."

Alex smiled, finally glancing at her. "I do. Even though he told me I'd never be as good a cook as you."

Regina burst out laughing. "That's my boy. But you know his plan, don't ya? He was gonna ask you about having y'all spend some time in Atlanta so I could teach you my secrets."

Alex's eyes narrowed. "He was?" She glanced back at the grave. "He never told me that."

"I'm sure he didn't want you to be nervous about learning from the best," Regina teased.

"Maybe." Alex couldn't help thinking that maybe Nate had never told her what he'd wanted in fear of her saying no. She'd been adamant that if they were going to settle down, it should be in Kansas. Why had she been that way? Had he wanted to move back to Atlanta? He'd thrown the idea out there, of course. But he'd never made a big deal about it, always just pretty happy to let her have her way for the most part. Would he have put off starting a family and moved to Virginia if she'd let him know it was important to her? She'd known having children was important to him, and yet, maybe there had been room for compromise. And maybe she was overthinking something that was no longer relevant.

Eventually they made their way back to the truck and Regina's car. Jake was leaning on the driver's side door, facing away from them, but when he heard footsteps he pushed off and waited for them to approach.

"He's awfully handsome," Regina whispered.

Alex just laughed awkwardly, no idea what to say.

"So what day are you leaving? Can you do Sunday supper after church tomorrow?"

"Ohh . . ." Alex glanced at Jake. "I don't know, Regina."

"Is supper, uh, lunch?" Jake said with a small smirk.

"Supper is lunch, yes you're right, son." Regina smiled and put a hand on Jake's arm. "And if you like barbecue chicken on the grill, potato salad, and coconut pie, then you will join us for supper at noon tomorrow."

Alex's mouth parted in shock as Jake grinned at her. "That sounds amazing. I think we can make it. Can't we, Alex?"

"Yes, of course, Regina. I would love to see everyone." At the thought, she suddenly felt very excited. She'd missed them all so much.

"Good." She gave Jake's arm one final pat, leaned over, and wrapped her arms around Alex once again, and then turned and waved at the grave. "Bye baby," she yelled. "I'll see you two tomorrow."

She walked over to her beige sedan, which had to be a decade old but was in pristine condition, and drove away with a wave.

"I'm so sorry about that," Alex said.

"Why are you sorry?" Jake asked. "She's very nice. And I can't, in good conscience, pass up a meal like that. Besides, there was no way you could have told her no."

"You're right." Alex smiled. "You're a good sport. But I know this is weird." Her shoulders sagged.

Jake stepped into her space and grabbed her chin, tilting it up. "Because we're sleeping together?"

"Well, yeah."

"It's not weird, Alex. This is Nate's family. Would have been your family. You're in town. I can be a little bit uncomfortable in order for you to spend some time with them."

"You need to stop being so sweet, Jake," she said.

That boyish smirk returned. "I can't help myself."

"Ha ha, I'm sure." They got in the truck, and she took a deep breath. Why did he have to keep being such a good guy? If he kept it up, he was going to make it really hard to keep this only physical, though that's exactly what she needed it to be. After this trip it would be over, and she'd be able to focus on preparing for her move to Virginia.

The rest of the day was hot and exhausting as they worked the booth at the festival. Luckily they were so busy it flew by. Once they were packed up that evening, they grabbed some fast food and then drove to a nearby RV park so they could hook up to sewer and electric. After they ate, Jake got in the shower, and by the time he got out Alex was asleep on the sofa.

He sat down near her head in only his underwear, and gently brushed her hair off her cheek and behind her ear. She shifted the slightest bit but didn't wake. She was so beautiful, this woman, and had endured so much. He knew her parents had died in a car wreck when she was a young teen, forcing her to have to move in with Dean and his ex-wife. Then to lose her fiancé . . . he couldn't even imagine.

But she remained kind, affectionate, loving. The last two times they'd had sex it had been intense. Nothing like he was used to when sleeping with a woman, where it was all about pleasure and release. This had felt . . . emotional. The night before, she'd sat right here on the floor, knelt between his legs and given him the most earth-shattering blow job he'd ever had, but it wasn't because he'd climaxed. Hell, he'd gotten off a thousand times in his life, but the way she'd looked at him, touched him, said his name.

He was *still* thinking about it.

"Jake," she whispered, adjusting her body. Her hand reached out to find him although her eyes remained shut. "My turn?" she asked.

He grabbed her wandering hand and held it. "Nah, babe. You sleep. You can shower in the morning."

"Mmm. Okay." She tucked in her chin, smacking her lips.

He couldn't help laughing quietly. Standing up, he reached down and scooped her into his arms, and damn, she wasn't light, his small but muscular girl. Especially not while asleep. But he managed to get her into the bedroom—not an easy feat carrying a grown woman in an RV—and laid her down on their bed.

It was going to be difficult to give this up when they were back in Maple Springs, but he would. He'd let her go, because if anyone deserved to be happy and get what she wanted, it was Alex.

Thirteen

The next afternoon Jake pulled the pickup up to a small-ish bungalow-style house about five minutes from the cemetery they'd been to. There were three cars parked out front, lots of kids' toys scattered around the yard, and a heavenly smell coming from the back.

On the way over they'd agreed that they'd stick to the coworkers story, which technically wasn't a lie, even if it didn't tell the entire truth. But the last thing he wanted was to upset Nate's family. Or Alex. Besides, there was no reason to make this something it wasn't, considering their time together was limited.

After asking if she thought it'd be appropriate, Jake had brought along a bottle of Stag Signature Bourbon for Nate's father, Leon. He grabbed it from the back seat and headed around to the front of the truck.

"You look nervous," she said.

"Do I? Well, I am." Why, he wasn't sure. It wasn't as if he necessarily needed to impress these people. Maybe it was more guilt. He felt as if he had a sign plastered on his face—*I'm screwing your dead son's fiancée.*

"Don't be. They're the nicest people, and you've already met Regina."

He nodded and then followed her to the front door. Halfway up the driveway, the door flew open and a girl of about six ran out.

"Aunty Alex!" she called, running down the drive.

"Juju!" Alex wrapped her arms around the small body and hugged her. "I've missed you."

"I've missed you, too."

Alex turned to Jake. "This is June. She's Nate's niece. June, this is my friend, Jake."

"Everyone calls me Juju," she said, her Southern drawl dramatic and adorable.

"Nice to meet you, Juju," Jake said.

"You Alex's new boyfriend?" Juju asked, eyeing him sternly.

Jake's mouth dropped open, but Alex saved him.

"Oh no, Juju. Jake's just my friend."

"Okay." Satisfied, she turned and ran back, beating them inside. "Aunty Alex is here!" She yelled into the depths of the house.

Once inside, they were greeted by a large man who instantly hugged Alex. "How are you, girl?" he asked quietly.

"I'm good," she said warmly. "How are you?"

"Taking it day by day. Sure is good to see you. I couldn't believe it when Regina came home and said she seen ya." He nodded at Jake. "Tell me about your friend."

Before Alex had a chance to respond, the man stepped around her and put out a hand to Jake. "Leon Williams."

"Hello, sir. I'm Jake Cooper. Alex and I work together." After shaking hands, he held up the bourbon. "I brought you a little something. Alex's brother, me, and another guy own a distillery outside of Kansas City. Thought you might enjoy one of our products. "

"You don't say." Leon took the bottle, holding his head back to read the label. "Stag Signature Bourbon."

Just then a female voice that sounded like Regina's called out. "Leon, why aren't you checkin' this grill? It's ready for the chicken."

Leon gave Jake a sly grin and held up the bourbon. "Don't mind if I do. Care to join me out back?"

Jake chuckled. "Happy to." He turned to Alex, who just smiled and nodded. Outside he was introduced to Stephen, Nathan's older brother and Juju's father, and Leon Sr., his grandfather. Apparently, a visit from Alex was worthy of getting the entire family together, which he understood. They hadn't seen her since the funeral.

While Leon put the chicken on the grill, Stephen went in and grabbed some glasses. It wasn't long until they were all toasting with the bourbon.

"To Nathan. God rest his soul," Leon Sr. said, raising his glass.

"To Alex," Stephen said.

"To you all, for having me over," Jake said awkwardly.

Leon gave him a quick, fatherly wink. "And to you, son, for bringing the liquor."

With that, they all drank.

Alex watched the men toast outside the kitchen window. Things seemed to be going well, and surprisingly, it didn't feel weird. Well, not too weird. She was here, in her late fiancé's house with another man. While they weren't technically here as a couple, it still kind of felt like they were.

"They better not get lit out there," Tiana, Stephen's wife said, looking over Alex's shoulder. "He's supposed to have bath duty tonight." She turned and looked at the eight-month-old sitting in the high chair. "Isn't he, sweet girl? Daddy gonna give you a bath?" she crooned.

Alex turned and smiled at the baby. "She's so beautiful, Tiana. I can't believe how big she is."

"I know, she's huge. Last time I saw you, *I* was huge."

"You were pregnant, and beautiful," Alex said, although she could barely remember Tiana being pregnant at Nate's funeral. Nothing else had mattered then.

"Girl, please. I gained forty pounds with that little stinker. She had me craving anything fried and covered in cheese."

Her husband had walked in behind her just as she said that and slapped her playfully on the butt. "Don't you dare blame Camille. You still craving anything fried and covered in cheese."

"You better hush," Tiana said. Alex watched as they pretended to smack at each other playfully, ending with a quick kiss as Regina yelled at them for nearly knocking over her potato salad bowl.

"Get out of here with that nonsense," Regina said, shoving Stephen toward the back screen door. "Tell your father to check on that chicken."

Her only son, Alex couldn't help thinking as she watched Regina joke with Stephen.

She glanced around the Williamses' kitchen, recalling mornings sitting at the table eating Regina's pancakes, or the Christmas Eve that she, Tiana, and Juju had made cookies—one of the few things she could cook—to set out for Santa. Alex hadn't felt this at home in a long time. This was to have been her family. Her future. So, what were they to her now? How long could she maintain a relationship that had no true identifying factor?

They were going to eat outside at a long picnic table, so Regina gathered up a tablecloth and a stack of paper plates and headed for the door. "Ti, give that potato salad another stir. Alex, will you start filling some cups with ice?" Then she was gone, outside to set up the table.

Alex loved that Regina still treated her like one of her children, the way she always had. They got to work on their jobs, but the minute Tiana was finished, she leaned against the counter where Alex had been lining up the glasses.

"So," she said, giving Alex a long look.

"So?" Alex replied. She'd always adored Tiana, and admired her. She could still remember attending her and Stephen's wedding many years ago when she and Nate were newly dating and on leave. It had been such a fun week here in Atlanta. Ever since then, they'd gotten along well, even as infrequently as they'd been able to see each other.

"You into this guy?" Tiana asked quietly.

"What?" Alex laughed awkwardly. "We work together."

"Look at me," Tiana said flatly. Alex did, to find her glaring at her with a don't-bullshit-me look. Tiana was always direct. "Try again. You've been looking out this window checking up on him."

Alex sighed, letting her hand fall to the counter. "It's not like that."

"Maybe not. But Regina thinks it might be."

"What did she say?" Alex asked, horrified.

"Says she drove up on y'all holding hands at the grave site."

"Shit," Alex muttered, grabbing another glass and adding ice. "Did it upset her?"

"I don't think so. But I think it surprised her."

"I hate that she saw that. It wasn't like that at all. Jake's a really nice guy. I've talked to him about Nate a lot. He was just being supportive."

"I believe you. But he can be supportive and into you at the same time."

Just then Regina came back in the kitchen followed by Tiana's two older children, Juju and Devon, who was four. "Tiana, pull the cornbread out of the oven. Alex, fruit in the fridge." Regina grabbed a platter from a cabinet and handed it to Juju. "Take this to Papa."

"Yes ma'am. And I'm sitting by Aunty Alex at the table," Juju called over her shoulder.

Alex winked at her. "Of course you are."

The next two hours passed by in a blur of laughs, photos, and funny stories about Nate as a child and as a teenager, and then several about him and Alex together. His family asked her several questions about their time in Afghanistan and Iraq, and Nate's short period of time in Syria.

Even Jake had occasionally joined in on the conversation, asking her questions. Juju had sat between them at lunch, which had probably been for the best. It was tempting to want to touch him, even if just for comfort, and she would have hated to slip and get too close in front of everyone here.

After the chatting died down—mainly because baby Camille was ready for a nap—and Papa Leon Sr. lit up his pipe, Regina asked everyone to help carry in the dirty dishes.

"We should probably get on the road if we're going

to start to Nashville this evening," Jake whispered to her as everyone dispersed.

"Okay. Give me ten minutes to help clean up?"

He nodded. "Sure. Take your time."

She headed inside to find Stephen helping his mother load up the dishwasher. Regina turned when Alex entered. "There you are. Come with me," she motioned toward the hallway and led Alex up the stairs and into her bedroom.

The butterflies in her stomach came to life, wondering what in the world Regina could want to say to her in private. It had to be about Jake, even though everything during lunch had seemed normal and fine.

"Sit, I'll fetch what I'm here for," Regina said, pointing at her bed. Alex sat down and watched her step into her small walk-in closet. While she waited she glanced around the small master bedroom. An antique chest of drawers anchored the far wall with Nate's Air Force portrait on top. Alex sucked in a breath at the sight of it. She'd purposely bypassed photos on the first floor, not wanting to get emotional today. Just being in his family home had been difficult enough.

The quilt on the bed was well worn but made of a lovely blue floral material that was so soft, Alex was tempted to lie down and inhale the scent of the Williams family. Leon and Regina Williams had raised their children in this modest home. Alex knew Nate's old bedroom was down the hall, even though it had been turned into a retreat for the grandchildren years ago. They didn't have a lot of money, but there was so much love in these walls she felt like she could almost touch it.

Regina walked out of the closet holding a small box.

"Found it." She sat down beside Alex and opened it. "This was my grandmother's."

She pulled out a beautiful gold chain with a dainty pendant hanging from it. Alex cupped it in her hand. There was an opal surrounded by tiny rubies. "It's beautiful, Regina."

"Isn't it? I was going to give it to you on your wedding day."

Alex froze, her eyes meeting the other woman's. "Oh Regina. That's okay. I'm glad to see it, though. It would have been beautiful with my dress."

"Silly, I still want you to have it."

"Oh no, I couldn't." Alex shook her head.

"Yes you can, and you will." She pulled the necklace back and gently laid it in the box before handing it to Alex. "I'd even told Nate my plan. And that woman, Charlotte, who was planning your wedding. She and I had emailed several times about tuxes and such."

"She never told me about the necklace."

"Well, it was to be a surprise."

"Regina, I just—"

"Alexis." Regina grabbed her hands and looked her right in the eye. "Tiana has another of my grandmother's necklaces."

"I bet she'd like this one, also," Alex countered. "Or Juju."

Regina shook her head. "No, doll. This one was always meant for Nathan's wife. And while that may not have happened, you're the closest I'm ever going to get. You carry my baby in your heart, and so this belongs with you."

"Thank you," she whispered, her chin trembling.

"You're always going to feel like my daughter, Alex. You belonged to Nathan and that means you belong to me too. You're one of the only parts of him I have left. And I'm talking about even when you fall in love with someone else. D'you understand?"

Alex nodded, but suddenly felt the need to make something clear. "Just so you know, I'm not in love with Jake. He's just a good guy."

Regina smirked, a sad but kind look in her eye. "Nate already taught you this lesson—good guys are the easiest to fall in love with."

Fourteen

The ride back to the RV park was quiet for a long time. Jake wasn't quite sure what to say because it wasn't entirely clear what was going on in Alex's head. It occurred to him that right now she may not be interested in talking to him at all after such an immersive reminder of Nate. He didn't want to upset her further if that's where her thoughts were, though he hoped that wasn't it.

"Thank you for coming and being such a good sport," she said, relieving him.

"It was my pleasure, Alex." He smiled at her, and he'd also meant what he'd said. "They're really great."

"I know. I miss them. I mean, we only saw them once or twice a year, but between email and care packages, there were always updates. Not so much these days. Partly my fault."

"How so?"

She shrugged. "I don't make as much of an effort I guess. I think Regina tries to follow my lead. Doesn't want to bug me."

"She really loves you though. They all do."

She was quiet for a moment, and he hoped he hadn't upset her. "Want to hear something stupid?" she asked.

"What?"

"Sometimes I'm angry that Nate didn't wait to die until we were married." She chuckled.

"I don't think any of your feelings are stupid, Alex." He tightened his grip on the wheel. As well as he'd gotten to know Alex at this point, in-person conversations like this made him nervous. When their interactions were all through messaging, he could really think out a response. Sometimes they were delayed by the time difference, so he was able to really put thought into them. But like this, he was afraid of saying the wrong thing.

"I actually had a woman say to me, 'at least you weren't married.'" She let out a sound of disgust. "What does that even mean? Like, I hadn't loved him as much as I would have a few weeks later? Like a legal document makes my pain any less?"

She shifted in her seat to face him, patting her chest as she went on. "If we'd been married, I would have had rights. I would have had his *name*. And that family. I would have had that family."

Jake breathed in deep, unable to look at her. Blowing out slowly, he finally replied. "From what I can tell, Alex, you *do* have that family. They adore you."

She turned and leaned back into her seat. "It will fade. I'm so far away. The kids will get older and not think about me. The only good thing is that today took some of the pressure off, in a way."

"What do you mean?" he asked, pulling into the park.

"Sometimes I feel this weight to keep Nate's memory in this world. To talk about him. To think of him, so he doesn't fade away to nothing like he never existed."

Putting the truck in park, he turned to look at her. He could tell when she'd come out of Regina's bedroom that she'd been crying—her eyes were still a little puffy.

"Seeing them today, looking at their photos, listening to their stories. I'm reminded that Nate is alive in their home. In their heads and hearts. It's not just up to me. I know that sounds crazy."

Jake reached out and grabbed her hand. "It doesn't sound crazy at all, Alex. I'd never thought about anything like what you're saying before, but when you say it, I get it. I saw it too. I've never met Nate and after today, I feel a little like I knew him."

"I'm glad." She smiled and squeezed his hand. "You know, I don't think we entirely fooled Regina."

His eyes went wide. "She say something?"

"Nothing direct. But Tiana told me she saw us holding hands at the cemetery."

"Shit, I'm sorry. Does that upset you?"

She tilted her head, looking back at him. "No. I thought it would, but it doesn't."

Relief hit him harder than he'd expected. "Good. Listen, you just want to chill tonight? We can get up early and head out in the morning." After today, he was kind of in the mood to spend some time with her alone. Time that he didn't have to spend driving.

"Yeah, that would be nice."

Unclasping their hands, she made to get out of the truck, so he did the same. Once they were inside, she went into the bedroom and pulled the door shut. He sat down on the sofa, unsure of what to do with himself. It was almost four, so they had the entire evening to kill. Maybe she'd want to watch a movie or something. Go get some takeout later.

When she came out of the bedroom in her running clothes, he was surprised and a little disappointed.

"I hope you don't mind. I just want to get this in. Clear my head a bit."

"Yeah, sure. Actually, I have some work I could do. Haven't looked at the Stag social accounts today."

"Okay. I'll be back soon."

"Be careful," he said.

She rolled her eyes but smiled. "I'll be fine."

When she was gone, he sat down and glanced around at the empty space. How had he ever done this alone before? He already missed her voice. Her presence.

Pulling out his laptop, he did the work he needed to do. Checked on their shipment that was sent to Nashville ahead of them, replied to a few Facebook posts and Twitter comments. He'd given Alex the job of posting some shots on their Instagram account, which he saw she'd done. The photos she'd taken on the trip so far were really good. She had a much better eye than he did, and her captions were a lot wittier. The proof was in the amount of likes and the increase in comments. And not a bikini in sight, so TJ should be pleased.

Glancing at the time, Jake stood up and looked out the window. She'd been gone about forty-five minutes. They seemed to be in a decent part of town, but he knew anything could happen anytime and anywhere.

Finally, he let his thoughts drift to the place he'd been avoiding. Would things be different after today? Because part of him felt like they should be. Yes, they'd discussed on multiple occasions that this was a short-lived affair. They were just enjoying each other, and it would come to an end once they returned to KC. But after spending an entire afternoon witnessing the results of the relationship she shared with Nate, he felt like a traitor.

That family loved her like crazy. That man had loved her like crazy. The evidence had been presented to him today through the photo albums that Regina had pulled out and shared. The stories that they'd all told, laughing and sometimes wiping away tears. Alex had lost her best friend. The love of her life. And here he was just casually having a fling with her.

It didn't feel right.

He ran a hand through his hair and clicked open a new internet window. Trying to think of anything else, he found himself mindlessly flipping from video to video. Reading the news.

Finally, he heard the steady pound of her footsteps outside, and then the RV door opened. He made to get up as she walked in, but she immediately put up a hand. Her skin shone with perspiration, tank top spotted and ponytail damp.

"Stay back," she said. "I stink."

Sitting back down, he smiled. "Little bit muggier down here in Hotlanta, huh?"

"Oh my Lord, and here I spent years in the desert. There's hot, and then there's Southern hot," she said. "I'm getting in the shower."

He nodded. "Want me to go grab some dinner?"

"Uh, sure. Whatever you want."

He went and picked up some sandwiches, making sure to get her extra lettuce and jalapeños—just like she ordered on just about everything she ate—and then got her a Dr Pepper. Her favorite drink, although she tried to drink it only every few days because of the sugar. He figured she deserved it today.

When he got back to the RV she was dressed in her

tiny shorts and tank top, her face bare and her hair damp. She looked beautiful. When he pulled out the Dr Pepper she smiled and took it from him.

"You know me too well."

"Yes I do." He handed her the sub. "Extra lettuce and jalapeños."

"Turkey and Pepper Jack?"

"Do I look like it's my first day on the job?" He asked, making her laugh.

They sat and ate while watching Netflix on the pull-out sofa, but by the end of the third episode of the show they'd chosen, she sat up.

"Hey," she said quietly.

"Yeah?"

"I don't want this to be weird, or for you to take this personally," she said, and he held his breath, frozen in place as he waited for her to finish her thought. "But . . . I think I want to sleep alone tonight." She sucked in her lip as she stared at him, obviously waiting for his response.

"Okay. Sure. I'll take this bed." His heart pounded in his chest as he tried really hard not to take it personally. He really should be used to rejection by now, but then again, he usually didn't put himself in situations to feel it. Yet, here he was.

"No, Jake. I don't want to do that to you. I can sleep out here."

He shook his head. "Alex, I'm not going to have you sleep on this pull-out. It's fine."

Her shoulders slumped. "Thank you, Jake."

They went back to watching the show for one more episode, but he couldn't help thinking that his concerns had been valid. Something had changed.

* * *

Day 419 Day 12 on tour
I don't know how I feel today. Things have been so confusing with Jake. I hadn't planned on asking him to sleep in a separate bed, but I just needed some space. I hate the thought it might have hurt his feelings. The most ridiculous part was that I'd missed him and almost called him back, but I didn't want to look like a flake. The last thing I want to do is mess with his head. Or my own. This is temporary.

Lunch with Nate's family was amazing, but sad. It's weird to be around them now. Am I trying to hold onto something that I have no business holding on to? Too many things feel uncertain now. I hope things are better when I move. Today I intend to feel optimistic. Again. I hope this time it sticks.

Alex slid her journal into her bag and looked ahead through the pickup windshield. Jake had gone into the truck stop to pay for the diesel. Once he was finished, he got into the truck and put on his seat belt.

"I was looking at our route this morning. We should be there by noon," she said.

"Perfect. I called the RV park yesterday, and our spot's available at noon, which means we can hook up and then get over to the liquor store around two. And then I was kind of thinking that after tomorrow's event in Olmstead, maybe we should just head out right away and drive through the night."

"Oh." She turned and looked out the windshield. "Okay. So, this will be our last night sleeping in the RV then?"

"Yeah," he said shortly. "I think I'm ready to get home."

Okay. That hurt a little. And it was official—she'd hurt his feelings.

"I'm ready to get home also. But . . . I think I'll just miss the RV," she said, hoping he'd take her meaning for what it was. A sign that she'd loved their time together.

He sent her a quick smile before looking back at the road. "You never want too much of a good thing."

That was a direct hit, and she didn't know how to respond to it. "We'll still see one another quite a bit before I leave. I agreed to come into the Stag a few times a week and help cover the desk."

His eyebrows went up. "I didn't realize that."

"Does it bother you?"

His chuckle had a bitter undertone. "Just another decision at work I had no part in making."

"Jake, I'm sorry. I . . ."

"It's fine, Alex. Has nothing to do with you. We need the help and you'll do a good job."

She was quiet as he started up the truck and pulled out of the filling station.

"Getting on Seventy-five, right?" he asked.

"Yeah. All the way to Chattanooga." She glanced at her phone just to verify she'd told him correctly. She hated this coolness between them so much, but she wasn't sure how to fix it. "Then we'll get on Twenty-four all the way to Nashville."

He nodded. "This is a pretty drive. You'll like it."

She couldn't help thinking that she'd like it a lot better if he wasn't acting so weird. Playing back yesterday, she tried to recall if she'd done or said anything that might have offended him—except the not-sleeping-together thing. Nothing came up, unless it was something someone at the Williams house said. But she couldn't imagine that. And he'd been totally fine until her request, so that had to be it. She'd ruined everything by telling him she didn't want him last night.

Trying to focus on the intention she made today—
to feel optimistic—she kindly asked him what kind
of music he wanted to listen to since she usually
picked and he just went along with whatever. Of
course, that had been his same response now. With a
sigh, she decided to put in an audiobook.

It had worked a little, because when they arrived in
Nashville three and a half hours later and pulled into
the RV park, they were so engrossed in the mystery they
were listening to that Jake didn't want to get out. When
it finally came to a reasonable place, she pushed PAUSE.

"It's the boyfriend," he said instantly.

"You think?" she said. "I think that seems too
obvious."

He shrugged. "It can't be her stepdad. He was in
Alaska when the sister was killed."

"Yeah, but how can you be certain?"

Obviously considering her statement, he narrowed
his eyes. "It could possibly be the stepdad, but to me that
seems more obvious than the boyfriend."

"It's probably neither of them."

They smiled at each other, holding the gaze for a moment too long. She really liked these moments with
him, when there was no overthinking or worry. They
just had fun. That's what she wanted for the rest of their
time together. That was what attracted her to him.

"Hey, I need to say something . . ." She licked her
lips before continuing. "Last night . . ."

He put up a hand. "No need to explain, Alex."

"I know that. But I want to. Yesterday was over-
whelming—"

"I get it."

"Will you let me finish," she snapped, and his eyes
went wide.

"I'm sorry. Yes, finish."

"Being in Atlanta was more difficult than I'd expected. Last night, I was afraid it was going to be a
cry-myself-to-sleep kind of night. I hadn't had one in a
while and I didn't want to do that to you."

He was quiet, glancing down at the console between
them.

"Look at me, Jake." Lifting his eyes, he stared back
at her. "If tonight is our last night, I'd really like us to
be . . . together. If you want. I know it's not fair to be
this way, so . . . uncertain. I don't want to make this
about me, but . . ."

"Yes," was all he said.

She met his eyes. "Yes, what?"

"I want you tonight."

Fifteen

That afternoon, Jake had told her they should dress up a bit so she'd worn some thin cropped pants, one of the tops she and Charlotte had chosen, and her favorite rose gold flats. Their first stop was with the owner of a very successful liquor store chain in Nashville. When they showed up at the large brick building in an obviously upper-middle-class part of town, she and Jake got out of the pickup, and she grabbed the bag full of Stag product samples.

As they walked toward the door, Jake spoke quietly. "This will be my third try to get an account with Peter Dunn's company."

"Really? What's the big deal?" She wondered if that was why he'd seemed a little nervous on their way over.

"Besides the fact that he owns eighteen liquor stores throughout Tennessee?" He gave her a long look.

"Okay, point taken. But obviously there's more. There are plenty of liquor store chains you guys work with."

"Yes, he's also a silent partner in a Sip, Bite, Match. They opened twelve new units this past year across the country. So now a total of thirty-two."

"Isn't that the Chuck E. Cheeses for grown-ups place?"

"Yes, and my hope is that if Dunn starts selling us in his liquor store, it will lead to an account with the restaurant."

They stepped onto the sidewalk that led to the front door. "I have a good feeling about today," she said.

He winked at her. "Thanks. I hope you're right."

They stepped inside, and after alerting the woman at the counter of who they were, a man finally came out from a back office. If Alex had to guess, he was closing in on sixty, but was still very handsome with an angular jaw, expertly cut thick hair, and a tan that said he probably had a big old pool in his backyard.

"Mr. Dunn." Jake stepped forward with a hand out. "Always good to see you."

"Likewise, Jake." Peter Dunn turned to Alex with a roguish grin, his eyes quickly looking her up and down. "And I see you brought your secret weapon here."

Huh. So *that* was the kind of guy they were dealing with. She put out her hand, but her smile was forced, for Jake's sake. "Alexis Parker. It's nice to meet you."

"So, you think you might be ready for the big time?" Mr. Dunn gave Jake a wink that Alex hated. She wanted to inform him that the Stag was already big time without his help, thank you very much.

"I'm certain we are. We're now selling in twenty-nine states," Jake said with just as much confidence.

"Very good," Mr. Dunn said, obviously impressed or a good faker. "Well, let me show you around the new store."

As they followed, Alex had to admit that Dunn's flagship store was impressive for a facility that sold alcohol. He spared them no detail, describing how he'd chosen the beautiful wood floor that was actually tile and not wood at all. They then discussed the intricacy of the layout for optimal browsing time, which he claimed was based on some extensive research his daughter had done throughout their seven locations in Nashville. Even the restrooms were gorgeous.

"Mr. Dunn, this really is a beautiful store," Alex said, feeling obligated to speak first since he'd directed a lot of his comments her way for some reason, as if pretty furnishings impressed only women.

"Thank you, Alexis. I really have my daughter to thank. Ever since she joined my company three years ago, our sales have nearly doubled. One thing about me, I never miss an opportunity to appreciate a woman's talents."

Alex didn't know if the comment warranted respect or for her to throw up in her mouth.

"Your daughter sounds very talented," Alex said.

"She is. I'm lucky to have her."

"I learned from the best," a smooth voice said behind them.

Alex and Jake turned in unison to find a gorgeous woman, probably around thirty or so, making her way down the aisle toward them.

"Jake Cooper?" she asked, putting out a hand to Jake.

He shook it. "Very nice to meet you. Vanessa, I assume?"

"You assume correctly."

Alex watched the two of them, stunned really, by how beautiful this Vanessa woman was. She was the photoshopped version of a centerfold photo, with the smoothest skin and shiniest brunette hair that curled in long coils over her shoulders. Alex had carefully chosen her outfit and done her hair and makeup, yet still felt like a troll next to this woman who somehow pulled off elegant and sophisticated in a pair of jeans and a linen blouse.

Vanessa turned to her this time, putting out a hand. Immediately Alex squared her shoulders and took it. "Alexis Parker."

"It's a pleasure, Ms. Parker," Vanessa said. She smiled at her father. "I'm sure Dad has spent a lot of time bragging about the new store."

Mr. Dunn smirked. "You know me. But I'll let you show them the best part."

Vanessa's grin was almost salacious as she turned to Jake. "I'm sure you'll appreciate what I have to show you, Jake."

He held out a hand toward the hallway they were standing near. "Then by all means."

Alex was tempted to reach out and grab his hand, which would have been ridiculous under any circumstances. They were here on business. Also, they weren't a couple.

"I've been following the growth of the Stag online," Vanessa said over her shoulder as they headed down the short hallway. "I was so impressed with how you capitalized on your gorgeous space by doing weddings."

"Thank you. We were hesitant, but it's been amazing, and is now a good part of our profit and brand recognition. We've been voted the most popular venue in Kansas City for the past three years."

"Impressive," Vanessa said, stopping at a closed door at the end of the hall. "You seem to be popular yourself, if the comments on Instagram are any indication."

Jake froze, his lips parted, eyes glancing toward

Alex. He let out an embarrassed chuckle and rubbed at the back of his neck.

Alex decided to butt in. "You know what they say. Never read the comments. Most of them are pure fabrication."

"*Most*?" Vanessa said with a quirk of her lips. "Anyway, I'll admit I was inspired by your business model."

"Oh?" Jake asked.

"When this store opened in January, we decided to add an event space."

"For weddings?" Alex asked, wishing her question hadn't come out so skeptical sounding. She didn't want to embarrass Jake, but something about this woman was rubbing her the wrong way. Plus, what was she saying? Weddings in a distillery were cool and hip. Weddings in a liquor store? Uh, no thanks.

"Not weddings, necessarily. Smaller scale. Showers, birthdays, small corporate events. And the best part is that there is a main entrance off the back, so no one has to go through the retail side."

"Smart," Jake said. "I'd like to see it."

"Absolutely." With a smile she opened the door.

Anxious to see why all the drama was necessary, Alex followed Jake into the space and immediately her eyes widened. The same wood-looking tile ran the length of the room and the ceiling was row after row of wood beams set amongst the ducting and industrial aspects. Somewhat similar to the main floor of the Stag building, but this was new construction, although it didn't appear to be with the far wall that was half dry-wall and half exposed brick. The front was made up entirely of windows and clear-glass garage doors. It was really lovely, although not very big.

"Wow. It's great," Jake said, walking into the center of the space. "How big is this?"

"Only about three thousand square feet. Four if you open the garage doors and utilize the patio."

Alex walked over to the windows and peeked outside. The patio had several seating vignettes, a fire pit, and a beautiful grilling station.

"This is gorgeous."

Vanessa beamed. "Thank you, Alexis. We love it. We just had our ninth event this weekend. A birthday party for Sidney Phillips."

"The country singer?" Jake asked, surprise in his voice.

"Yes. It turned out really well. I'm fairly certain the photographer has a deal with *People* magazine, so we should get some buzz. We've already had some high profile inquiries since then."

"Good for you," Jake said. He glanced at Alex, and she could tell he was getting antsy. She felt the same. Cool story, but it was time to get down to business. "So is it *you* I need to convince to carry Stag products?"

Vanessa smiled. "This time, yes. But I have to tell you, I'm an even harder sell than my father."

Jake nodded. "Understood. I'll start by pointing out that our Signature Bourbon—one of our premium aged offerings—was awarded a Platinum Sip Award this year."

"That's impressive." Vanessa tilted her head to the side. "Did you bring some to taste?"

"We did," Alex said, interjecting herself. They'd left it at the counter when they'd come in. "I'll go get it."

Jake shoved his hands in his pockets, anxious. There was not a doubt in his mind that Vanessa Dunn was coming on to him. It was in the way she looked at him, the way she stood a little too close.

Now that they were alone, he stepped toward the garage doors along the wall and looked at the patio.

"The garage doors are a nice touch."

"I agree. Having alfresco events is very appealing to people."

"I bet." *Where was Alex?*

The feeling of Vanessa stepping a little closer made him anxious. When she spoke, there was no mistaking the interest in her voice. "I'm looking forward to sampling what you have to offer, especially since it seems to be so popular."

He turned and looked at her. Would he have taken this bait on previous tours? Quite possibly, but right now the thought made him sick to his stomach.

"Well," he said with a smile, shoving his hands in his pockets. He'd worn dark jeans today but with a button-up shirt and sports jacket, which right now felt like a vise. "Alex should be right back and we can get to it."

"Hmm." She linked her hands together loosely, tilting her head to the side. "Do you have plans for this evening?"

He eyed her warily. Technically, no. He didn't have any official plans. "Not necessarily. What do you have in mind?"

"After her birthday party, Sidney Phillips gave me two tickets to a show she's doing tonight downtown." She walked closer to him. "I thought maybe we could go together and then get some dinner. Discuss the Stag. Your liquor. Maybe let me pick your brain a bit on your event-space marketing."

Staring at her for a moment, he considered her offer.

He wanted this account. Wanted it badly. But he was here with Alexis. There was no way he could leave her alone while he went out with another woman. "I appreciate the offer. But Alex—"

"Can find something else to do this evening," Alex finished for him.

He turned to see Alex walking back in the room carrying the bag of Stag liquor bottles.

"Alex . . ." he started, but she just shook her head.

"I'm fine. And I wasn't trying to eavesdrop. With the room so empty I could hear you in the hall."

Vanessa smiled. "It is loud in here. Are you sure you don't mind, Alex?"

"Not at all," she said. Her smile appeared sincere. It even warmed when she looked over at him. "Honestly, I have some things I could get done this evening. A night alone sounds nice."

What was she doing? And did she mean what she was saying, or was she just reacting to him revealing how much he wanted this account before they'd walked in?

Jake turned back to Vanessa, who looked as though things were settled.

They weren't. Not by a long shot. Yes, he wanted this account. Wanted to call his business partners and tell them he'd finally signed with Dunn. Prove to them that he did more than play around on these tours and that his part in this business was critical.

But in the past thirty minutes he'd watched Peter leer at Dean's sister and then suffered through this completely unnecessary brag fest by him and his daughter. All after a day where Alex had taken him along without question to her almost-in-laws' home, where they'd treated him with such kindness it ate him up inside.

No, there was not a chance in hell he was leaving her alone tonight. Not for a potential lay with a beautiful woman. Not to mingle with celebrities. Not for a profitable contract. Not for any reason at all.

"I'm sorry, Vanessa. Alexis is being polite because she knows how much I want you to stock Stag products in Dunn Liquor stores. But I think I'll just leave these here for you and your father to try." He walked over and handed her the bag. "I know you'll enjoy them. And I hope I'll be hearing from you."

He backed away from her, closer to Alex. "If not, I'll accept that maybe this partnership isn't meant to be." With a quick smile he looked around the room. "And good luck with this space."

With that he turned, put a hand on Alex's lower back to gently steer her from the room, down the hall, and through the liquor store.

"What the hell was that?" she hissed, as they headed for the door.

"Keep moving."

She did, squaring her shoulders. The minute they were outside he kept walking, grateful that Alex did the same. But as soon as they got into the pickup she turned on him.

"What the hell is wrong with you?"

Leaning over the console, he wrapped a hand around the back of her head, tugged her toward him gently, and then kissed her hard. For a split second, he could feel her resist. She wanted to argue. Make him explain himself as she'd asked him to do. But he didn't let up, and then she was kissing him back. A quiet moan coming from her throat as she angled her head, dipping her tongue into his mouth.

They were at it for several long moments until she

finally pulled away. "You are so stupid, Jake Cooper. You had that contract. All you had to do was go out with her tonight."

"And you'd have really been cool with that?" he asked. *Say no.*

She gave him a confused long look. "You wanted this."

"But I didn't want her."

"She was very pretty."

"You're very pretty."

Alex stared back at him, eyes wide. "This is temporary, Jake. That contract could last a long time."

He swallowed, not liking that she wasn't only not willing to drop this, but also didn't seem to appreciate what he'd done. "Are you implying that I should have gone out with her—maybe even slept with her—in order to close this deal?"

She shook her head. "No."

"Let me say this: if this contract legitimately hinged on me going out with this woman, then it wasn't a contract worth having."

"If I hadn't been here, you'd have gone."

"Possibly."

Her lips pursed. "I hate the thought that you gave this up because you felt bad for me."

"I don't feel bad for you, Alex. You are strong, independent, incredibly intelligent, and attract people wherever you go just by being yourself. I have no doubt that you'd have been just fine tonight if I'd chosen to go." He touched her face with the back of his fingers. "It's me I feel sorry for, because tonight's my last night with you. . . . And I don't know how I'm supposed to stop wanting you when this trip is over."

* * *

That night they lay in the back of the RV, naked bodies loosely twined after mind-blowing sex. Her head was rested in the crook of his arm. "I don't want things to be awkward between us when we're back home," she said quietly.

"We won't let it be." Jake was playing with her hair, and she angled her head up to look at him.

"Promise? Because you became my best friend over the past year, and I don't want to lose you."

Jake dipped his chin and looked down at where she was nestled against his side, her fingers sliding back and forth in his chest hair. He smiled at her. "You won't. I can't wait until you can text me all the top-secret stuff that happens inside the CIA."

She laughed and slapped at him. "I can't do that, and you know it."

"I guess not. But don't worry, you won't lose me."

He closed his eyes, relaxing into the pillow. She could just lie here and stare at him, his long lashes, full lips, and five-o'clock shadow. He was the most beautiful man, and if things were different, she could fall for him so hard. But she had plans, and loving another man was not in the cards for her right now. Maybe not ever.

"Do me one favor."

His right eye peeked open and he looked at her. "What?"

"Don't start dating anyone until I move away."

Both eyes opened at that, his lips quirking. "You're not asking much, are you?"

Her lips pouted. "I'll be jealous," she whispered.

The lines between his brows deepened and he stared at her for a long moment before finally responding. "Okay deal, but you better do the same."

"Because you'd be jealous?" she asked.

"Crazy jealous."

Why did she feel like crying? Instead she smiled. "Don't worry. I have no desire for a relationship. None."

He nodded, a sad smile on his lips. "That's too bad, Alex. Because you'd make a man really happy."

Sixteen

The following Friday morning, Alex carried her last bag into Joel's spare bedroom and sighed. Moving in with Dean's father was the right thing for her, she knew that, but she also knew her brother was skeptical.

"Alex, Dad snores. He's only a wall away. Maybe we should get you a white noise machine."

She dropped her shoulders and gave him a long look. "Do you hear yourself? I've slept surrounded by multiple people for years. I can handle snoring. I can handle his daily television rituals. I can handle it all. Besides, this is temporary."

Charlotte tugged on his arm. "Chill out, babe. You're giving us all anxiety."

Dean glared down at her and she gave him a wide-eyed "what are you gonna do about it" look in return. "Alex and Joel are going to get along like peas and carrots," Charlotte said.

"I hate peas and carrots," Joel said as he came down the hallway. He peeked into the room. "We'll get along like Cheez-Its and Cheese Whiz."

They all cringed, and Alex laughed. "As long as I'm the whiz."

Joel nodded. "I'll be the it."

Alex and Charlotte grinned. Dean sighed. Alex and Joel had always loved to joke like this and just be silly. It was why she knew living with him for a couple months would be easy, and he'd been excited about the idea. At the ripe age of eighty-four, he was like the cool grandfather.

She knew that here she could come and go as she pleased without anyone asking questions or offering advice. And watching a happy, in-love couple make out in the kitchen would no longer be a problem.

"Don't forget to put that key on your ring," Joel said.

"Already done." Alex held up her keys and jangled them. The older man gave her a thumbs-up and then was gone.

"I'm gonna head home and get back to editing," Charlotte said. They'd driven two cars over. "You still cutting your dad's grass?"

Dean nodded. "Yeah. I'll be home in a few hours. Want me to pick up some dinner?"

"Burritos?" Charlotte said excitedly, scrunching her nose as if she knew Dean wouldn't be crazy about the idea.

"Fine. But you owe me."

Chuckling, Charlotte leaned in and kissed his cheek. Then she turned to Alex and wrapped her in a hug. "I'm going to miss you in the house. So is Fernando."

Alex pulled back and smiled. "Maybe he can come have a sleepover."

"Anytime," Dean said. The dog was a little high maintenance.

Charlotte just rolled her eyes and pointed at him playfully. "Don't forget my guacamole this time. Or else."

"Mind like a steel trap," Dean called to her as she walked away.

"Sure!" Her voice echoed down the hall.

Every time Alex witnessed them teasing each other she felt a little . . . off. Before her trip with Jake it had made her sad. Now, it just made her jealous. It had been fun to have someone to tease and joke with every day, and she'd missed him over the past week like crazy. To her surprise, neither one of them had really texted since arriving back in Maple Springs a week ago.

"Need help getting things set up?" Dean asked. He looked lost, as if he were dropping a child off at summer camp and didn't know how to leave. God, he was such a dad of a brother. With that thought, she was reminded of the struggle that he and Charlotte had to deal with: his sterility.

The past year had been tough on him. He'd been working his ass off at the Stag, fallen for a beautiful, younger woman who wanted children, and then had to tell her he couldn't give her any. His little sister—who he'd helped to raise—had lost her fiancé and then left for a foreign country. All he wanted to do was make everything right. Take care of those around him. That was his way, and Alex needed to give him a break because, in reality, he was the one person in her life that she could always, without fail, count on.

Tears suddenly pooling in her eyes, she rushed over and wrapped her arms around his waist. He caught her with a mumbled curse of surprise, but immediately hugged her back.

"I'm sorry I've been a pain, Bean." She'd been calling him that since she could speak. Being a toddler with a teenage brother meant she always thought he was the coolest thing that existed. She hated that she'd been annoyed with him lately.

"Don't apologize, Alex. I'm the pain in the ass."

She laughed, but it only made her tears come faster. "Yes, you are. But I love you."

"Ah, Buzz." He nearly choked on the words, which was unusual for him. Dean rarely let vulnerable emotions show. Well, except for fear and worry. Those were his defaults. "I love you too. Which is why I'm always stressed out about you. All I want is for you to be happy."

"I know that."

She pulled away and looked up at him. "I know me moving away disappoints you, but it will make me happy."

He stared at her. "You sure? It's so far."

"It's an amazing opportunity, and now I have nothing holding me back."

He let out a deep breath through his nose before finally nodding. "I understand, Alex. I do. And Charlotte's right, we can visit."

"Yes."

He glanced around at her three bags and two boxes, most of which they'd recently pulled out of a storage unit she'd had nearby for several years. It will still full of things she'd amassed throughout her life that Dean hadn't been able to store in the apartment he lived in before moving in with Charlotte.

"I guess I'll get started on the lawn then," Dean said. Alex followed him down the hall and into the living room where Joel was seated in his favorite old recliner watching baseball.

"You outta here?" Joel said without taking his eyes off the TV.

"No, I'm mowing your yard."

"That's not necessary you know."

"You always say that," Dean replied. "And yet, every time I get here, it's waiting for me."

Joel shrugged. "I know you like to do it your way. Right, Alex?" He winked, and she just chuckled.

Dean headed outside, and she went back to her new room to start getting comfortable. The closet was empty and ready, so she hung all of her clothes and laid out her few pairs of shoes. She really needed to do another shopping trip to get some more necessities, but maybe she should wait until she started her new job to see what everyone else was wearing.

After her clothes were all unpacked she took her bag of toiletries to the hall bath. It was small, but thankfully Joel had his own small master bath, so she could have this one pretty much to herself while she was here.

As she worked, her thoughts wandered to Jake. She found herself thinking of him frequently. She missed him like crazy, and it had been weird to go from constant togetherness to barely speaking. Much to her surprise, she was excited to start working a few days at the Stag in a week. They'd told her they didn't need her until Jen officially moved upstairs, but she'd be going in next Friday to train and she was looking forward to seeing him. Speaking of the Stag, she had been curious about one thing. Picking up her phone, she texted him.

ALEX: Did you ever hear from the Dunns? I keep hoping they started an account.

She followed it with the fingers-crossed emoji. After a few moments he responded.

JAKE: No. Not a surprise.

She frowned at her phone. She'd really hoped they would come through.

ALEX: Sorry.

He didn't respond so she went to watch TV with Joel. She refused to feel sad.

Seventeen

The following Monday Alex answered her first phone call all alone, her heart pounding. "The Stag, this is Alex speaking."

The woman on the other line was inquiring about wedding packages, so thankfully she could transfer it up to Jen. Easy. Hopefully they'd all be like that. After hanging up, she took another glance at the cheat sheet Jen had left her for reference.

There was general info on the company, product pricing, their hours, and tour info.

She leaned back in her chair just in time to see Jake walking toward the front desk. She smiled. "Hi."

"Hey, you," he said, leaning his arms on the counter. "First day on the job."

She groaned. "I'm terrified of the phone ringing."

He laughed. "And here you were hired by the CIA."

"I know! But my skillset has absolutely nothing to do with being a receptionist."

"Well, you look cute sitting here," he said quietly.

She glanced around. "You better be careful."

"Nobody's out here."

"Yeah, but voices carry in this building."

He smirked. "Sorry. How've you been?"

She shrugged. "Okay. You?"

"Good."

They were quiet for a moment, and she could have sworn he'd glanced at her chest. Had he missed her body as much as she'd missed his?

"We said we weren't going to let this be weird," she whispered.

His eyes creased with humor. "We're not."

She tilted her head to the side. "Then why are you still standing there?"

He glanced around like he wanted to say something, but then leaned down over the counter, grabbed a sticky note and a pen, and scratched out a quick message. He dropped the pad back down on her desk, then walked away.

She turned it over and read his note. *I was picturing you naked.* Immediately she slapped her hand down on the pad and then ripped it off. Instead of throwing it away she dropped it into her purse.

Shit. He *was* going to make this difficult. Stupid thing was, she wasn't upset about it.

Friday afternoon Jake leaned back in his chair in the Stag conference room. Much to his frustration, he, Dean, and TJ had just interviewed someone for the front desk job.

"I liked her," TJ said. "She had a great personality, and I like that she came recommended by Tara." Tara had been their original receptionist who'd ended up quitting to stay home with her first baby.

"I agree. And she has experience," Dean added. He looked at Jake. "Thoughts?"

Jake shrugged. "She was okay. But obviously we

don't need to make any rash decisions since Alex is helping out for a while." She'd been there for five days and he already wished she'd stay. He loved being able to see her. Flirt with her, and yeah, he'd broken the rules they'd set up on their tour, but he couldn't help himself.

And she'd flirted back, dammit. Notes on one another's desk, sexy emails full of innuendo. They'd yet to touch each other, but something about the flirting and subterfuge was like foreplay. At some point soon they wouldn't be able to hold back anymore, and he already had his reasoning worked out. If they'd been fine with doing it on the trip, why not be fine doing it until she left town? What was the difference, really?

"I agree, we shouldn't feel rushed," Dean said. "But I know Alex would like to wrap this part-time gig up sooner rather than later."

"She said that?" Jake's brows furrowed.

"Well, not exactly, but she still needs to make a trip to D.C. to find a place to live. I just don't want to keep her here any longer than necessary."

Jake blew out a breath, meeting TJ's wary gaze. The two of them hadn't entirely been the same since their argument over a month ago, but things were okay. He kind of missed talking to his friend the way they used to, but he figured this was just part of how a male friendship evolved when one party eventually joined into a committed relationship with a partner. How could it be like it used to be when they were both single?

"Well, the good news," Jake said, "is that she's here for now, and we still have three interviews to go this week, so let's keep an open mind. But let's all agree that today's interview is a definite contender."

They all nodded their agreement. Jake began to rise

out of his seat when Dean spoke up. "You leaving? We were just getting to the good part."

Jake dropped back down and glanced at TJ, who had a smirk on his face.

"What?" Jake asked, annoyed. Were they keeping something else from him?

In response, TJ pulled a stack of stapled invoices from the bottom of his paper pile and slid it across the table. Jake picked up the first one. It was from a bar he and Alex had visited in Pensacola that owned multiple locations along the Gulf. The invoice was for a nine-hundred-dollar order.

"Nice," he said, moving onto the next document. Twelve hundred dollars from a place in New Orleans. Wow. The next two were similar orders from places he and Alex had visited. The last one, he stared at for a long moment. He looked at TJ who raised his eyebrows. "You're shitting me," Jake said.

"Crazy, right?"

"Whatever you did or said, this time it worked," Dean added.

"I turned down a night out with the daughter. *That's* what I did."

"You're kidding," TJ said. "And you didn't even tell me about that?"

Jake shrugged. "Didn't seem important." And also because they weren't talking as frequently as they'd been before.

"She ugly or something?" Dean asked.

Jake shook his head. "No, she was hot. I just . . . I don't know. Wasn't feeling it. Plus I didn't want to ditch Alex to go out with her that night. She'd have been alone."

"Good man," Dean said. "And she obviously didn't hold a grudge."

"Yeah. I'm shocked," Jake said, looking over the thirty-six-hundred-dollar invoice. "When did this come in?"

"This morning. This tour seriously paid off. This makes thirteen orders total that have come in since you got back."

Jake leaned back in his chair. "Must have been your sister," he said to Dean. "She charmed everyone she met."

"Of that I have no doubt." Dean pushed back his chair but didn't stand up. "But we know this is you. All of your tours have helped this business grow, but this one takes the cake."

Jake looked up at Dean. Had he heard him correctly? "Thank you."

Dean smirked. "You got plans tonight?"

Jake narrowed his brow. "No. Why?"

"I thought we could go out and celebrate."

There was a small knock at the door. They all turned to find Alex peeking in. "Sorry to bother you," she said quietly.

"No problem. Come on in," TJ said.

She quickly met eyes with Jake as she stepped in. "Uh, Dean, Farmer Ben is here to pick up the mash?" Her lips grimaced as if she'd said it wrong. Jake smiled. Clearly she didn't realize they bought their rye from Ben. He cut him a good deal because he came back and picked up the cooked mash to feed his pigs. This kind of relationship was part of the beauty of running a small-batch, locally sourced distillery.

"Okay, thanks."

She gave a quick smile, and Jake and Dean both

called her back at the same time. "Sorry," Dean said. "Alex I just wanted to ask you if you could call Julie's down the street and make a reservation for dinner tonight. For seven people."

"Oh, okay."

"We're celebrating," Jake said, standing up. He walked around the conference table and handed her the invoice.

He watched her scan the contents, her mouth sliding into a smile. "Oh my God! No way!"

Jake laughed. "Can you believe it?"

Her arms flew around his neck in a tight squeeze. His hands settled on her back as he glanced over her shoulder at TJ and Dean, who were both looking on in surprise.

Alex pulled back and looked at the other two guys. "This is amazing. You guys have no idea how hard Jake works on these tours. He's incredible."

Dean's eyebrow went up. "We actually *do* know, and we're grateful."

"Yeah, well, you better." She gave Jake one last smile and left the conference room.

When she was gone, Jake turned back to his friends, who still looked like they wanted to say something, but thankfully neither did. Jake took that as an opportunity to escape. "Thanks for the good news, guys. I've got work to do. Can't wait to celebrate tonight."

He walked out of the conference room and into his office, his heart pounding. Right now it was difficult to know which he was more excited about, the order from Peter Dunn's company, or the fact that he finally found the nerve to ask Alex to come over tonight.

No, that was bullshit. There wasn't an order or an account in the world that would compare to spending a night with Alex. Now he just had to convince her.

He picked up his phone and sent her a text.

JAKE: Go in the women's bathroom in two minutes.
ALEX: Jake!! You're insane.
JAKE: You gonna be there?
ALEX: Yes.

He grinned down at his phone, startled when a knock came at the door. Glancing up, he found TJ standing there.

"Can I come in?"

"Yeah." He glanced at the time. "I've got a minute."

TJ's eyebrow raised as he closed the door and then sat down. "So, you and Alex."

Jake sighed. Of course he couldn't hide anything from his best friend. Honestly, he was surprised it had taken TJ this long. "What about it?"

The look of resignation on TJ's face said he was hoping he'd been wrong. "Dude."

"It's fine, man."

"Is it? Dean will . . . hell, I don't even know. Gut you."

"And why is that? Would it be because he doesn't want anyone with his sister or would it be because I wouldn't meet his standards?"

TJ frowned. "Come on, man. We all know that you've never been one for serious relationships. No guy wants that for his sister."

"What if that's not what's going on here?" Jake asked, defensively.

"Is it not? Because the last I heard, she's moving in November. Am I mistaken?"

Jake's lips pursed and he rested his chin in the crook

of his hand as he leaned on his armrest. "No. You're not mistaken."

TJ muttered a curse. "You've fallen for her. Haven't you?"

Their eyes met. "I don't know."

"Does she know that?"

Jake shook his head. "No. And she won't. Ever." Did he just admit to falling for her? Did he even know himself? He knew that he thought about her constantly. Her smile, her taste, the way he felt inside her. The way she laughed at her own jokes, and teased him when he wasn't sure how to do something.

"Why won't she know? Are you crazy?"

"She's moving, just like you said. And she wants that. Sees it as her opportunity to finally follow her dreams."

TJ looked confused, then laughed, shaking his head.

"What the hell's so goddamn funny," Jake asked.

"I seem to recall being the jackass on the other end of almost this exact conversation with you several times last year. Now I know how stupid I sounded."

Jake should be offended, but instead he found himself laughing. "You're right. Damn, you pissed me off. Everyone knew you and Jen were hot for each other."

"Yeah, well, that little display you and Alex just put on in the conference room . . ."

"Did Dean say anything?"

"Not yet, but you better prepare yourself for the third degree if anything else happens. I just happen to know you a little better than he does."

Jake's phone buzzed and he glanced down. Alex had texted him a stopwatch emoji. He smiled. "I gotta go," he said, getting up from his desk.

"Jake," TJ said, stopping him. "If you're into Alex, let her know. Don't let a good thing get away without trying. I speak from experience."

"We'll see, man." He walked out of his office and headed for the bathroom. Right now he wasn't sure about the future, all he had on his mind was finally getting his hands on Alex.

He glanced around the hallway and ducked into the ladies' restroom. It was empty. Leaning down, he scanned the floor under the two stalls, grinning when he saw her little beige ballet shoes in the last one. Walking down the short row, he gently pressed on the door. It swung open to reveal her standing there biting her lip.

"This is insane," she said.

He locked the stall door and turned to her. "But it's exciting, isn't it."

"Yes," she whispered.

Slowly he stalked toward her, taking in her full lips, flushed cheeks, and bright eyes. "You're so beautiful I can hardly stand it."

The minute his hands settled on her hips, she tilted her face up to his. "Kiss me."

"I plan on it. But tonight, you're coming home with me, and we're going to do a lot more then kissing. Deal?"

She nodded. "Deal."

Eighteen

Alex had never been so hyperaware of another person's body. It was a rather small restaurant, and they were seated at a tightly packed round table, which meant she was nearly shoulder to shoulder to Jake. It also meant he'd been able to discreetly put his hand on her upper thigh, his fingers sliding over her skin back and forth.

It was driving her mad in the best possible way.

After kissing in the ladies' restroom today, she'd gone back and forth on telling him tonight was a bad idea. But the minute he'd walked into the restaurant sporting the most well-fitted slacks and button-up shirt stretched across his chest, she knew she'd been fooling herself. She was pretty sure he'd liked what he saw when he'd looked at her if the smoldering look he'd given her had been any indication. Exactly what she'd hoped for when she'd chosen this navy dress that rode a little high and dipped a little low.

And yet, even with electricity zinging between them, they'd only said hello briefly before taking a seat beside each other. Once their lower extremities had been concealed, it hadn't taken him long to start touching her, and she hadn't minded a bit.

Having roving fingers on her thighs hadn't stopped her from chatting with John, who sat to her right. It was a little odd that he was Charlotte's ex, but Alex could certainly see why Charlotte, and eventually Dean, liked him. He was handsome, funny, and charming. He'd very politely asked her about her job with the CIA, which she'd discussed as well as she could, considering she hadn't yet started. He seemed to be very interested in the kind of work she did, and she realized how much she enjoyed talking about it.

On her other side she could feel Jake listening to their conversation, slightly leaning in her direction, his thumb drawing pictures on her bare skin below the table.

Everyone was in good spirits and several toasts were made around the table, about celebrating six years in business, about the tour, and Jen's new position that would hopefully take the wedding-planning part of the Stag to the next level. They'd even discussed Charlotte and Dean's upcoming wedding.

"That reminds me," Charlotte said, looking at Alex. "Next week I'm going to choose our wedding cake. I'd love you to come with me."

"Oh my gosh, I'd love that. But . . ." she glanced at Dean. "Don't you want to go?"

"We have ten barrels that need bottling this week. Besides, I went last year. I think you'll enjoy it." He gave her a smile, and she understood that he meant he'd gone last year when he'd been planning *her* wedding. The thought sobered her up a bit.

"Only if you want to, Alex," Charlotte said.

"I want to. Definitely."

"Good. I'll text you the time. I can pick you up."

Alex nodded and found herself glancing over at Jake. He winked at her, squeezing her thigh quickly and then pulling his hand up onto the table so he could eat. Immediately she missed his touch, and as soon as she was finished with her chicken, she moved her arm in order to put her hand on him.

She started on his thigh, just resting her hand there. Before long, he'd casually leaned a bit in his chair as everyone continued to drink and converse. It wasn't long before he placed his own hand on hers and moved it . . . right . . . there.

Oh God. His penis jumped under her hand and she gave it a gentle squeeze. He gave the slightest jerk, which delighted her to no end. She glanced around the table to see if anyone seemed to notice, but they were all caught up in their own conversations.

Their group continued to talk, nearly closing Julie's Bistro down. All the other tables were empty, but Ian the manager—who knew the guys well since the Stag was down the road—told them to take their time and enjoy themselves.

She was trying, but at some point, over the past twenty minutes they'd been sitting there . . . something about her had felt off. Very, very off.

Jake leaned to his right and spoke quietly. "You okay?" he asked Alex.

She turned to him, her face and the tops of her breasts were flushed, and her eyes bright. "Yeah. Why?"

"You've had a lot to drink."

Her eyes narrowed, and he hoped he hadn't offended her. He knew how she hated to be made to feel like she needed someone keeping tabs on her. But something wasn't right about how she was swaying.

"Not really. You counting?" she asked.

Grateful she'd spoken quietly and not drawn attention,

he shook his head. "No." And he hadn't been—she'd just gotten quiet, in addition to the physical symptoms.

Then again, it was getting late. They'd been here over three hours. Deciding to drop it, he turned back to the table to find Charlotte watching them. He gave her a tight-lipped smile.

Did she know? It was possible that Alex had confided in her, but he wasn't certain that Alex would have trusted that Charlotte could keep from telling Dean, so maybe it was just her sharp observational skills. Nothing got by Charlotte, and he figured it was partly because she was a photographer. He'd seen enough of her work to note how she managed to take photos of people in intimate moments that others around them would probably never have noticed.

Twenty minutes later John announced he was heading out. Everyone said goodbye, then Charlotte spoke up. "This was fun, everyone. We should do it more often."

"We should. In fact, TJ and I were thinking that we should have another cookout. Like we did in the spring," Jen said.

"That's such a good idea. Especially now that Alex is home for a while," Charlotte said. Jake couldn't help notice Alex didn't really respond with anything more than a smile. Something wasn't right. An hour ago she'd been slowly trying to rub out a situation below the table. He'd had to stop her, reluctantly. They could finish it later. Maybe—because now she was eerily quiet, her hands folded in her lap.

"You feeling okay?" Dean asked, his eyes narrowed on Alex.

Thank you. Someone else was seeing it.

Alex balked, an annoyed chuckle coming out. "Why is everyone asking me that?"

"Sweetie your face is red." Jen's face was full of sympathy.

Without thinking, Jake reached over and held the back of his hand to her forehead. She jerked back at first, but then relaxed when she realized what he was doing.

"You're really warm, Alex." Now he was worried. He wasn't imagining this.

"I guess I do feel kind of shitty." Alex looked at all of them. "But it's not because I'm drunk. My stomach hurts." She put a hand on her stomach. "Maybe it was my chicken."

"Could have been," Charlotte glanced at everyone. "Anyone else get chicken tonight?"

Everyone shook their heads. Dean and TJ and even John had gotten the same as Jake, steak. And he was pretty sure the other two women had gotten salmon because they'd discussed it at length while they ate.

Alex's shoulders sagged. "We need to stop talking about it. I feel worse with every second that goes by."

"Why don't I take you home?" Jake said, moving to get up.

"No!" Her eyes got wide and she looked at her brother. "Can we go? Like, right now. Please."

Everyone looked at one another for a second, and then moved all at once. Jake watched Alex stand up and bolt to the front of the restaurant without speaking to anyone. Charlotte rushed after her.

"She's so going to christen the sidewalk out front," Jen said as they gathered their things. "I know it when I see it."

"Are you serious?" Jake said frantically, fearing that she was probably right.

"Should we tell Ian we think she may have food poisoning?" TJ asked quietly.

"I don't know. Shit, this sucks," Dean muttered as he scratched his signature onto the credit card receipt. "What if that's not what it is."

"Seems likely." Jake glanced down and saw Alex's purse on the floor near her chair. He picked it up. "She was fine until a little bit ago."

"Maybe she's just drunk," Dean said.

"She didn't drink more than I did," Jen added.

"Yeah, I don't think that's it," Jake said. And he didn't. It had come on too suddenly. He'd seen her drink before and she hadn't gotten sick like this. Plus she wasn't acting intoxicated. "But I think we should tell Ian. He'd be better off erring on the side of safety and throwing out the chicken. We're his friends and we won't make a big deal about this. Someone else might take it to the news."

"He's right," TJ said. He looked at Dean. "You take her home. I'll talk to him."

Dean nodded. "Thanks, man."

Jake followed Dean outside, Alex's purse in his hand. The minute they were on the sidewalk, he heard it.

"Shit," Jake muttered, his heart pounding. It was dark out, but the Maple Springs town square perimeter was dotted with vintage-style street lamps, giving them a clear view of Alex bent over near a park bench on the square puking her guts out. Charlotte stood next to her, rubbing her back. She looked over and saw them all on the sidewalk.

"Dean, bring me some napkins from the car," Charlotte called.

He moved quickly, heading for his vehicle parked along the side of the road. Jake didn't know what to do with himself, so he began to cross the street just as Alex stood up and looked over her shoulder.

"No!" she called out instantly. "Go away!"

He froze, eyes locking with Charlotte, who gave him a sad smile. "It's okay Jake, we'll call you and let you know how she is."

Nodding, and feeling a little stupid, he held up Alex's purse. "I'll put this in Dean's car."

"Thanks," Charlotte said, rubbing Alex's shoulder. She'd sat down on the metal bench and had her head resting on the back. She looked horrible, and it was killing him. Couldn't people die from salmonella or E. coli? He didn't know what was wrong with her, but there was no way to guarantee it was just something that would work itself out.

On the way over to Dean's car, he met him in the street. "Hey," he said, stopping his friend. "You may need to take her to the hospital."

Dean's eyes narrowed. "I realize that."

"You keep me updated. Okay?"

"Okay. I will."

Jake put a hand on Dean's arm. "I mean it. Let me know how she is."

Dean hesitated a moment and then finally responded. "I will, man. I promise."

Somewhat satisfied, Jake walked to Dean's SUV and put Alex's purse in the back seat. As he laid it down, he noticed her journal inside. Shaking his head, he shut the door and headed for his own car. He'd already snooped once, but now more than ever, he was dying to know if she was thinking of him the way he was thinking of her.

Nineteen

When Alex woke up, she was in a hospital bed, with an IV in her arm. How long had she been here? Her eyes could barely make out the giant clock on the opposite wall. Finally, she focused and saw that it was almost nine. In the morning? What day?

She had a vague memory of going back to Dean's house after vomiting in the park. She'd then thrown up again in the bathroom, Fernando sitting beside her on the cold tile. A groan came from her lips as she recalled things turning violent after that, her body letting go of fluid in every possible way. *Oh God*. It had been so bad.

Moving her head to the side, she tried to find clues to who might be here with her and saw Charlotte's purse on the chair. But no Charlotte.

Lying back on the pillow, she closed her eyes. She remembered walking into the ER, getting hooked up to an IV, but beyond that, things were a bit of a blur. Had admitting her really been necessary?

She lay there for a while, wondering what was going on. Finally the door opened and a nurse walked in, her smile bright. "Good morning. How are you feeling?"

She checked a monitor beside the bed, waiting for Alex to answer. "Okay. Tired."

"I bet. How's your tummy feel?"

Alex put a hand on her abdomen. "Like I did a hundred sit-ups."

"Not surprised. You were one sick woman. I think the worst of it has passed. The fluids should be helping a lot."

"It was food poisoning, right?"

The nurse nodded as she put a thermometer in Alex's mouth. "Dr. Benson is on her way in. She'll discuss it with you."

Alex opened her mouth when the thermometer beeped. "Okay."

Her head pounded as she relaxed into the pillow. She felt like she'd been in a car accident. Where was her brother?

A few moments later the door opened again and a middle-aged woman with red lipstick came in. She smiled back. "Morning."

"Morning," Alex said, giving a weak smile.

"I'm Dr. Benson. How are you feeling?"

"Like garbage, honestly."

"I can imagine. Do you recall talking with the ER doctor last night?"

Alex tried to think and finally shook her head. "No. All I can remember is puking and going to the bathroom at the same time. TMI, sorry."

Dr. Benson raised an eyebrow and chuckled. "No such thing in a hospital, I'm afraid."

Alex laughed, but it hurt her stomach so she moaned. "I'm sore everywhere."

"I'm sure. Your body was traumatized by this. You'll

need to take it easy for a while." Dr. Benson stepped closer. "Alexis, we ran a stool test and blood work last night. I need to ask you . . . are you aware that you're pregnant?"

Alex inhaled, her breath stuttering. Opening her mouth, she felt her heart beating in her head. "What?" she whispered.

"Your blood work revealed that you're pregnant, which is why we went ahead and admitted you for observation. The severity of your symptoms, in addition to the bacterial infection itself, and the alcohol in your system. Well, all of that combined could negatively affect a growing fetus. It will probably be fine, but we didn't want to take any chances."

"What?" she repeated.

"When was your last period, Alex?" Dr. Benson asked, her face a mix of business and sympathy.

Alex whimpered. "I don't know." Shit, she hadn't even thought about it. She'd used protection. And life had been so busy. She tried to think back. It had definitely been before the trip. "At least five or six weeks." *Oh God.* "This can't be happening. Are you sure?"

"I'm afraid I am."

Alex closed her eyes, the pounding in her forehead making her feel nauseous again. "I think I might be sick."

She could hear the doctor moving around and then gently placing something near her. "Here you go. I'm sorry to have to tell you this news like this. But it's better that we know so we can help you and your baby the best way possible."

As Alex's thoughts warred in her head, something occurred to her. Her eyes shot open. "Does my family know this?"

Dr. Benson shook her head. "No. Dr. Ellis, who treated you last night, chose not to tell anyone until you were coherent enough to discuss this. He made the judgment call that you probably weren't that far along, and that you may not have even been aware yet. So only the staff who helped you know right now."

She sighed in relief. "Okay. Thank you. Please don't say anything to them."

"No one will. That will be up to you. I'm going to recommend you stay here today. Possibly until tomorrow. Once the antibiotics start to work and the fluids help you feel better, than we'll reevaluate this afternoon. Sound good?"

"Sure," Alex said, tears pooling in her eyes.

Dr. Benson nodded. "I'll be back in a few hours. And Alex, everything will be okay."

Alex wasn't so sure, but she just nodded. The minute the woman left, she sucked in a hard breath. How had this happened? Dammit, she knew exactly how it had happened. But how? They'd always used a condom. Every single time.

Rolling slowly, holding her stomach tight against her, she maneuvered herself onto her side. That's when the tears fell, sliding down her temple and onto the pillow. What was she going to tell her brother? What was she going to do? What about her job?

A baby? She didn't want a baby. It wasn't part of her plan. Not at all. How had she been so stupid to let herself get knocked up? And how in the world was she going to tell Jake?

She lay there for what seemed like an hour, her mind racing, when a quick knock sounded on the door before opening. Charlotte peeked her head in smiling. The minute she saw Alex, it turned into a look of concern.

"What's wrong? Did you get sick again?" She asked, glancing down at the bedpan resting near Alex's arm.

"No, I just . . ." Dean walked into the room, a cup of coffee in hand, his brows narrowed. "I don't feel great. That's all."

Charlotte scooted a chair closer to Alex's bed. "I bet. Last night was awful for you."

"I don't think I've ever been that sick in my life."

"I'm so sorry." Charlotte reached up and grabbed Alex's hand. "Do you still feel like anything needs to come out?"

Alex shook her head. "Not at the moment." Her lip began to quiver again. The weight of the news she'd just received was so heavy, she was tempted to just scream it out. But another part of her wanted to just pretend every word out of Dr. Benson's mouth had been a dream. How could your life change so much in a matter of moments?

A stupid question. She'd already survived several life-altering moments. Ones she'd been certain would destroy her.

The image of Nate that popped into her head had her tears coming fresh. She pinched her eyes shut, embarrassed to be losing it in front of her brother and Charlotte. Nate had wanted children so badly. Talked about it constantly, even going as far as telling her he wanted a son named after his father and grandfather. They'd waited, because they had big plans for their future. How could she do this to him? Just let herself be so careless as to get pregnant by accident?

"It's okay, Alex," Charlotte said quietly. "You'll feel better soon."

She shook her head. Now she just wanted them to go

away. "You guys can go if you want," she said, her voice teary.

"No way," Dean said. "We're not leaving you."

"I'm fine, Dean."

"Should I tell Jake to go?" Charlotte asked. "He came by to check on you a while ago. He's been really worried, sitting in the waiting room all morning."

Alex nearly groaned. Was now the time to drop this bomb on him? She hadn't even had time to process the news or what she was going to do about it. "Yes. Please tell him to go. I don't want to see anyone."

"Okay," Charlotte said, her voice full of concern.

"I'll go tell him," Dean said before leaving.

Alex could feel Charlotte's presence beside her but she couldn't open her eyes. Between the pain in her head and ache in her heart, she wasn't strong enough to make eye contact. Charlotte was easy to talk to, and Alex was afraid she'd spill.

"Jake really cares about you, Alex." Charlotte said. "I know you don't feel up to it now, but if you need to talk about what happened between the two of you, I'm here for you."

Alex breathed deep. That was so typical of Charlotte, who was too perceptive and kind for her own good. Eventually Alex would have to deal with what was happening to her. When she was ready she'd turn to her future sister-in-law, but until then, she just wanted to wallow in her sadness.

Jake watched Dean come down the hall toward the third-floor waiting room. His face looked serious, and that was when Jake knew what he was about to say.

"She doesn't want me to come back. Does she?"

"Nah. Sorry man." Dean eyed the items in Jake's hands. On a whim, he'd picked up a stuffed giraffe with big eyes wearing a pink T-shirt in the gift shop along with a balloon that said GET WELL. He was pretty sure the stuffed animal was intended to be a new baby gift, but for some reason it had made him think of her, so he'd grabbed it, not even questioning the twenty-dollar price tag or the tiny diaper it was wearing.

He held the items out to Dean. "Uh, I just . . . got these. You can give them to her."

"Cute," Dean said. He flipped over the tag on the giraffe's ear and raised an eyebrow. "'It's a Girl'?"

"I just liked its face, okay? I thought she'd like it," Jake said defensively.

Dean laughed. "She will. You're right."

"So it's officially food poisoning, right? She gonna be okay?"

"Yeah, that's what they say. IV fluids and antibiotics."

"Seems weird they admitted her. Could it be more serious?"

"I don't think so. I think they're just being cautious." Dean shifted on his feet. "She wouldn't appreciate me getting graphic or anything, but last night when we went home, it was really bad. I don't think she had any fluid left in her body. About three in the morning she was so weak she couldn't stand up to leave the bathroom. That's when we brought her here."

Jake winced, his head hammering with worry and fear.

"I appreciate you coming, man. I know you guys got to be close friends on that trip. She'll be ready to see you when she's feeling better."

Jake nodded. "I know. I understand."

Dean gave him a tight smile and held up the giraffe

and balloon. "I'll go tell her it's a girl. That might cheer her up."

Jake just shook his head and backed up toward the elevator. "Call me if anything changes."

"Will do."

Twenty

A week later, Alex poured herself a big glass of water in Joel's kitchen. He was in the living room reading, so she quietly walked back to her room, grabbed the plastic bowl she'd just barfed into, and sneaked back into the kitchen.

After washing it out, she grabbed a paper towel to dry it off, intent on taking it back to her room and shoving it under the bed before she climbed back into it to sleep most of the day away. The excuse of needing to recover from her illness had been an excellent cover for the kind of depression that made it difficult to function like a normal person.

The minute she turned around she jumped at finding Joel sitting at the kitchen table.

"Jeez, you scared me," she said.

"Sorry, didn't mean to." He smiled. "Sit, Alex."

She sighed, put the bowl on the counter, and sat across from him at the little breakfast table. "Everything okay?" she asked brightly, attempting to redirect.

He gave her a long look. "You tell me. I've seen you tiptoe into this kitchen with that bowl for the past four mornings."

She sagged into her chair. So much for him being old and aloof. "I thought I was flying under the radar."

"Close. I'm not the most perceptive guy, but I heard you the other day. And you turned down my bacon this morning."

She groaned, "Oh God, the smell. I can still smell it."

Joel nodded in understanding, then went silent for a moment. "Who else knows?"

"No one."

His graying eyebrows went up. "Not even the father?"

She shook her head.

"How come? You're a grown woman. You have no reason to keep this a secret."

"I don't know, Joel. I'm not handling it well."

"That's understandable. Have you considered what you are going to do?"

With a long-suffering sigh, she leaned on the table. "Live here forever, sleep the days away, and pretend this isn't happening?"

"If only life were so grand," he teased. "Who's the father, Alex? You're obviously not going to have to be alone in the decision making."

She pinched her lips together and looked down at her fingers. "Jake Cooper."

When she looked up and risked a glance at Joel, she didn't see even the smallest trace of surprise or even judgment on his face. "Well, you've got one thing going for you then."

Her eyes narrowed. "What's that?"

"You'll have one good-lookin' kid."

She couldn't help smiling. Probably for the first time in a week.

"And what do you think Jake will say?"

"I have no idea. I considered not telling him," she said, wincing.

"Alex," Joel chided, then sighed. "He deserves to know. Sooner rather than later."

"How do you inform someone you've ruined their life?"

Joel's head jerked back, and he let out a chuckle. "That's quite a bold statement, young lady. Babies don't ruin lives. Are they difficult and sometimes unexpected?" He shrugged. "Of course. Also, it's been a while I'll admit, but if I recall, this isn't something *you* did to *him*. You did it together."

Ugh, what a conversation. But she had to admit, talking about it took a weight off her chest. But she still wasn't convinced by what he was saying. "This news will absolutely blindside him."

"Did it blindside you?"

"Of course. I nearly passed out."

"Then why spare him? You don't need to go through this alone."

Alex considered that. "I know you're right. But part of me still isn't ready to deal with it. It's like, I can just keep pretending it's possibly not really happening."

He nodded to the bowl on the counter. "The consistent reoccurrence of that bowl tells me it's definitely happening. And pretty soon you won't be able to hide it."

"I know that." She looked at him. "I'm scared. And angry. And sad. And guilty."

"*Guilty?* What for?"

Her lips twisted, and she glanced out the window. "Joel . . . I don't want this baby. I'm a horrible person, but I don't want to be a mother."

The look of sympathy on his face was disarming and she had to look away. Why did he have to have faith in her? She didn't have any in herself. Not when it came to this. "How do you know that, Alex? The news is still brand new."

"Having a family was no longer part of my plan. That was something I was going to do with Nate. Not on my own. What about my job? What about . . . everything?"

"I can't answer these questions for you. You've got to tell Jake, though. He might surprise you. Hell, you might surprise yourself. I think you'd be surprised how everything might be okay if you open your mind up to the possibilities. There are too many people who love you for this to be bad."

She shook her head. "I don't know. Right now it feels like . . . the end."

"Well, the only thing to do at the end of something, is start a new beginning," he said.

Alex slumped in her chair. "Thanks, Joel." Although she wasn't sure if she felt better.

"Anytime, darlin'. Now." He tilted his chin and gave her a serious look. "Start going in the bathroom and vomiting like a civilized person. No more bowl."

She couldn't help laughing as she got up and went over to give him a hug. He hugged her back and then she went into her room and lay down on the bed.

Her hands instinctively sought out the "It's a Girl" giraffe stuffed animal. Her first thought when Dean had given it to her and said it was from Jake had been to throw it in the trash. What kind of sick jokester was the universe for doing that to her? But then, she hadn't been able to let it go, cuddling with it in the hospital and sleeping with it every night since she'd been home.

She'd only talked to Jake once, briefly, to assure him she was recovering. The worry in his voice had only made her more depressed. He'd been up to the hospital twice. Each time she'd turned him away, which she felt bad about, but how was she supposed to face him without telling him the horrible news?

First, she'd needed time to process it herself. Not that the seclusion had helped. In fact, she was more confused and angry than ever. It also hadn't helped that recovering from the food poisoning and night from hell—as she liked to call it—had been harder on her body than she'd anticipated. Add in some awesome morning sickness and a bleak outlook on the future, and she was basically a bedridden head case.

Rolling over, she grabbed her journal from the bedside table. She'd avoided it for the past week because she hadn't known how to face her own thoughts. In many ways, this journal had been her way of communicating with Nate's spirit when she felt the need, and part of her felt like if she didn't write it down, she could keep the truth and the shame from consuming her.

But now that she'd talked with Joel, the secret was out in the universe. It had penetrated her bubble of denial.

Day 446
I'm pregnant. I'm terrified. What will happen now? Everything I had planned is ruined. What am I going to do with myself? I don't want to be a mother. It wasn't supposed to be this way.

I'm so sorry, Nate. So, so sorry.

Today I intend to feel, I have no idea. But I do need to tell Jake. Soon.

Her phone buzzed on the bed and she picked up, revealing a text from Charlotte.

CHARLOTTE: How you feeling? Up to sampling cake today?

Oh God. She wasn't sure if she could, but damn, she was going to try.

A shower had gone a long way in making Alex feel better. The tea that Joel had made her had also helped. By the time Charlotte pulled up to the house, she felt somewhat normal.

"How are you doing?" Charlotte asked as Alex buckled her seat belt.

She turned and forced a smile. "Better."

"Good. We've all been a wreck worrying about you this week. Especially Jake. He has worked out that I know about you two and has been texting me constantly for updates."

"You're kidding. Why doesn't he text *me*?" Or maybe he had and she hadn't always replied. Yeah, that was it.

"I don't know. But you should call him now that you're feeling better."

"I will. Promise," she said as they headed toward the highway. "This illness has just taken a lot more out of me than I expected."

"Oh my God, I can imagine. Girl, you were wrecked that night. I'd never seen anything like it. Salmonella is no joke."

"Seriously. I wouldn't wish it on my worst enemy." Except she'd go through it again to not be dealing with what she was right now. God, she was horrible. *Horrible*.

Thankfully for the rest of the drive to the cake decorators, Charlotte rambled on about ideas she had for her and Dean's wedding. Alex actually enjoyed listening and even giving her thoughts. For a few minutes she could just pretend life was going on as normal.

When they pulled up to a small house she was surprised. "This is the baker?"

"Yes. And just wait until you see the kitchen she has in the back. Jill's cakes are legendary. However, we're using her granddaughter Julia. I'm pretty sure Jill is priming her to take over her business so she can retire."

They got out of the car and headed around the side of the house. They went through a tall wooden gate and sure enough, there was an addition built on to the back of the house. Next to the door was a sign: JILL & JULIA'S CAKES. BY APPOINTMENT ONLY.

Charlotte pointed at the sign. "Ooh, look. She's made it official and put Julia's name on the sign." Just then the door opened and an older woman with shoulder-length grayish blonde hair stood inside.

"Charlotte, so good to see you," she said, stepping aside so they could enter. She immediately turned to Alex. "I'm Jill."

"So nice to meet you. Alexis."

"Jill, Alexis is my fiancé's younger sister. The one we were here choosing for last year."

Jill immediately turned and grabbed Alex's hand. "Of course. Oh sweetie, I was just heartbroken to hear of your loss. How are you?"

Did she have a moment? Or six hundred? Alex thought. But instead, she just smiled and replied kindly. "Much better. Thank you. I'm really excited to be here myself and help Charlotte pick her cake."

Giving her hand a quick pat, Jill turned and led them

into the packed room. But what a room it was—lined ovens, shelves filled with cake pans, mixers, and all manner of cake-decorating paraphernalia. The giant island in the center took up most of the room. And it smelled divine, like butter and vanilla.

"Julia will be right out," Jill said. "She just got back from a party delivery for this evening." Just as she said it, a young woman with a brunette ponytail and a pink apron stepped through a door that obviously connected the cake kitchen to the house.

"Sorry to keep you waiting," she said. "So good to see you both." Alex was glad they didn't repeat the sad introduction, but instead got right to the business of cake tasting and looking at cake photos. It made her realize how much fun she'd missed out on by not being able to plan her own wedding. Then again, maybe it was for the best.

After nearly eating their weight in cake samples, Charlotte and Alex had come to a mutual decision on two flavors. Chocolate-chip cake with chocolate-fudge filling for one layer and carrot cake with cream-cheese filling for the other. Alex had verified Charlotte's suspicions that, although Dean never got that excited about sweets, he really liked carrot cake.

By the time they left, Alex had actually started to feel happy. Spending time laughing with other women had helped tremendously. Once they were back in the car, Charlotte turned to her. "How about some coffee? There's a great place down the street from here."

Alex nodded. "Sure."

Before long they were seated outside, sipping lattes and soaking up the sun.

"It's such a gorgeous day," Charlotte said, angling her head up to the sky.

"It is."

"I'm so happy to have you doing some of this with me. We really need to discuss what color bridesmaid's dress you'd like to wear."

Alex's eyes went wide. How had she not thought of that yet? How pregnant would she be in April? *Would* she be pregnant in April? Just thinking the question to herself made her feel dizzy.

"Alex, are you okay?" Charlotte asked, touching her arm.

She looked up. "Yeah, why?"

"You just suddenly looked . . . green. And your eyelids sort of fluttered."

"No, I'm fine. Sorry."

Charlotte's eyes narrowed. "Are you sure you're feeling better? Did the hospital tell you to follow up with a primary care doctor? You should go to mine."

Alex shook her head. "No, no. I'm okay."

"Is it too much wedding talk? I'm sorry, I should have known."

"No, Charlotte. I promise, it's okay. I'm excited to be in the wedding, and help you plan. But . . ." Their eyes met, and suddenly the weight of her secret, and the pain of the unknown was so intense she felt like she could no longer shoulder it on her own. "Charlotte, I need to tell you something. But you can't tell anyone else."

"What is it?" The concern in her voice was obvious.

"I'm pregnant."

Charlotte's lips parted, her eyes widening. "Oh my. Is it . . . Jake's?"

Alex nodded.

"Oh honey . . ." Alex could tell Charlotte was searching for words. Finally she grabbed Alex's hand and smiled before finishing. "That's the most amazing news."

Alex's chin dipped and her eyebrows went up. That was not the reaction she was expecting. In fact, it was so sincere and kind, she immediately started to cry.

The look of panic on Charlotte's face made Alex cry even harder. She could feel the eyes of coffee shop patrons on her but right now she didn't care, she just wanted to sob and let out all of her frustration.

She wiped at her eyes as Charlotte sent an awkward smile to the people around them. "Excuse us. Sorry," she said as she stood, stuffed one coffee in her elbow, the other in her hand, and then grabbed Alex. "Come on, sweetie."

She shuffled them into the parking lot and over to the car. By the time they were sitting inside, Alex had somewhat pulled herself together.

"I'm so sorry, I don't know what just happened."

Charlotte smirked. "You're pregnant. That's what happened."

"Oh God." Alex cried out, letting her head fall back on the headrest. "I can't believe this, Charlotte."

"How is Jake taking this? I mean, no wonder he's been so worried about you. I'm surprised he hasn't knocked down Joel's door."

Slowly, Alex looked at her friend. "He doesn't know."

"What?"

"The only people who know are Joel and now you."

Charlotte's head jerked back. "You told Joel?"

Alex shrugged. "Apparently the sound of daily yakking is a dead giveaway. Who knew?"

Charlotte frowned. "You poor thing. How far do you think you are?"

"Maybe seven weeks or so. To be honest, I've tried not to think about it."

"Why not? This is amazing."

"No, it's not. Charlotte, I don't want to have a baby. I want to move to Virginia and work for the CIA. I was not meant to have a family . . . my chance died."

They were silent for a moment and Alex wiped a tear from her eye.

"Alex, a pregnancy is an incredible gift. I hope you realize that."

Oh no. She met Charlotte's eyes, feeling like the biggest asshole in the world. "I'm so sorry, Charlotte. I can't believe how insensitive that was."

She gave her a small smile. "No it wasn't. You're dealing with something huge right now. Your feelings are normal. I just hope you can try and look at it a different way. There are people desperate to get pregnant. It's a miracle. Truly."

Alex wished she could see it that way. She really did. But right now it felt like a tragedy, and every single fear she possessed come to life. How in the world could she keep a human life safe? Every person she'd loved that much—except one, her brother—had died and left her alone. How could she handle being a mother? Loving something so fiercely and also being responsible for caring for it all alone? It was unthinkable.

"Maybe this was exactly what was meant to happen," Charlotte said. "Maybe Jake was meant to happen to you. There is no doubt that he cares for you a lot."

Alex shook her head. "Not like that. Even if he did . . . a baby, Charlotte?" she pleaded. "This is Jake we're talking about. The man who has slept with women all over the South."

Charlotte hesitated. "Is that what this is about? That you don't want a baby with Jake?"

Was that it? "No. I don't even know why I said that."

"I think you need to tell him. Right away. Things always seem more difficult when you feel alone. I promise you. And you won't be alone, no matter what. Dean and I are here for you. Always."

Twenty-One

Jake shut the door to their storage building across the back alley of the Stag. He and John had just moved a few more barrels over to the main building to begin the bottling process. Since they were still a small operation, it was all hands on deck when it was time to process a finished product. The bottling, labeling, packaging, was all them. Over the past year or so, they occasionally enlisted the help of Charlotte and Jen. Sometimes even friends, but for the most part, the four of them—Jake, TJ, Dean, and John—did the work.

His phone buzzed in his pocket and he pulled it out, surprised and decidedly happy to see Alex's name attached to a text. He opened it up.

ALEX: Busy today?
JAKE: Barrel-processing. Want to come help?
ALEX: Sounds like a blast. But I was thinking more along the lines of lunch.

He stared at the screen in shock. She wanted to get together. Immediately he replied.

JAKE: Yes.

They hadn't seen each other since the night she'd gotten sick, well over a week ago. She'd texted a couple of days later to thank him for the giraffe, but that was it. Every other time he'd tried to reach out, he'd been met with silence. Several times he'd tried to get information through Charlotte, but she'd assured him that Alex had just been through a lot and was resting. The wait had been killing him, and he'd been close to showing up on Joel's doorstep more than once. He'd even driven by. Twice.

ALEX: I still don't have a car and Joel went to the
  doctor. Can you pick me up?
JAKE: Of course.

He glanced at his watch. It was already 10:45.

JAKE: I can be there at 11:00. Is that too soon?
ALEX: No. That's fine.

He shoved his phone into his pocket and looked at John. "Hey, man. Can we pick this up after lunch? Something came up."

"Sure. Everything okay?"

"Yeah, everything's great." He glanced at his watch and thought through all the possibilities. "I'll probably be back around one or so. Actually, I don't know when I'll be back."

John smirked. "Take your time, man."

Jake just laughed and headed for the front of the building. He went into the restroom and checked his face in the mirror. He looked tired and he was a week short of a legitimate beard, but there was nothing to be done about it now.

Heading to the alley, he got in his Jeep and made the short trip across Maple Springs to where Dean's father lived. When he pulled up, Alex was sitting outside on the front step.

She stood up as soon as she spotted him, and his heart lodged in his throat. She always looked beautiful, but today her hair was in a ponytail, there were dark circles under her eyes, and she had on a pair of cutoffs with a baggy shirt. This wasn't the Alex he'd spent two weeks on the road with, and all he wanted to do was hold her.

He pulled in, and before he had a chance to get out, she walked straight to the passenger door and got in.

"Hi," she said with a smile.

"Hey," he said, reaching out to grab her hand. "It's so damn good to see you."

Her eyes widened, her cheeks blushing. "Good to see you too."

His eyes ran over her body. "You feeling better? I've been out of my mind worrying about you."

"I'm better, yeah."

But something was wrong. No doubt in his mind. He began to back out of the drive. "Where do you want to eat?"

"Actually, before we do that, can we just maybe go somewhere and talk. Like the lake?"

Before he took off, he stopped in the middle of the street. He turned and looked at her. "Alex, is something wrong?"

She gave him a pretty smile and squeezed his hand. "I just missed you. And I'm really not that hungry."

He wasn't entirely convinced she was being honest with him, but he nodded and took off toward the Maple Springs lake on the west side of town. It wasn't very big, but he found an area to park near some playground equipment and a couple of picnic tables. There was also a dock with a bench, and he figured she might like to sit out there since it was such a nice day.

"I haven't been out here since high school," he said as they walked out to the dock.

"I can only imagine what you were doing out here in high school."

"You're better off not trying," he said, and she laughed.

The sound was like a balm to the anxiety he'd been suffering from for the past couple of weeks without her close by.

There was a slight breeze coming off the water, but luckily the air was still warm enough that it was pleasant. Alex sat down on the bench, pulled up her legs, and crisscrossed them.

"Now be honest with me, Alex. How have you been feeling?" he asked, resting an arm around her back.

"Okay. Thank you for the giraffe, by the way," she said, smiling.

He chuckled. "I hoped you'd like it."

"I did." She looked down at her legs. "You know, it was kind of funny because . . ."

When she didn't finish her sentence, his brow furrowed. Finally, he dipped his head and touched her chin. "Alex, look at me."

She shook her head, not allowing him to lift her face up to his. He inhaled, panic settling into his chest. What was going on? Was she seeing someone else? Moving away early? Did they find out that it wasn't food poisoning she had, but something worse?

A tear fell on her bare leg and he instantly went down to his knees on the dock in front of her, grabbing each side of her waist, trying to look up into her face. "Alex, babe, talk to me."

She wiped at her eyes and looked away from him, out at the lake. "I can't," she whispered through tears.

"Alexis, you're killing me right now. Tell me what's wrong. Is it me? Did I do something?" His voice was frantic, but he didn't care. All he wanted to know was what was wrong, and how he could make it right if possible.

She shook her head and finally met his eyes. "Jake," she whispered.

"What? Tell me."

"I'm pregnant."

He froze there, on his knees, his arms resting on her legs, his hands on her waist. Slowly the earth began to spin around them. He registered cold air on his face and then goose bumps broke out on his skin.

"You're pregnant?" he heard himself ask quietly.

She nodded. "I found out in the hospital. They did blood work in the ER."

"So . . ." He looked down at her soft hands resting in her lap, and then his eyes ran up her torso, her baggy shirt. He wanted to touch her, hold her. Lifting his head, he repeated his earlier statement. "You're pregnant. With my baby?"

Her lips trembled. "Yes. I'm sorry."

"Why are you sorry?" he asked. They'd done everything right—he thought. They'd used a condom every time, even though it had obviously failed them somehow. This wasn't her fault.

"I'm sorry because this was not supposed to happen,

Jake. We had a plan. I had a plan. What in the world are we going to do?"

He sucked in a breath, completely at a loss for words to say. One thought kept running through his head. *My baby. She's pregnant with . . . my baby. Inside of her.* A gut-wrenching, raw and protective feeling came over him as he looked at her. How did he make her understand that there was no reason to cry?

"Alex, everything will be okay. I promise. I mean— I'm in shock, I think—but it will be okay."

She bit at her lip and could barely meet his eyes. "I've been thinking," she said. "It's crazy, but . . . you know, Charlotte and Dean can't have children so they've started looking into adoption, and—"

"Stop," he said, dread and fury washing through him. The sudden look of fear in her eyes let him know it had come out more forcefully than he'd intended. But the words that were coming out of her mouth were so unimaginable he felt like he could demolish something.

Pushing up from his knees, he stood, suddenly unsure of what to do with himself. He turned and looked down at her. "Alexis, if you think for one fucking minute, I'd let you give our baby to your brother, then you don't know me very well."

"So then what? We just have it? Pretend we're a family with me living halfway across the country? How would that work?"

"Halfway across the—" He stared at her in confusion and then it dawned on him. "Are you kidding me? You're still gonna do it? You're going to still take this job. *Pregnant?*"

She stood now, her body rigid with frustration. "Why

wouldn't I? It's what I want. You know that, Jake. You've always known."

"Of course I know what you want, Alex. We talk about you all the goddamn time. But what about what *I* want?" he yelled, pointing at himself. "I'm not sure if you realize this, but I sure as fuck have feelings too."

Her mouth formed a perfect O, before her eyes narrowed in anger. "You asshole. I asked you about your feelings all the time."

"Did you, Alex? And if I answered, did you listen?"

"That's not fair," she whispered.

He knew it wasn't fair. Right now he *was* being an ass, turning the table on her, because he *had* deflected every time she tried to probe too deeply into his emotions. He'd never wanted to share how hard it had been to be the kid who had needed special classes in school just to learn to read, or how his parents used to tell people that they just needed to "get Jake through high school," when his siblings were getting straight *A*'s. Those things lingered with him, whispering in his ear that he wasn't smart enough, that if anything good happened to him, he was just lucky or got by with his charm.

While she was busy crying over her dead fiancé, would it really have seemed appropriate for him to share how his brothers teased him that he'd be the one that would never marry? Sometimes he tried to figure out if they based those assumptions on the fact that he always tried to appear uninterested, or did they believe he truly wasn't capable of supporting a family?

No, it had been easier to be her go-to. Her safe space. That's what he'd wanted because it had made him feel good. Feel needed.

They stood there staring at each other for a long

moment, and the look of pain in her eyes was like a knife in his heart. This woman had been through so much, and now this. He held out a hand. "Come here," he said quietly.

She hesitated a beat, her lips trembling. Her shoulders slumped and she stepped forward. The minute she was close enough, he grabbed her and pulled her into his chest. He closed his eyes and rested his temple on her head, relieved when her arms wrapped around his waist.

"I'm sorry," he said.

"I'm sorry too."

They stood like that a long time, the sound of water hitting the dock below and the breeze on their skin. He knew this moment was only the beginning of a tough road ahead of them, but for just this moment, he wanted to hold onto her and not let go.

Twenty-Two

By the time Jake got back to the Stag, he was a mess. He was just glad that Dean appeared to have left already. Heading into TJ's office, he shut the door.

"What's wrong?" TJ asked, looking up, brow furrowed.

Jake sat down hard in the chair across from his friend and leaned forward.

"I'm about to tell you something that you cannot repeat outside of this room."

TJ frowned.

"At least, not yet."

"Okay," TJ said. They'd been best friends a long time. Played sports together. Went camping together. They didn't ever go to the same schools, but that had almost made their bond stronger because they'd had to work to stay close friends. And they had, even starting this business—along with Dean—together. Jake would take a bullet for TJ and he knew his friend felt the same way, even if they did sometimes bitch like siblings and have disagreements.

Jake took a deep breath and blew it out slowly. "Alex is pregnant."

TJ's eyes immediately went wide. "Shit, seriously?"

"Seriously." Jake said, willing his friend to get it. It was obvious when he did. His eyes narrowing.

"Wait. Do you mean . . ."

"It's mine."

"You're kidding me." He shook his head and lowered his voice. "What the hell were you thinking?"

"What do you mean what was I thinking? It was an accident."

"I figured that much. I mean what were you thinking hooking up with Alex?"

"Well, I was thinking that she's an adult who can make her own decisions. We were in an RV together for two weeks. It happened."

"Damn, man." TJ said. "Does Dean know?"

"No."

"When are you going to tell him?"

"I don't know yet."

"Wouldn't it be better to tell him right away?"

"I wanted to, but Alex isn't ready."

TJ sighed. "Wow. I'm just . . . I don't even know what to say."

Jake scrubbed a hand down his face. "TJ, she's . . . struggling. Still doesn't know how to accept this. I think she's scared."

"Who could blame her?"

"Here's the thing . . ." Jake looked down at the floor for a minute, considering his words, then looked back up at his friend. "I want this."

"You want a baby?"

"The baby, her. All of it. I know it sounds insane."

TJ's lips parted, and Jake could tell he was considering his words. "Are you in love with her?"

Jake sighed. "I don't know. Maybe. But I do know

that the thought of her having my baby does not terrify me like I thought it would. I feel overwhelmed by the idea, but also . . . excited."

"Shit, dude," TJ said. He smiled. "You're right. This is insane. Who would have thought you'd be the one to have a kid first?"

Jake chuckled. "Maybe the reality of it hasn't hit me yet."

"It'll hit ya when Dean finds out. That's for sure."

They were both quiet for a moment. "I've got to convince her to stay, TJ. She's still talking about moving to Virginia."

TJ sighed. "Give her some time, man. This is a lot to deal with."

Jake nodded. "Yeah. You're right." But it was a lot for him to deal with also, and yet he wouldn't consider anything that didn't include them together. Several times he'd thought back to that single mother at the airport. How much she'd appeared to struggle all on her own. Alex didn't have to do this by herself, he was more than willing to raise this baby with her. That's what he wanted. Suddenly he couldn't understand why she didn't.

Charlotte had convinced Alex to get out of the house that Sunday and go to the Labor Day cookout at TJ and Jen's. Now that the four of them—Alex, Joel, Dean, and Charlotte—were in the car on the way over, she was glad.

It was a gorgeous day. She'd put on a cute outfit that made her feel somewhat normal, and even she had to admit that she'd gotten tired of staring at the four walls of her bedroom. The best part of today, so far, was that she hadn't been sick, although the thought of smelling grilled hot dogs made her want to gag.

If she was being honest with herself, she was also really excited to see Jake. It was a weird thing, to long for someone, to miss them, yet also fear and dread their presence. She wasn't even sure why she felt that way. He'd called her several times since she'd told him about being pregnant, but they never talked for long, just enough for her to fill him in on how she was feeling. She could tell he wanted to talk more, and even see her again, but she'd kept things brief between them.

They pulled into TJ's long country driveway, and Alex searched for Jake's Jeep but didn't see it. She frowned. They'd texted this morning and he'd said he was heading out here around noon. It was now quarter after.

"This is a beautiful house," she said. It was obviously newer construction, but was made to look like an older two-story farmhouse with a porch running the expanse of the front.

"Isn't it?" Charlotte said from the front. "TJ built it a couple of years ago. Wait until you see the inside. The kitchen is to die for."

She was right. The minute they walked in, Alex was in awe. The entryway was bright and airy with the most gorgeous house plants and grand staircase. Jen greeted them excitedly in a red tank top that showed off her bright tattoo sleeve and navy shorts. Her dark hair was in a ponytail, showcasing a red streak of highlighted hair peeking out beneath her ear.

"Your hair is fantastic," Alex said when Jen came over to give her a hug. "I love the red."

"Thank you. I just did it a couple of days ago." Jen

pulled back and looked her over. "How are you after your bout with the plague?"

Alex laughed. "I'm fine. But it was ugly."

"I heard. Damn, you poor thing. Out all ends, huh?"

"Jen, good Lord," Charlotte said with a laugh. "Go show Alex your kitchen."

Within no time she'd had a tour of the entire house, from the pantry to the gorgeous tub in the master bedroom, where Alex now sat, wishing it was full of water and bubbles.

"This house is insane, Jen. I could spend days in this tub alone."

"I practically do. It's one of my favorite things." She looked around the design magazine worthy bathroom. "But I definitely got lucky."

"What do you mean?" Alex asked.

Jen shrugged. "I would have never had this house on my own. I grew up poor as hell. Sometimes homeless. I was shit with money. Hell, I'm still shit with money. I got lucky that TJ fell in love with me. I mean, we don't necessarily make sense on paper, you know?"

Alex frowned. "But you make sense when I see you two together."

"Thanks," Jen smiled. "Thankfully he has the patience of a saint. I'm kind of a pain in the ass."

"Kind of?" A deep voice called out from the bedroom.

Jen laughed and rolled her eyes as TJ joined them in the bathroom. He walked in, put an arm around Jen's waist, pulled her against him and kissed her forehead.

A sharp ache sliced through Alex at the sight of such tenderness. Such easy happiness. Jen was right, they were a bit of an odd match—Jen's boldness contrasted with TJ's polish. How did two people get so lucky? And did they realize that all of this could be yanked away from them at any second?

"This isn't weird at all. The three of us in your bathroom, you two kissing and me in the tub," Alex joked.

"Oh my God, it's not weird." Jen said. "I swear, I bring every person I know up here and tell them to sit in the tub."

"She does," TJ said, winking at Jen. "Anyway, I'll leave you two alone, but food's about ready."

"Okay," Jen said, watching him leave. "See, that. That's why I'm lucky. He made this happen."

"You kind of made it happen too, Jen. By being so awesome he couldn't help but want you."

"True," she said, and they both laughed. "But I had a tendency to push good things away, and luckily he forced me to see that I deserved it."

Alex got quiet, suddenly wondering if Jen knew about her being pregnant. It wouldn't surprise her if she did. Jake and TJ were best friends, and it was unlikely that TJ would keep it from Jen. If she did know, Alex appreciated that she wasn't giving her the third degree.

She rose up out of the tub and stepped out. "Thanks for showing me around."

"Absolutely. I'm sure the novelty of living here will wear off someday. Then again, I kind of hope it doesn't. I'm grateful for everything I have because of TJ. Sometimes you don't know how much you want something until you have it."

"I bet," Alex said, making her way down the main staircase. She worked Jen's words over in her head as they headed to the back deck. The minute Alex walked outside she met eyes with Jake's, whose stance visibly relaxed when he saw her. She didn't miss the way his eyes ran up and down her body.

He met her eyes again, and their gaze held a little too long—until he leaned down to listen to something Joel was telling him. She watched him laugh and nod his head, his eyes darting warily back to her.

She sat down next to Charlotte and her photography assistant, Lauren. The conversation was about Dean and Charlotte's wedding, and she tried to join in as much as she could, especially when Charlotte told Lauren about them going to taste cakes.

"Weren't Jill's cakes to die for?" Lauren asked Alex.

"They really were. And her little kitchen was so cool."

"I need a man to propose just so I can go in and order a cake," Lauren said, laughing.

Alex smiled as a shadow came over her. She looked up to find Jake standing there quietly.

"Lauren, let's go make a plate. I'm starving," Charlotte said, standing up. She winked at Alex. "Can I bring you a burger?"

"Sure," Alex nodded.

"What do you like on it?" Charlotte asked.

"Lots of lettuce and jalapeños," Jake answered for her.

Charlotte smirked, her eyes darting back and forth between the two of them, finally landing on Alex.

She nodded. "He's right, but maybe this time pickles instead of jalapeños."

"Got it," Charlotte said, heading inside.

Jake sat down in her vacated chair, pulling it closer, but not enough to draw attention. Thankfully everyone was busy chatting, eating, or inside getting their lunch from the spread that had been laid out on the big island in the kitchen. Dean was thankfully busy manning the grill and wasn't paying them any attention.

"How are you?" he asked, leaning forward, elbows on his knees.

"I'm okay."

"You look amazing today."

"Thanks," she said, adjusting her sundress in her lap.

"Jalapeños make you sick?"

She smiled. "I'm afraid they might. My stomach's been a little sensitive."

He nodded. "I want to touch you," he muttered.

"Jake."

He sat up with a sigh and looked around the yard. TJ's house sat on a giant lot surrounded by farmland. Crop fields on one side, cows on the other. It was surprisingly beautiful and very serene.

"I love it out here," she said.

"Do you?" Jake asked.

She looked at him. "It's so peaceful."

When he didn't respond, she looked back to find him staring at her intently, elbows now settled on the arm-rests of the lawn chair.

"What?" she asked.

"Let me give you this, Alex."

She laughed, shaking her head. "A giant home in the country?"

He shrugged. "A home. Peace."

Her eyes went wide. "Is that what you want? For us to just play house?"

"No, I don't mean to play."

"Well, that doesn't sound like peace to me at all. Do you know what happens when you make happy plans, Jake? People die."

Leaning forward, he narrowed his eyes. "Is that what you're afraid of, Alex? Because you can't live life wait-ing for tragedy."

"Are you really saying that to me? I lost my par-ents in a car wreck and the man I love in a helicopter accident." She noticed the way his jaw tightened when she mentioned loving Nate. Tough—she would never *not* say it. And those losses she'd mentioned, that didn't even include the pain of losing her second real family to divorce. When her parents had died, Dean and his now ex-wife Amy had treated her like she was their own. That, too, had been taken from her. Loss and grief were a constant in her life. "Jake, every time I have a family, or try to, I lose someone I love. I'm tired of hurting."

"I understand that, Alex. Do you not think this scares me too?"

She glanced around the deck to find Dean watching them. There was no way he could hear their conversation, but it had to look odd, the way Jake was leaning toward her with a scowl on his face.

"Stop," she said. "We're not alone."

He relaxed, sitting back a bit in the chair, but still leaning to the side to be close enough to talk. "We need to tell everyone soon, Alex. I want to be free to touch you whenever I want."

She frowned. "What do you mean, Jake? You seem to think once we tell everyone, it will just be a happy thing."

"It could be, Alex. If you let it."

"Don't you think this is hard enough as it is?"

He shook his head and put his hands on the edge of the chair as if he was going to stand up. "Say the word, and I'll tell your brother right here and now. We can do this together. Fuck anyone who gives us a problem."

What was he saying? Did he really mean that he wanted them to be a couple? What, get married? She could never put herself in that position again, it was too painful. That kind of love, that kind of commitment, it was terrifying. "Why are you doing this to me, Jake? This was my chance. I made a plan. I have a job. If I couldn't have a family with Nate, then I don't want one."

He stared into her eyes, his jaw rigid, nostrils flaring as he breathed in and out deeply. Finally he stood up and went inside without another word.

She sat there, her heart pounding in her chest. What had she done? Was she shivering? How could she have said those words to him? Immediately she stood up but was stopped by someone grabbing her arm.

"What the hell was that about?"

Alex turned to see Dean, eyes narrowed.

"Nothing. Let go of me." She yanked her arm from his, easy to do because he hadn't really gripped her that hard, but her anger concerned him. She could tell by the shock on his face.

"What was he saying to you, Alex?"

"It's none of your business, Dean," she pushed her chair in and made her way into the house. Rushing through the kitchen, down the hallway, and into the entryway, she flung open the front door just in time to see Jake's Jeep peeling out of the driveway and down the road.

Twenty-Three

Alex hadn't heard from Jake since the day of the cook-out. Nearly a week, considering it was Friday morning. She'd managed to get out of working at the Stag front desk another week by convincing Dean she still didn't feel good.

She knew he was skeptical and worried, but he hadn't pushed. Thank goodness, because there was no way she could be around Jake and just pretend everything was normal. Every time she thought of the look on his face that day she wanted to cry. But then sometimes she told herself that it was for the best. Right now, she'd just wanted to wallow in her own self-pity and didn't want anyone trying to make it better for her.

The last thing she wanted was a man to offer her a commitment out of obligation. Jake had been a happy bachelor up until she came along and wanted a road-trip fling. He might think he was being a good guy—because that's what he did, especially when it came to her—but how could she do that to him? Wrangle him into being a father.

She still didn't know if she wanted to be a mother. And that thought alone kept her up at night. Wasn't some kind of maternal instinct supposed to kick in by now?

Rolling out of bed, she decided to take a shower. It usually made her feel better. Going into the bathroom, she began to undress. When she pulled her underwear down, she gasped.

It was dotted with blood. "Oh my God," she whispered.

In a panic, she grabbed some toilet paper and checked to see how much came away. Not a ton, but she knew this couldn't be ignored.

Taking a deep shaky breath, she washed her hands, put her nightgown back on, and went into her room. Picking up her phone, she called Charlotte, who answered right away.

"Where are you at?" Alex asked.

"Just left the grocery store. Is everything alright?"

"I'm okay," Alex said, not wanting her to panic. Except, she was about to panic herself. "No, wait. I'm not okay, Charlotte. I'm bleeding."

"I'm on my way, Alex," Charlotte said without hesitation.

"Okay, thank you."

When they disconnected, Alex began pacing the floor, uncertain of what to think. What to do. A few minutes later she heard the front door open and Charlotte saying hello to Joel. Finally there was a knock on her bedroom door. She pulled it open and Charlotte rushed in.

"How are you feeling?"

"Scared."

Charlotte nodded. "I know. But chances are everything is fine. Are you cramping?"

Alex shook her head. "No. I really haven't felt

anything except nauseous, and my boobs have hurt a little."

"That's good, I think," Charlotte said. "As soon as you told me, I called my own OB office. The nurse there is one of my former brides. She can get you in today."

Alex mouth dropped open. "Oh my God."

"I know this is sudden, Alex. But you really do need to see a doctor, and this office is great. They offer you lots of options, they have a midwife, I think—"

Alex put out a hand. "Please, I just . . . need a minute." She sat down on the bed. Had she believed that she could just keep going on like nothing was going to happen? She was pregnant. There was a human growing inside her. Decisions had to be made.

And the thought that maybe something was already robbing her of the choice made her want to cry. She looked up at Charlotte and nodded. "Okay, let's go."

Jake stood behind TJ's desk chair looking over his shoulder as they discussed the new updates he'd made to their website that morning. Now that they were going all in on the wedding planning services, they'd created a complimentary and dedicated site to the wedding aspect of their business: Stag Weddings. He'd been working on it for days with Jen's input, and was really proud of it.

"I love it," TJ said. "Don't tell Jen this, but I thought she was crazy with that logo idea. But it totally works. It's slightly more feminine, but not too much. I think it will appeal to anyone, but it's still definitely our branding."

Jake chuckled. "I felt the same way, but yeah, she was right."

Jen had talked them into creating a logo for all of the

wedding-related correspondence and website. It was their same Stag head, but it had a wreath of flowers around its neck. All three of them had been horrified when she'd brought it up, but she'd asked them just to let her have a graphic designer show them some samples, and crazy enough, she'd won them over.

So now the website for the liquor was a background of wood paneling with a white Stag outline and name, and the wedding site was the same except the paneling was white wood with a flower-adorned beige Stag. The two looked really good together.

"Who would have thought that someday we'd be discussing our wedding business website?" TJ said, chuckling.

Jake agreed, just as his phone rang. It was Alex. He hadn't spoken to her since their discussion at TJ's. His heart skipped as he answered it.

"Hello," he said.

"Hi, it's me."

"What's wrong?" He could tell by the sound of her voice that everything was not okay.

"I'm sure it's not a big deal, but I was bleeding a little bit."

"Shit." He turned away from TJ, whose eyes were searching for answers. "That's not good, right? What does it mean?"

He felt sick to his stomach. The thought of anything happening to her, to this baby, gutted him.

"It could be nothing, but I'm going to the doctor right now to check. I just thought you'd want to know."

He ran a hand through his hair. "Hell, Alex, of course I want to know. I want to go with you."

"Charlotte's with me."

"Why?" he said into the phone. "Why would you call

Charlotte and not me? I should be taking you to the doctor." He'd missed her like crazy this week, but damn, her comments at the cookout had ripped him apart. Now she wouldn't even let him be there for her.

"I'm sorry, Jake. I guess . . ."

He could hear Charlotte in the background telling Alex to tell him to meet them there.

"Yes," he said. "I'm meeting you there. Where do I go?" he asked, waving off TJ who had walked around into his line of sight and was trying to get his attention. He waved him off and turned in the other direction, only to look up and see Dean standing in the doorway of TJ's office.

Fuck.

"What's going on?" Dean asked.

"Are you ready? I'll tell you how to get here," Alex said on the phone.

Jake was silent, staring at his friend.

"Jake, you there?" Alex asked through the phone.

"Is that Alex?" Dean asked. "Why is Charlotte taking her to the doctor?"

"Is that my brother?" Alex said quietly.

Jake swallowed hard. "Yeah," he replied.

"Shit. Did he hear you?" Alex muttered.

"Yes. I'm gonna have to let you go, Alex," Jake said, looking at Dean, whose eyes narrowed at the sound of his sister's name.

"Jake, no. Wait," she said frantically.

"There's no other option, Alex. Text me the address."

He disconnected, and immediately held up a hand. "Listen to me, Dean."

"What's wrong with my sister? And why was she calling to tell you?" His voice was menacing.

"Calm down, Dean," TJ interjected. "Everything is okay."

"Is it?" Dean looked around Jake to TJ. "Because clearly everyone here knows something I don't."

There was no other option than to spit it out. "Alex is pregnant," Jake said.

The expression on Dean's face didn't change at first, and all the air in the room seemed to stand still. Finally, his brow furrowed.

"Are you telling me, my sister is pregnant . . . because of you?"

"Yes. That's what I'm telling you."

Jake heard TJ move behind him, and then his best friend was standing beside him. "Dean, let's stay cool here, man. They didn't do anything wrong. Alex is an adult."

Dean gave TJ a stunned look. "And this guy is supposed to be my friend." He looked back at Jake. "You promised me you'd take care of her. In what fucking universe does that mean knocking her up?" he said calmly. So calm it was chilling.

TJ stepped forward, a hand out, even though Dean hadn't moved. "Come on, Dean. You know Jake would never do Alex wrong."

"Do I? Because the Jake I know doesn't do relationships. He just sleeps around." He pointed at Jake. "You were not, under any circumstances, supposed to sleep with my sister. Two weeks. Two goddamn weeks and you couldn't keep your dick in your pants."

"Fuck you, Dean," Jake said, fuming inside. It was all he could do to keep his cool. His body hummed with fury at the situation, at himself, and with fear at the idea that Alex might be losing their baby as they spoke.

"Alex is important to me too. And if you don't know me better than that, then we don't have anything else to discuss here."

His phone buzzed in his hand, hopefully with the doctor's office address, so he pushed past his two friends and left the room. It wasn't five seconds before he heard footsteps behind him. Turning hard, he put out a hand to stop Dean.

"Where do you think you're going?" he asked.

Dean stopped short. "I'm going with you."

"Like hell you are. Alex is going to the doctor because she may be losing this baby. *Our* baby." Jake didn't miss the subtle look of pain that shadowed Dean's eyes at the comment. "I will not allow you to march in there like a fucking barbarian and upset her. She's mine to worry about now. Not yours."

With that, he turned and left. Dean didn't follow.

Twenty-Four

Alex had filled out some paperwork, trying not to be sick the entire time, and then been shown to a room. She was seated on the exam table, pants off, with a paper cloth over her lap. It was cold in the room, and she kept trying to keep her teeth from rattling.

"I can't believe he hasn't called either of us yet," she said to Charlotte who was sitting in a chair.

"I can't either. Maybe Jake didn't tell him," Charlotte said. There was a clear hint of worry in her voice.

"I don't know how he couldn't have. I heard Dean ask him in the background. Something happened. I feel it."

"It will be okay, Alex. I'll handle Dean. The last thing you need is to be worrying."

"I can't stop. My heart feels like something's clamping down on it." She touched her chest and tried to take several deep breaths, but the scent of astringent made her feel like gagging every time she inhaled. "This sucks," she whined.

"It's just anxiety. Keep taking slow deep breaths," Charlotte said soothingly. Just then, her phone rang.

"Oh shit," Alex said. "Who is it?"

"It's him," Charlotte said. "I'm gonna go in the hall."

Alex nodded. "Tell him I love him. Please. And hurry back."

Charlotte gave her a warm smile, then ducked out of the room. Alex blew out a shaky breath. She swung a leg up, realizing her red toenail polish looked like shit. And why the hell was she worried about such nonsense right now? She could have a dead fetus inside of her.

Please, no. Please be okay.

A knock at the door sounded and she sat up straight. A middle-aged woman in pale blue scrubs and a low, slightly messy ponytail walked in. Her smile was warm and her voice calming. "Good afternoon. I'm Dr. Mendoza."

Alex shook her hand and introduced herself. "My sister-in-law Charlotte is in the hall. I was hoping she could be in here."

The doctor peeked outside quickly. "I don't see her."

Alex let out a breath, shoulders sagging. "Okay, that's fine. I'm sure she'll be back."

The doctor sat down on a stool and they discussed the same things she'd gone over with the nurse—last period, symptoms, and her food-poisoning episode.

"That's horrible," Dr. Mendoza said. "But the good news is, I don't think it will have any negative effect on your pregnancy." She stood up. "If you could lie back, we're gonna go ahead and take a look inside."

There was a knock at the door, and Alex was relieved to know Charlotte was coming back. Instead it was a nurse. She peeked her head in. "I have a . . . Jake, out here? Can he come in?"

Alex's heart bloomed in her chest. "Yes. He can come in."

The nurse nodded and stepped back, and then Alex

saw him. His eyes immediately finding hers, his expression hard and scared. She could tell.

"Are you the father?" Dr. Mendoza asked casually as the door closed behind him.

Jake cleared his throat. "Yes. I am."

"Come on over. We're just about to see what's going on in here. You can see best if you stand right up by her head." She tapped Alex's leg. "Let's get one foot in each stirrup."

Alex maneuvered her legs and, without thought, reached out and grabbed Jake's hand. He took it, squeezing a little too hard for a second. She stared up at him as the doctor arranged her sheet and then began typing onto a machine with a black screen.

Jake ran a hand over her forehead. "How are you?" he asked quietly.

"Nervous."

His lips quirked. "No matter what, it's gonna be okay."

She nodded. "How's my brother?"

Jake sighed. "Hating me."

"Oh no. He'll get over it."

"I think so too. But don't worry about that. You're all that matters."

"Okay," Dr. Mendoza said, kindly pretending she wasn't listening to their conversation as she held up a massive wand. Jake squeezed Alex's hand again and she heard him swallow. "I'm just going to insert this inside—it shouldn't really hurt, but might be uncomfortable. If you feel any pain, speak up."

Alex nodded. She squeezed Jake back as the wand slid inside. It didn't hurt, but she could certainly feel it.

"Okay?" Jake asked, looking down at her.

She could only nod.

"This should only take a minute." Dr. Mendoza

began to move the wand around, taking some measurements of a round space with her free hand on the mouse. "I'm measuring your gestational sack."

She moved the wand again, everything on the screen changed, and then they saw a tiny gray blob in the gestational sack. Clicking the mouse again, Dr. Mendoza took more measurements. "And this is the yolk sack."

Alex couldn't take her eyes from the screen although part of her wanted to look up at Jake. She could hear his breath. His hand still gripping hers, the paper sheet crinkling every time he tightened it.

"And this little part here," Dr. Mendoza said, "is your baby."

The paper crinkled again, their hands holding so tight she thought they'd lose circulation.

"Is it okay?" Jake asked.

"See this little flipper right here?" Dr. Mendoza touched her cursor near the gray blob. There was what appeared to be a tiny valve flapping back and forth, almost like on a pinball machine.

"Yes," Alex said.

"That's its heart beating. Everything looks just as it should."

Alex let out a wispy laugh, and then her eyes closed as she sucked in a shaky breath. She felt the warmth of Jake's mouth as he kissed her forehead. He stayed there for several seconds, and she reached up with her left hand, resting it on the back of his head.

The sound of the doctor cleaning up had them pulling apart. Alex cleared her throat and awkwardly sat up. "Why was I bleeding then?"

"A little spotting is usually no reason for alarm. If it doesn't stop or you're cramping, then definitely call."

Alex nodded. "Okay."

"Otherwise, I'd like to see you back here in about three or four weeks. Maybe then we can *hear* the heartbeat."

Jake reached up and wiped at a tear on her temple. "Thank you so much," he said to the doctor.

"Of course. And Adrianne will be back in with a little bag of goodies for you. Samples, coupons for maternity clothes, and a book you may find helpful. It will answer some of your questions."

"Thank you."

When they were alone, she turned to Jake and whispered. "Maternity clothes?"

He grinned, putting a hand on each side of her face. "I can't wait to see you in maternity clothes. It will be sexy as hell."

Her eyes flew open. "You're crazy."

His lips touched hers and she went still. He kissed her again and then whispered against her mouth. "Kiss me, Alex."

She did, allowing him to part her lips and take it deeper. Reaching up she touched his face as they angled the other way. He felt and tasted so good, she hadn't realized how much she'd missed this.

When he finally looked at her, there was a crease between his brows. "This is happening, Alex. We're having a baby, and I don't want you to pull away from me again. Please."

"Aren't you scared?"

"Terrified. But you know, you *know*, you can trust me. I've been your person for the past year." He reached between them and touched her stomach. "And now this is mine. Ours. Don't stop needing me now."

"I've needed you so bad, Jake. But I'm so afraid," she

said, tears beginning to fall. "I'd come so far. Made such good progress."

He pulled back and looked at her fiercely. "Listen to me. This has nothing to do with what you've been through before. This is now. This is us. You and me. Don't tell me this is a step backward, Alex."

She sighed deeply, trying not to panic.

"I know you, and right now you're telling yourself that if you don't take that job, you've failed. And that's bullshit. We'll get through this and we'll figure it out. Whatever you want after that, I'll do everything in my power to give it to you. Just give me until this baby is born, and then we'll decide what to do."

Everything he was saying felt right. It was almost a relief for him to tell her what they should do and that that it would be okay. That wanting this was okay, because after today's scare—the thought that she may be losing this tiny life inside of her—she knew she did want it.

Maybe this was one of those opportunities to take a new path. To sacrifice something she wanted because of her love for someone else. This baby. Maybe this was what she was meant to do. Become a mother. And Jake would be a good father, even if they weren't together. He was such a good man.

"Okay," she said. "I will."

His eyes closed, and he leaned in to place a soft kiss on her nose. "Thank you."

Fifteen minutes later, they were heading down the elevator, looking for where Charlotte had gone. As they left the office and made their way to the courtyard near the parking lot, they saw her. She was sitting beside Dean on a bench. As soon as she saw them she stood, anticipation on her face.

"Everything okay?" Charlotte asked.

"Yes, we saw its heart flapping." Alex laughed and then looked around Charlotte at Dean, who'd stood up. His hands were shoved into his pockets, but as soon as she headed for him he took them out and let her walk into his arms.

Until now, she hadn't realized how much she'd needed him through this. He'd always meant everything to her. The handsome teenage brother all her friends had been in love with and who had taught her how to ride a bike. The man who had held her after her parents had died and soothed her as she'd cried herself to sleep. And the same man who'd done the exact same thing when her fiancé had died a little over a year ago. How many times had he just let her cry on his shoulder? Could anyone really blame him for being overprotective after witnessing her go through so many heart-aching moments?

She'd never had any doubt that he would be supportive of her being pregnant. But she'd been concerned about the man who'd done the impregnating. His best friend—she knew that had to sting. Jake had described it perfectly when he said that Dean would feel betrayed, even though that was silly. She and Jake were both adults who could make their own decisions.

"Don't be mad, Bean," she said against his chest.

"Oh, Alex. I'm not mad at you."

She angled her face to him. "Don't be mad at *anyone*. Please."

"I'm trying." He stepped back and looked at her. "How are you?"

"A little better. I've been pretty sick."

"Charlotte told me you've known for a few weeks."

"I have. I wasn't ready to talk about it though. I still

wasn't today, but this kind of rushed things along." She glanced over at Charlotte. "Thanks for being here with me."

"Anytime." Charlotte gave her a weak smile. "I'm just glad everything is okay."

Alex stepped back and stood next to Jake. He reached out and grabbed her hand, and Alex didn't miss the way Dean's eyes tracked their movements.

"We're doing this," she said to her brother. "We're having a baby. Together."

Jake gave her hand a squeeze.

"I'm going to continue to stay at Joel's. He's already offered."

"What?" Dean asked. He looked at Jake. "Why can't she stay with you?"

"Because," she said, cutting Jake off, "I don't want to. We're not going to start shacking up just because we're having a baby."

"Even though I did offer," Jake said tersely.

"What about the job in Virginia?" Charlotte asked.

"I'm going to inform them that I'm declining the offer," Alex said.

Dean's eyes widened in shock, but Alex could tell that the news made him happy. "Okay. Then what are you going to do for the next . . . seven months."

"Well, have you hired a new front-desk person yet?" Had that just come out of her mouth? She felt Jake turn and look down at her.

"Alex," he whispered. "Are you sure?"

"Well, have you?" she repeated.

Dean's mouth quirked. "Nope. Not yet. If you want the job, it's yours."

Twenty-Five

Eight Weeks Later

Alex opened her desk drawer and pulled out her jars of peanut butter and Nutella. Taking her plastic spoon, she dipped first into the peanut butter, coming up with a dollop. Then into the Nutella, topping the peanut butter with it. Carefully, using one hand, she screwed the lids back on and dropped both jars back into the drawer before taking her first lick of the spoon.

"New favorite treat?" A voice came from the other side of the counter.

She jumped and looked up to see Jake grinning down at her.

"How do you manage to walk across these floors so quietly? It's not nice to sneak up on a lady while she's raiding her secret snack stash."

He stood up straight and walked around the counter and behind her desk. It had taken her a while to get used to them seeing each other so frequently. She worked three, sometimes four, days a week at the Stag. And the two of them had tried to keep things professional, but sometimes it was difficult. Especially since pregnancy hormones made for some surprising and naughty urges.

It didn't help that he was so damn handsome.

"Stand up," he said, motioning with his finger.

"Do you not see how degrading that request is? You want to inspect me like livestock."

"Yes I do," he said with a grin. "Stand."

She sighed dramatically but did as he said. The minute his eyes zeroed in on her melon-sized pooch, his hands instantly framed her waist.

"God, I can't get enough of this."

"You're so weird," she said, laughing when he hunched down and kissed her belly button.

He tilted his head up to look at her. "Come over tonight. Please?"

He'd been trying to get her to have sex with him for a month. And it wasn't that she didn't want to. She did. They hadn't been intimate in that way since Nashville, which felt like ages ago. They'd kissed a lot, but she'd held back on anything more for some reason. The idea of letting herself go too much, playing this game to the point of no return, scared her.

But damn, these pregnancy sex dreams were making it harder and harder to say no.

"Fine."

He popped up from the floor, eyes wide. "You mean it? Please, mean it. I even have a surprise for you," he said, leaning into her forehead.

"You do? What?" Now she was excited about more than just sex.

He smirked. "You have to come over to find out. I'll pick you up at six."

"Okay, fine. Now go away before someone sees us," she said, shoving him out of her desk area.

* * *

Alex put some lip gloss on in the hall bathroom at Joel's house.

"Somebody here," he called from the living room.

"Be right out. It's Jake."

"You sure? It's a white SUV."

Alex frowned at the mirror and then looked at her phone. 5:58. It had to be him. Putting her lip gloss away, she turned off the light and headed for the front door. "It's him, all right," she said.

"He must have gotten a new car," Joel said, staring at the TV.

"Not sure. Bye, Joel. I'll probably, uh . . ."

"See you tomorrow," he said, still staring at the screen.

She bit back a laugh and left. By the time she got into the driveway Jake was standing outside the shiny SUV grinning.

"What's this?" she asked.

"Well," he put out a hand. "It's my baby mama's new ride."

She stopped short, her eyes roaming back over the vehicle. "What do you mean?" And why had he called her his baby mama? Why had the sound of it made her so . . . sad?

"I got this car. For you." His excitement had quickly turned to wariness.

"Jake." She stepped forward and touched the front hood. It was so smooth, so new. "Where's the Wrangler?"

"I traded it in."

Alex jerked her eyes back to him. "For this? What will *you* drive?"

"I got you this and me a smaller used car." He shrugged. "No big deal."

"You can't be serious." She walked around to the

side, and he moved so she could see inside. "Oh my God. It's gorgeous."

"Sit down."

She did, her hands instantly going to the steering wheel. "I haven't had a car in years. I can't believe this." She'd sold the car she and Dean had gotten her in high school when she'd first been deployed. She'd never needed it when she'd been stationed stateside either, so it hadn't made sense to have it sit and pay property taxes for nothing. When she'd gotten back she'd assumed she'd be living in the D.C. area and that she wouldn't need a vehicle that badly. But now . . .

"I don't know what to say," she said, her fingers trailing over the console buttons.

"Say you love it."

Alex turned her head to find him leaning against the doorframe, face rather close to hers. She lifted her hand and touched his jaw. "I love it," she said quietly.

His lips quirked and then he leaned in and kissed her softly. "Drive us home," he said, pulling back and closing the driver door.

Home.

He walked around the front and got in, so Alex started up the engine. She let out a little squeal of excitement. "How old is this car? It's amazing!"

"Brand new. You're the first owner."

"Jake," she said. "You should not have done this."

"Alex, you're going to have our baby. I can't, in good conscience, leave you without transportation. And I certainly can't let my baby ride around in a piece of shit. It's not safe."

"I'm going to help you make the payments."

He shook his head. "Fine, then get us home. I'll show you how you can make your first payment."

She laughed as she backed out of the driveway. "I bet you will."

Sex with Alex had been amazing every time. But sex with the woman carrying his baby . . . Good God, it was something else, Jake thought as he looked up at Alex riding him.

She had a hand on each breast, her eyelids fluttering. "Squeeze them," he groaned. Nearly coming right then as he watched her fingers pinch her nipples. "Shit, baby, yes. Just like that. Come here."

She fell forward, her tits falling into his face. They were so much fuller and rounder than they had been before, her nipples a dark rose color, and every time he sucked on one she moaned as if it was the best thing that had ever happened to her.

At this angle he could feel her tummy between their bodies, and he swore the idea of it made him grow even harder inside of her. Was that normal? To be so insanely turned on by the idea of a woman carrying your baby? If not, he was fine to be labeled a freak, because he fucking loved it.

As she picked up speed, bouncing on top of him, he grabbed her ass, trying to slow her down. "Hold up, Alex. You're gonna make me come."

They hadn't bothered with condoms tonight. He'd gone to the doctor recently, and she was already good and knocked up, so hell, why bother? And holy shit, the pleasure of being skin on skin inside of her was so raw and intense he could die a happy man right here.

She let out a guttural moan and he knew she was coming. Again. He began to piston up inside of her, meeting her grind as they both finally came together.

After a moment she sat up and swiped her hair off

her face before leaning back down to kiss him. "Four times. It's a record."

He chuckled against her lips, loving how into it she'd been tonight. They'd had intercourse twice, but yeah, she'd come four times. He felt good about that, although, whatever this pregnancy horniness she'd mentioned was doing to her, he was into it. Who would have thought he'd have the best sex of his life with a pregnant woman? Then again, he knew it was more than that. It was sex with Alex. *His* pregnant woman.

The next morning Alex crawled out of Jake's giant king-sized bed early. She was parched, something she'd been dealing with frequently the past few weeks. Thankfully he didn't stir as she got up and walked quietly into the kitchen in a T-shirt and panties.

She was still surprised by how nice and homey Jake's duplex was. It was painted a light gray and all of the furnishings were neutral and simple, but comfortable and attractive. According to him, one of his sisters-in-law worked at a furniture store and had helped him. Whatever the reason, Alex had liked it immediately.

She was so thirsty she grabbed a glass out of the cabinet and just filled it from the tap. As she drank, she wandered into the living room snooping around at his books, photos of his family and friends, and what he had laying on his coffee table. Surprisingly, nothing but a remote. He was amazingly tidy.

Even the kitchen had been pristine. The sun was coming up so she peeked out the front curtains, smiling when she caught sight of her new car. She still couldn't believe he'd done that for her. No one had ever done anything so huge.

The sight of the shiny white SUV made her wonder.

What kind of car had he gotten himself in place of the Jeep Wrangler, which she'd known he'd loved a lot if the amount of custom work on it was any indication?

She stepped back into the kitchen and opened a door she assumed went to the garage. It was dark inside, so she searched for a light switch. The minute she located it and flicked it on, she sucked in a breath.

Inside the one car garage set a black two-door . . . something. She couldn't even place what brand it was. It was clearly several years old. Not junky, but so far removed from the chick magnet, bachelor ride that the Wrangler was, she almost couldn't breathe.

Footsteps sounded behind her and she stepped out from the garage door and shut it.

"What are you doing? You feeling okay?" Jake stood there in baggy pajama pants, eyes squinted, hair mussed.

She instantly set her water glass down and walked into his arms. "Yes, I'm okay. I'm just sad."

"Why?" he asked, wrapping his arms around her.

"Your car."

His gravelly chuckle had her looking up at him.

"You don't dig it?"

"Why did you get rid of the Wrangler?"

"So I could get the other one?"

"But why? You could have just gotten me the car in the garage. I don't need something so nice."

He narrowed his eyes, obviously confused. "Alex, I already explained this. You are pregnant with our child. When it's born you will be driving the two of you around. I need you to be safe. That's all that matters."

"But you loved the Wrangler."

He looked at her as if she was speaking another language. "You're more important than that, Alex. I'd never been so excited to buy a car in my life than when I drove that car off the lot for you."

Her lips parted. "You're unbelievable, Jake Cooper."

He smirked. "You're damn right. Don't forget it."

There was no way she could, because it scared her to death.

Twenty-Six

Day 534 Twenty weeks pregnant
Apparently, the baby is the length of a large banana.
It's so weird to imagine. I've actually felt great lately,
but I keep hoping I'm going to feel him moving. Every
night I lay in bed waiting, but so far, nothing. Today I'm
meeting Jake's family, and I'm so nervous. He told them
about me being pregnant a month ago, but we've put
off the intros because of me. I don't know why I keep
stalling. What if they don't like me? What if I like them
too much?

I think I'm going to wear the opal necklace Regina
gave me. I don't know why. Today I choose to feel ex-
cited.

Alex took a deep breath as Jake pulled into the driveway of a modest middle-class two-story home. The
lawn was deep green and meticulously manicured, the
landscaping around the home mature but also cared for
with the same detailed hand. "You grew up here, right?"

"I did," he said before getting out of the car. They'd
taken her SUV, but he'd driven. She clumsily slid out of
her side, her gut seeming to come out of nowhere over
the last couple of days. She'd officially had to switch to

maternity pants only about two weeks ago, and it was odd to feel like she was starting to get front heavy.

"Do I look okay?" she asked. She'd worn dark jeans, a striped cotton top, and brown boots. She hadn't really known how to dress, still trying to figure out dressing in maternity clothes.

"You look gorgeous, Alex. Just like you did the last time you asked." He winked at her before they walked up the driveway. She'd noticed there were several other cars parked in the street, which only added to her nerves.

"Did you get the box?" she asked. He held up a wrapped box in his left hand.

When they got up to the front door he knocked and then immediately opened it and stepped inside. "We're here," he called out into the entryway.

Voices came from the back of the house, presumably the kitchen, and then a woman came down the hall grinning. "Hello," she said in a singsong voice.

"Hi, Mom," Jake said. He wrapped an arm around her, giving her a quick hug before turning back to Alex. "Mom, this is Alexis Parker."

"Hello, Mrs. Cooper," Alex said. She'd considered putting her hand out, but immediately the woman wrapped her in a giant hug.

"Alex, I can't even tell you how excited I am to meet you. And please call me Sharon. Or Gamma, that's what the other grandkids call me. Not that you're a grandkid, but, well . . . you'll be having one." She let out a little squeal of excitement, still holding onto Alex's hand. "You're going to have to excuse us for being a little excited, but we had resigned ourselves to the idea that there would never be any baby Jakes in our lives." She grinned.

Alex smiled and looked at Jake, who raised an

eyebrow. "Told you," he said. "I'll try not to be insulted by that, Mom. Again."

"Oh, honey, you know we tease." She looked at Alex and whispered loudly. "But I was truly worried."

Alex laughed as Sharon led her down the hallway. The kitchen and dining area was filled with people. She met Jake's two brothers, one of their wives—the other was a doctor and was on call—several nieces and nephews, and then finally his father, Ken.

"It's nice to meet you," he said in a soft voice. It was obvious that Ken was not the dominant partner in the relationship, and Alex liked him immediately.

"You two sit down, I've got some things to show you." Sharon said, shushing everyone.

Glancing around the warm and slightly dated kitchen, Alex noted that Sharon had set out plenty of food, including a few pies, and had several wrapped gifts on the end of the counter.

She instructed Alex and Jake to sit at the table, and everyone else found a seat.

"Jake told me not to go crazy, but I just couldn't help myself when he told me." Sharon placed the presents in front of Alex. "But this is what Gammas do. You'll have to get used to it."

Alex smiled at Jake. "Go ahead," she said.

"I think these are for you," he said.

"They're for both of you," Sharon said. "You're the daddy, Jake. Why don't you both open one?"

Jake and Alex glanced at each other and then laughed awkwardly. They'd yet to call him Daddy or any fatherly endearment, but she liked the sound of it. She wondered if he did. They proceeded to open the gifts, which were several newborn outfits. All gender neutral, but all adorable. The sight of them sent a little tingle through her body. Even this far along, she hadn't really let herself look at baby things. She wasn't sure why. But holding these tiny onesies and itty-bitty socks made her feel excited. More so than she had up until this point.

The final gift was a small bag, and the only thing inside was an envelope tucked inside the tissue paper. Alex opened it and pulled out the card.

Dear Alexis, We are so excited to welcome you to our family. Love, Sharon and Ken

There was a gift card to a local baby boutique for a thousand dollars.

"Oh my goodness," Alex said breathlessly.

"Mom, wow," Jake said, looking over her shoulder. "Thank you."

"Well, we bought your brothers each a baby bed set when they had their first kids. Bed and dresser. I wasn't sure what you'd like so you two can go and pick it out."

Alex looked up at Jake, his gaze on her so intense, and so full of . . . something. It made her want to melt into him. They hadn't even thought that far ahead or talked about where she would live when the baby was born. Had he been thinking about it? Right now, she was trying to take one day at a time.

She turned back to everyone. "Thank you so much. This is so generous I don't even know what to say."

"Oh, I'm so glad you like it. I can't wait to see what you pick out. They have so much cute stuff in that shop. I could have bought it all. I can't wait to find out if it's a boy or a girl."

Grinning, Alex nodded at Jake. "Give her the box."

He reached down toward the floor, picked up the small box with a bow on it, and handed it to his mother. She took it, her mouth dropping open for a moment as she read the sticker that identified it was from a bakery. "Is this what I think it is?"

Jake shrugged. "Open it and find out."

Sharon pulled off the ribbon and peeked inside. "Oh my God!" she squealed.

"Well, what the heck is it?" Ken said in frustration.

Alex loved their interactions.

Sharon opened the box and pulled out a giant cupcake, big enough for three people. It immediately got the five children excited.

"Kyle, get a plate and knife," Sharon instructed one of Jake's brothers. She shushed the children gathered around her and then took the offered utensils and sat the cake on the plate. "Okay, you all ready? I'm gonna cut it open."

Alex and Jake smiled at each other, and under the table he clasped his hand with hers.

"Here we go," Sharon held the knife up over the cupcake. It was loaded with an inch of frosting on top. She slid the knife down dramatically and then paused and let out a little scream, which made Alex laugh. She was quite a character. Slowly she pulled the knife back to reveal blue filling. "A boy!" she screamed, and everyone got excited.

Alex and Jake had already found out that morning at their sonogram appointment. They'd then taken a cupcake over to Joel, Dean, and Charlotte, who had all been patiently waiting to find out.

"I had a feeling it might be a boy," Sharon said.

"How?" Jake asked.

"I dreamed about it." She looked at Alex. "You know, after two boys, we wanted Jake to be a girl. I was so devastated when I saw that penis on the screen."

One of the kids let out a loud "Ewwww, Gamma."

"We know this story, Mom. You've told me a million times," Jake said. Alex looked at him. Did that bother him? His mother clearly loved him—that much was obvious, especially when she leaned down and kissed him on the cheek.

"Oh honey," she said. "You're perfect. Especially now that you finally gave me another grandbaby."

Alex grinned at him. A strapping, handsome man being kissed by his mommy was a special sight. It was hard to believe that she was going to have one of those one day.

By the time they left the Coopers' house two hours later, she was loaded with gifts, stuffed, and exhausted. But she felt happy and content. Something she hadn't felt in a long time. This family was now, sort of, hers. No matter what happened between them, these would be her child's grandparents, aunts, uncles, and cousins.

In the car Alex buckled up and glanced over at Jake. His profile was strong and gorgeous, his shoulders broad. She couldn't wait to see how handsome their son would be.

"Your family is great," she said as he started the car.

He turned to her. "Yeah, they're not bad."

"They're clearly really proud of you."

"You think?" he asked.

"What does that mean? Of course I think. Did you hear your dad showing me all your baseball trophies? Good grief, they must have a million anchors in the wall to hold those shelves up."

"Well, honestly, tonight was the first night in a long damn time that I've been with my family and felt . . . part of them. Not like the outsider."

"What do you mean?"

"I'm thirty-two, Alex. Single. I've never brought a woman home. Not once. And my family has loved to give me shit about it for a decade. I've been to a hundred birthday parties for my nieces and nephews, been here for countless holidays where everything is focused on the kids, the families. It got old being the bachelor uncle who would never settle down. But tonight . . . I had you." He reached over and touched her belly. "And this guy. And for once it was about us. For the first time it was my baby that had my mom excited."

He looked into her eyes. "Thank you for that."

Alex leaned over and kissed him softly. "You're welcome."

They stayed like that, leaned into each other, staring into each other's eyes in the moonlight.

"Can I come home with you?" she whispered.

Jake reached up and touched her face. "Alex, my home is your home."

Twenty-Seven

Alex knew this day was not about her, but she felt like a whale, standing near the officiant in her light blue bridesmaid dress in front of about thirty people set up in chairs in the upstairs of the Stag. Everything did look lovely though. One half of the large room was set up for the small ceremony, the other half held six round tables with white table cloths.

She, Charlotte, and Jen had been busy the past couple of months getting everything ready. Making centerpieces, shopping for jewelry, going to dress fittings. It had kept Alex's mind off the stress of her daily life. Where would she live, what would she name this baby, was she in love with Jake?

She glanced over at him, standing next to TJ opposite her and Jen. How did one human manage to be so handsome? Instead of tuxes, the guys were in dark gray three-piece suits, and the look made her want to pull Jake into a dark corner and eat him up from top to bottom. He'd even slicked back his hair a bit, something she'd never seen him do before, but damn, it was hot.

As if he could feel her eyes on him, he glanced over and waggled his eyebrows at her. She bit back a laugh.

His eyes ran down the length of her massive thirty-six-week-pregnant body and then back up to her face. He winked at her, that same look in his eyes that he gave frequently lately. Ever since she'd gotten pregnant. The one that made her feel so cherished and protected she wanted to cry.

Suddenly Dean stepped out of Jen's office, which was off to the side, and made his way toward them. He took his spot next to Jake and TJ and then looked over at Alex. Her brother looked so handsome today, and for a moment she was reminded of him as teenager. Her hero.

"Love you," she mouthed to him.

He mouthed it back and smiled at her before turning to look down the aisle.

Jake's eyes caught hers again, just behind her brother. Part of her was tempted to mouth him the same words. She wanted to. Felt it. But they'd yet to say it to each other.

She looked down the aisle as the music Charlotte had chosen began. Lauren, Charlotte's good friend and photo assistant, stood in the small aisle with her camera ready to capture Charlotte's approach. Alex stood up straight, but she was starting to feel the strain. Everything ached these days. Her back, her feet, her crotch.

The first thing that trotted down the aisle was Fernando, sporting a bowtie. Everyone laughed as he walked up, then plopped down at Alex's feet and rolled over on his back.

"Good boy, Fernie," Alex whispered. He sat up and gave her a panting smile, tongue hanging out. The loud intake of Dean's breath across from her had Alex looking back up at the rear of the room.

Tears pricked at her eyes as she took in the sight of a happy, smiling Charlotte walking slowly toward her brother. Her dress was a fitted but very simple satin number, and she wore her hair down with pin-curl waves. Her bouquet—as all the flowers adorning the room—was a visually striking collection of wisteria, blue hydrangea, and white peonies. Charlotte's florist friend, Mark, had seriously outdone himself while also giving them a great deal. Everything, including Charlotte, looked so elegant and classic, Alex knew Dean had to be losing his mind at the sight of her. No one deserved this moment more than these two people.

Instantly Alex's gaze searched out John, the man who had once—many years ago—stood Charlotte up on their wedding day. Alex smirked as she found him in the crowd staring at Charlotte with wide eyes. *Eat your heart out, sucker.*

Thankfully for Alex's poor pelvic bone, the ceremony was short and sweet, and it wasn't long before Dean was kissing his new bride along to the ABBA song "Honey, Honey" blasting out of the speakers. Everyone cheered as the two of them walked down the aisle grinning, followed by Alex and Jake, along with Fernando—aptly named after an ABBA song—and then TJ and Jen.

The reception got started immediately with Stag cocktails. After rushing to the restroom to relieve herself for the twentieth time today, Alex was happy when she walked out to find Jake waiting for her. She smiled up at him, touching the vest under his jacket. This was really the first time they'd gotten to see each other. The ladies had gotten ready at Charlotte's parents' house while the guys had gotten ready here.

"This vest is really doing it for me," she said, running a finger down his torso.

"Yeah?" he asked, fisting his lapels and looking down at himself. "I'm feeling pretty dapper. Not gonna lie."

"Not fair a man can be expecting a baby and still be so hot."

"Ah, babe," he leaned down and put his arms around her. "You have no idea how sexy you look today." His arms slid back until he was cupping her belly in his hands. "In fact, I'd like to drag you out of this place right now and down into my office. Nobody has to know."

She slapped him away. "Charlotte and Dean would never forgive us if we ditched their wedding. Besides, Jen has something totally amazing planned for later. It's a surprise."

Jake's brows went up. "She gonna sing?"

Alex smiled. "Something like that."

"Hmm. Well, right now all I can think about, besides you naked, is eating. I'm starving, and you're *always* starving so—"

"Hey!" She said. "You better watch yourself."

He grabbed her hand and they headed for the buffet table. The next hour passed quickly as they ate and chatted with friends. Alex watched everyone dance. She just wasn't really feeling up to getting out there, but watching Joel dance with Charlotte was proving to be plenty entertaining. When the band switched to a slow song, Jake came over from talking to someone across the room and held out a hand to Alex.

"I'd love to dance with a beautiful pregnant woman," he said.

She placed her hand in his and let him pull her up out of her chair. "You'll have to keep me steady. I'm front heavy," she said as he drew her into his body on the dance floor.

"Me too," he whispered, pretending to adjust his crotch.

"Oh my gosh, what's gotten into you lately?" she asked, grinning.

He shrugged as their bodies swayed to the music. Her large belly kept them from getting too close. "I guess I'm just really happy."

Alex tilted her head to the side and stared up at him, her fingers threading into his hair. She didn't care if she messed up his perfectly styled do, she liked how the short strands felt against her skin. "I'm happy too, Jake. Happier than I've been . . . in so long. I didn't think it was possible for me."

He leaned down and kissed her, although it was a little awkward. Just then she felt the baby roll over in her stomach. Jake pulled back, his mouth wide open with excitement. "Okay, I felt that one!"

Alex laughed. The past several weeks he'd been obsessed with feeling the baby move. "I felt that one too. He's now getting comfortable on my bladder."

Jake nodded toward the restroom. "You need to go?"

She shook her head. "Nah, I've got a few more minutes to dance with you."

He angled his body around her stomach, so they could get closer, which required them to switch things up. They grasped hands on one side, and he pulled her tight with one of his hands around her waist on the other. Thankfully she still had one free arm to wrap around his shoulders and rest her fingers on his neck.

After a few moments he let go of her hand so he could rub her belly softly back and forth as if he was dancing with it. Alex leaned her forehead into his temple. "What are you doing?"

"Teaching my son how to dance."

She bit at her lip, suddenly emotional. It had been a while since Nate's face had entered her mind. She'd been so busy, and it had been so long.

And she just didn't think about him as much.

Taking a deep breath, she blew it out slowly against Jake's neck. Feeling it, he lifted his head and looked down at her. "You okay?"

She nodded. Could he tell she had tears in her eyes? She stared up at him, and his eyes didn't leave hers. Since his hand was still rubbing her stomach, she took her free one and lifted it to palm his jaw. "I love you so much, Jake Cooper."

His eyes widened a bit and the corner of his mouth lifted. "I love you, Alexis Parker."

"You do?" she whispered.

"I do." He nodded. "I have for a long time."

"It scares me to love someone as much as I love you."

She could tell by the way his eyes lit up that he loved hearing that. "I know, babe. But you know better than anyone, no matter what happens, you'll never regret loving someone."

Her heart nearly stopped beating. How did this man always know just what to say to make her feel reassured? Safe.

The song came to an end and there was a commotion at the front of the room. Alex jerked her head around to see Jen and her friend Ant—the lead singer of the band—pick up microphones. They were quickly followed by about six kids who were amazing singers from Jen's theater program.

"What are they going to do?" Jake asked quietly.

"Just watch. Charlotte's going to flip her lid."

"Charlotte," Jen said into her microphone.

Charlotte was rushing up to the stage, the hugest

smile on her face, Dean being dragged along behind her. "What are you doing?" Charlotte yelled in excitement.

Everyone's attention was on the stage and the kids who were lined up around a microphone.

"This is a gift from your new husband," Jen said before nodding at the kid choir. They immediately belted out the first couple of lines of ABBA's *Lay All Your Love on Me*—the movie version—and Charlotte screamed and began jumping up and down.

"What is this?" Jake asked, clearly confused.

Alex turned to him. "Charlotte is obsessed with *Mamma Mia*."

They turned to see Ant singing the first verse. Jen would obviously kill it on the female verses. And Charlotte was singing along with all of it like it was the most amazing thing she'd ever seen. Alex couldn't help laughing at the whole scene. This might be the happiest day of her life. She was in love, she was expecting a baby, and she was surrounded by the most amazing people.

Twenty-Eight

Alex rolled over in bed and let her head flop back down on her pillow when she found Jake's side of the bed empty. She'd almost forgotten that he'd left the day before to attend an event in Nashville. It was the big grand opening of the newest Sip, Bite, Match. Peter Dunn had asked if they'd be willing to have the Stag Wagon parked outside. There would be bouncy houses for the kids, drinks for the parents, and a news crew for publicity.

Jake, Dean, and TJ had all decided it would be best if they passed, but Charlotte and Alex had talked them into doing it. They'd only recently started working with the Sip, Bite, Match franchise, and it didn't make sense to turn down this offer. Besides, Nashville wasn't that far, it was only for two nights, and Alex still had a week until her due date. Dr. Mendoza had told her it was unlikely she would go into labor before then.

After dozing on and off for an hour, Alex finally pulled herself out of bed, rubbing at her stomach. She'd had a few stomach pains the past couple of days, but they weren't bad, so she hadn't worried too much. From everything she'd read, that was normal and could go on for weeks before real labor kicked in.

As she did every morning for the past week, she went into the nursery first. Standing in the doorway, she flipped on the light and smiled.

The bed and dresser they'd ordered with Sharon's gift card had been delivered a couple of weeks ago, and Jake had just finished putting it all together last weekend. Alex was in love with it. They'd chosen to decorate in neutral colors, but the room was full of giraffes. A nod to the "It's a Girl" gift Jake had given her, which was prominently seated in the baby's crib. The only pink in the room.

Charlotte had gotten a kick out of telling that story at the shower she, Sharon, and Amy had thrown her a couple of weeks ago. Every time Alex thought about how her new sister-in-law had allowed Dean's ex-wife to help her plan Alex's shower it made her smile. Charlotte had known that Amy was still important to Alex, and she'd been the bigger person. And shockingly, Charlotte and Amy had gotten along just fine throughout the planning. Although when it had come up in front of Sharon, she just raised an eyebrow and mimicked zipping up her lips and throwing the key over her shoulder.

That Charlotte, she was something else.

Alex walked over to the closet and opened it up to admire all the baby boy clothes hanging on tiny hangers. She only opened that closet up about ten times a day.

She'd moved in with Jake the week after Charlotte and Dean's wedding, and she had no regrets about it. Part of her wondered why she hadn't just done it sooner, but then she'd remember that her best decisions had always been the ones she hadn't rushed into. They had the rest of their lives to be together, and she didn't regret the months she'd gotten to spend with Joel. Someday he'd be gone, and she'd always have those memories of them sitting around the TV and yelling at contestants on *The Price Is Right* about how stupid they were for thinking that croutons were more expensive than almonds.

Alex closed the door to the closet and headed downstairs to the kitchen. She still woke up thirsty every morning, so she proceeded to go through her morning routine of filling up a giant water glass, adding a straw, and then making oatmeal covered with pecans, maple syrup, and chocolate chips.

When she was finished, she sat down at the kitchen table and was then irritated when she realized she'd left her phone upstairs. Glancing at the stove, she checked the time and sighed. Jake would probably be calling soon, and if she didn't answer, he would send a search-and-rescue team over.

With another sigh, she pushed up out of her chair, and instantly a trickle of liquid ran down her legs. "Oh shit," she said, glancing down to see it rolling down toward her bare feet.

She couldn't believe this was happening right now. She hadn't even gotten to eat her oatmeal. Turning around, she waddled over to the counter and grabbed a wad of paper towels and shoved them down her shorts and between her legs.

As quickly as she could, she made her way into the hall and up the stairs. She could feel herself leaking a bit the entire way. The minute she grabbed her phone she called Charlotte to come pick her up. There was no way she was driving herself like this.

"Hello."

"Charlotte, my water just broke."

"Oh my God, okay." Alex could tell Charlotte was

moving through the house. "I'm on my way right now. Did you call Jake?"

"I will now." Suddenly tears and reality set in. "I can't believe this is happening when he's gone."

Charlotte sighed. "I know. Call him right now. Get him on the road."

The minute they disconnected, she pushed Jake's contact. While the phone rang she moved around the room trying to get her wet shorts off and pull some new ones on, which was difficult to do with one hand, a giant belly and a giant belly. She sat on the bed and turned off the phone.

He hadn't answered. Dammit.

As soon as she dressed and brushed her teeth, Alex carefully went back down the stairs. She'd had her hospital bag packed and waiting by the front door for two weeks. Jake also had one sitting beside it. The sight of it made her want to cry.

There was a knock at the door, and Alex let Charlotte in.

"You okay?" Charlotte asked immediately

Alex nodded. "Jake didn't answer though."

"Don't worry, I'll get Dean working on that. Let's just get you to the hospital."

"Your car," Alex said. "I'm leaking."

Charlotte shook her head. "I already put two towels down. Don't worry."

"Those are our bags," Alex said, pointing to the things gathered by the door.

Charlotte picked them up, and within moments they were on the road. Alex tried Jake's phone again and still got no answer. This time she left a voice mail.

"Jake, it's me. My water broke. Charlotte's driving

me to the hospital. Please hurry and come home." She disconnected and looked over at Charlotte. "What if something happened to him?"

"Oh honey, no. Don't think like that. He's just busy, I'm sure. Dean will get a hold of him and he'll head home right away. I even told Dean to start checking flights out."

"That might not be faster," Alex said, holding her stomach. She could feel a slight tightening in her lower belly.

"We'll get him home, Alex, don't you worry."

Jake glanced up at the antenna on the news van that had parked near the Stag Wagon for the past hour. He had a feeling it was jacking with his cell phone signal because he'd been trying to call Alex without success. It kept dropping the call every time he dialed.

And here he was all alone serving up drinks. There was no way he could walk away and leave with all these people milling about. When there was finally a break in the crowd he stepped into the RV and tried to use it in there. No such luck.

When he came back out, Vanessa Dunn was standing there. "Hi, Jake," she said.

"Vanessa, hello. I didn't realize you were also part of this."

"Whatever my father is a part of, I'm a part of. I'm now co-owner of Dunn Enterprises."

"Congratulations." He looked around. Things had thinned out even more. "Hey, could I ask you a favor?"

Her perfectly lined eyebrow rose. "Okay."

"I'm not getting any cell service. I think it's this jack-ass's fault"—he nodded toward the news van—"but my girlfriend at home is pregnant and I haven't spoken to her yet today. Think you could cover me here for a moment while I go and call her?"

Vanessa's eyes were round. "Your girlfriend is pregnant?"

"Yeah," he said grinning. "Actually you met her last year. Alex."

"Yes, I recall."

"Okay, thanks for doing this. I appreciate it." He took off through the parking lot before she could argue. Glancing at his phone, he kept walking until he had enough bars that he figured he could make a call. Almost before he stopped walking, notifications started pouring in. Calls from Alex, voice mails, calls from Dean, from TJ, from his mother.

"Shit," he muttered, his heart beginning to hammer in his chest. His fingers began to shake as he tried to process whom he should call first. He pushed Alex's name. After two rings, a voice said hello but it wasn't her.

"Charlotte," he said. "Where is she?"

"She's right here, Jake. We're at the hospital, she just got into a room."

"Oh God," he said, running a hand through his hair. "Can I talk to her?"

"Okay, hang on, she's getting her blood pressure taken."

Jake turned around, suddenly raging that he was what . . . eight fucking hours away. He needed to get on the road, but he couldn't head back to the RV or he'd lose his connection. After a second, he heard Alex's voice.

"Jake?" she said, her voice full of fear. The sound broke his heart.

"Baby, what's going on?" He felt like sitting down in the parking lot so he wouldn't fall down.

"My water broke, Jake. Please come home. I need you. I can't do this alone."

"You're not going to do this alone, Alex. I'm sorry I had no reception. I'm going to leave and start back, okay?"

"Dean's trying to find you a flight."

"Okay, good. That's good." Although he had no clue how to get to the airport from here. He needed his navigator, Alex. His world. "I'm gonna get there, Alex. You hear me?"

"Okay. Hurry."

"I love you."

"I love you," she said, her voice breaking.

"Everything is going to be okay. Hear me?"

"I hear you."

As soon as they disconnected, he called Dean.

"Hey, man," Dean said upon answering.

"Hey, did you find me a flight?"

"No. Unfortunately the next one from Nashville to Kansas City isn't until three. By the time it's all said and done, you'd be better off driving."

"Shit," Jake said, turning around. He caught sight of the Stag Wagon. The thing was massive. It was a pain to drive and he certainly couldn't easily speed in it. "Dean, I'm going to have to unhitch the RV and leave it here."

"Do it. TJ and I can drive down and pick it up in a few days."

"You sure?"

"Hell yes. Just get home. My sister needs you here."

* * *

Alex faintly heard Charlotte's voice in the distance. She was in so much pain it was difficult to discern if she was dreaming, in a coma, or maybe dead. They'd put something in her IV to help with the pain, but she'd been adamant she wanted to try to get through without an epidural. Why had she decided that?

"Alex?" Someone was rubbing her arm. "Open your mouth, sweetie."

It was a nurse. Alex tried to open her mouth only to get two wet ice cubes placed on her tongue. Instinctively she bit down, and enjoyed the coolness. She opened her mouth again and, sure enough, more ice was miraculously placed there.

"It's been seven hours." That was definitely Charlotte. "How long can she safely go with her water broken?"

"We've got plenty of time. She's doing great. Things are progressing steadily. She's dilated to a five and is in active labor, but she could move into transition at any time. Just keep on reassuring her. You're doing exactly what you should be doing."

"Okay. But you know we're trying to wait for the father. He's on his way."

"It will probably be fine if he gets here in the next hour or so. But there's no way to tell."

"Thank you," Charlotte said.

Alex forced her eyes open again and focused on Charlotte. "Where is he?"

"He's on his way, Alex. I promise. You're doing such a good job." She felt a cool hand on her forehead, swiping her damp hair off her face.

For the past several hours she'd walked the halls with either Charlotte or Sharon, sat in a chair, squatted, walked some more, and now she was in so much pain she didn't want to move.

Jake was about a half-hour away, on the east side of Kansas City when Dean called. "What's happening?"

"Where are you?" Dean asked.

"I should be there in about a half hour."

"Okay, because she's dilated to nine. It could happen at any time."

Jake punched the steering wheel with so much force he thought he might have broken something. He could not believe he'd let this happen. The event in Nashville hadn't even really been worth it. Nothing was worth not being there for Alex. He'd known she was terrified to go into labor. The thought of anything happening to her baby kept her up at night a few times.

And here he was driving nearly eighty down the highway trying to get to her.

"I'm trying, Dean," he said, getting on a ramp to merge onto another highway. The sun was now low in the sky, and although there were less cars on the road, some of them were difficult to see without their lights on.

By the time he pulled off I-35 and headed down the road toward the highway, his heart was beating to the point of pain. Every driver who slowed down in front of him made him want to rage. He was nearly frantic with anxiety and excitement. All he wanted was to get to Alex. It was the only thing on his mind, which was probably why he didn't see the truck coming at him from the other direction as he took off to go through a stop sign.

"You're doing great, Alex. You're breathing beautifully," the nurse said. Alex inhaled deep, watching the nurse, who was watching the monitor. "Now try to blow it out slowly."

Instead she opened her mouth and screamed. "Where is Jake?!" She glanced around the room realizing that everyone was gone. "Where is Charlotte?"

"Relax, Alex." The nurse's eyes darted back and forth from Alex to the door. Something had felt wrong over the past few moments.

"What's happening?" She said, suddenly panicking. Just a few moments ago Charlotte had been right by her side, talking her through her contractions, rubbing her back. Then she'd just disappeared with another nurse.

The woman standing near Charlotte's bedside turned and yelled toward the door at the same time she pushed the call button. "Someone come in here!"

Another nurse came around the corner a second later, a weird fake smile on her face. "How's it going, Alex?"

Was she kidding? "Where's Jake? Is he here?"

"Not yet, hon, but Dr. Mendoza is putting her gloves on."

Alex's eyes widened. "No! I'm waiting for Jake. He's supposed to be here." She let her head fall back and she wailed in desperation. "Charlotte!"

Right now she felt insensible, paranoid, and enraged. Right then another contraction began to radiate up her uterus, the pain forcing her to crunch into a ball, pulling her legs toward her chest. The minute it passed she let out a hard breath as if she'd just come up from being underwater. "Oh my God. I'm scared."

She fell back onto the pillow just as Charlotte walked in the room. The minute Alex saw her face, she knew something was truly wrong.

"Dr. Mendoza is here, Alex," Charlotte said, trying to smile. "Are you ready to have this beautiful baby?"

Alex began to shake her head frantically. "No, not yet, please."

"Everything will be fine, sweetie," Charlotte said, rubbing Alex's arm.

Tears fell from Alex's eyes, rolling down her temples. Her body began to vibrate, just a bit at first, but quickly led to a violent shiver. She was so cold. Her teeth began to chatter, and Charlotte looked at the nurse.

"What's happening?" she asked, her voice frantic.

"It's normal. It's time," the nurse said. She was messing with things at the foot of the bed, and Alex, with her teeth still chattering, began to cry harder.

"Charlotte," she said, almost unable to talk. "Where is Jake? I need him here."

"I know, honey." Was Charlotte crying also?

What the hell was happening? She wasn't even sure if she'd screamed that out loud or in her head. Alex watched as her sister-in-law darted a look toward the nurse who returned it with a quick shake of her head. Time began to stand still; sounds started to muffle.

"Someone tell me, what the fuck is happening. Where is Jake?"

"He'll be here soon," Charlotte said. "I promise."

"You're lying to me, Charlotte," Alex said weakly as Dr. Mendoza came in the room.

"Alexis," the doctor said in a soothing voice. "I need you to calm down. Your panicking is causing your baby's heartbeat to accelerate even more and that's not good."

"Oh God, no," she whispered. She tried to suck in a deep breath, but all she wanted to do was cry. Between the pain, the shivering, and the fear, she was nearing hysteria.

"Alex, hold my hand," Dr. Mendoza said.

Alex shook her head and locked onto a gloved hand. "Look at me."

Opening her eyes as wide as she could, Alex focused on the deep brown eyes of her doctor. "I'm scared to push."

"I understand, but believe me, your body was made for this."

She shook her head, feeling out of control. "No, it wasn't."

Dr. Mendoza gave her a weak smile. "We're going to deliver this baby now. Okay? But I can't do it without your help. I need you to think about your baby. He needs you to calm down."

"But can you please tell me where Jake is? Please?"

"Alex, right now, I need you to focus on pushing this baby out. Everything will be okay. Trust me."

Twenty-Nine

Alex hadn't dreamed about Nate in so long she'd almost forgotten what his voice sounded like. She knew she was dreaming for some reason, because she kept wanting to wake up. They were in the desert driving in a convertible, and she was angry with him. He just wouldn't pull over so she could get out.

Finally he did, and when she stepped out of the car, she looked around and realized she was in Munich, Germany. She began to run as fast as she could, calling for Jake. Where was he? She'd been searching for him all night. She stopped short when the Stag Wagon came into view. Smiling, she called out his name. He had to be here. He told her he would be.

Trust me, Alex. Everything will be fine.

She remembered hearing those words.

A low beeping sounded once. Twice. And then something was clamping down on her arm. She looked over. A stuffed giraffe was squeezing her arm. It got tighter. Tighter. So tight she began to twist around to try and get it off.

"Alex," a feminine voice said. "It's okay, Alex. Are you awake?"

She tried opening her eyes, but they felt like they'd been glued shut. Finally, she could make out Charlotte, and suddenly things began to come back to her in rapid succession. She was in the hospital.

"Jake," she said, feeling the tears begin to fall immediately.

"I'm right here, babe."

Her eyes flew open in time to see Charlotte stand up, and then her view was filled with the most beautiful sight she'd ever seen. Jake. He was smiling down at her. And he was holding their baby, who was wrapped in a blanket, a tiny cap on his head.

"Look what you did." he said, grinning. "I'm so proud of you, Alex."

"I was afraid something happened to you," she said through her tears. She felt so weak, and numb, and she hated that she didn't have the strength to sit up and hug both of them like she wanted to.

"I'm so sorry, Alex. I was in an accident just down the street. They took me into the ER afraid I'd had a concussion."

"Oh my God!"

"I'm okay. I promise."

He held up the little bundle in his arms just as a nurse walked up behind him. "There you are," she said with a smile. "Let's get this sweet boy in there with you for some more skin time."

Another nurse came in also and suddenly there was a flurry of activity. They were pulling down her gown and setting her naked baby on her chest. The entire time Alex didn't know where to look. She was so overcome with emotion and confusion, she wanted to take in every tiny detail of this body resting on hers, his big beautiful eyes and tiny pouted lips, but she also didn't want Jake to leave her sight.

When the baby started to cry, that was all it took to make her choose where to place her attention. In that moment she wrapped her arms around him and held him close. She pressed her nose into his skin—the softest skin she'd ever touched—and inhaled his sweet baby scent. This was everything she'd ever wanted. Heaven. Finally, she knew that everything was going to be okay.

For the next few minutes, Jake sat on one side of the hospital bed trying to help Alex as she attempted to nurse their baby for the first time. Once she'd fully come to, she touched and held their baby with such tenderness, such love, he felt like crying. Again. The minute he'd been introduced to his son, he'd lost it. After the stress of the day, the sadness of not being there for her, and then the accident, it had been almost too much emotion for him to handle. God, how he wished he and Alex could have shared that moment together. But they were together now—alive, healthy, and perfect.

Finally, their son's tiny mouth latched onto Alex's nipple and began to suck. Her head jerked up to him, and the look of joy and excitement on her face was so beautiful he felt as if his heart had been ripped out and was laying right there in the bed. This. This was what he'd needed all along. He'd only had to wait for her.

An hour ago, when he'd bullied his way out of the ER and up to the maternity ward, he'd been nearing a full-blown panic attack. He'd called Dean from the truck to tell him he'd been in an accident, and under no circumstances was he to tell Alex. He'd known he hit his head, and sure enough they'd driven him the rest of the way to his destination in an ambulance.

But it hadn't taken him long to realize that it was nothing serious, and he'd nearly beat the walls down to get out of there with a promise that he'd come back in the morning for a CT scan. He knew full well that if they'd been that concerned, they wouldn't have let him go.

He hated that he hadn't made it in time to be in the operating room when she had her surgery, but he'd seen the baby almost immediately and had been able to hold him the entire time they waited for Alex to wake up in her room.

"He has your hair," Alex said, petting their baby's tiny round head.

"Maybe. But he's got your eyes."

"You think?" she asked, looking down at the most beautiful little face Jake had ever seen. "I don't know."

"I've been staring at him for an hour," Jake said.

Alex looked up. "You have?" she whispered.

He nodded. "I was telling him all about you while you slept. Even the bad stuff."

She opened her mouth. "The bad stuff?"

Jake laughed. "Yeah. I told him that he'd have to get used to folk music and chick movies." He pulled a face and she laughed.

They both looked down when he squirmed and began to cry a little. Alex immediately began to soothe him, talking to him in a soft voice and trying to get him to latch on again. She was a natural.

"Thank you," Jake heard himself saying.

"For what?" Alex asked.

"For this. You. Our family."

"We *are* a family," she said.

Jake nodded. "Yes we are. Forever."

"I was beginning to think I'd never have a family," she whispered.

"Me too. But then a beautiful woman stepped off an elevator and my heart stopped."

She tilted her head and gave him a wry look. "You didn't know then."

"Maybe not. But damn, I knew you looked good that night."

Her quiet laugh made him smile.

"We haven't chosen a name yet," she said, running a finger over the fine baby hairs.

"He and I were talking that over also while you were asleep. I think we came up with a good one," Jake said.

"What is it?" she asked, a look of surprise on her face.

Jake hesitated for a moment, but not because he doubted what he was about to say. He knew in his heart, without a doubt, it was the right name. But he didn't want Alex to be sad. He decided to just say it.

"Nathan. He should be named Nathan."

She didn't reply for a moment, but her lip began to quiver.

"Do you like it?" Jake asked.

She nodded, tears falling from her eyes. Unable to stop himself from touching her, Jake leaned forward and kissed her forehead, their baby—baby Nathan—quietly suckling between them.

"Thank you," she whispered.

He kissed his way down her temple, her cheek, and then her lips. "I love you, Alex," he said against her mouth.

"I love you too. So much."

Epilogue

"How about this one?" Jake asked, holding up another outfit.

Alex looked up from the diaper she'd just put on Nate. "Yes. I like that one."

Once she dressed him in the little shirt and overalls, she passed him to Jake who immediately raised him up in the air and blew on his little stomach.

"Do that at your own peril," Alex said, taking the dirty diaper to the trash can in their hotel room. "He hasn't burped yet."

"Oh shit," Jake said, laughing and lowering Nate down into his car seat. "Sorry, little dude. I'm not looking to be puked on again."

Alex laughed and grabbed her purse and the diaper bag. In the past four months she and Jake had each been barfed on, peed on, and pooped on.

And she wouldn't change it for anything.

"Ready?" Jake asked, looking at her.

"Yep."

They loaded up their rental car, locking the car seat into the base, and headed down the road.

"You're sure they're home?" Jake asked.

"It's Sunday afternoon. They always do Sunday supper."

"I hope you're right," Jake said.

The minute they pulled into the Williams driveway, Alex knew she'd been right. Juju and a now toddling Camille were playing in a sprinkler out front.

Her heart began to race as she undid her seat belt and got out.

"Aunty Alex!" Juju screamed. Within seconds Alex was hugging a soaking-wet little girl while Jake got Nathan's car seat out of the back of the car.

"Let's go inside and surprise Grammy Regina," Alex said.

"Otay," Camille said before running up to the front door.

Alex followed the two little girls inside, holding her breath in the living room while she listened to Juju run into the kitchen calling for her grandmother. "Grammy Regina!"

"What?" Regina said.

"Aunty Alex is here with her baby."

There was commotion as everyone in the house came into the front room.

"Oh Lord, Alexis." Regina threw her arms up in the air and rushed over, pulling her into a hug. "What do you have against a phone, young lady?" she asked, chuckling.

Alex grinned as she squeezed her hard. "I wanted to surprise you."

"Well, you did that," Regina said. And as if she realized there was something better to see, she pulled away from Alex and peeked behind her. "Where is he?"

Alex stepped aside and turned to see Jake set down the baby carrier and pull back the cloth cover.

"Oh my goodness," Regina said in a hushed tone. "Isn't he just the thing."

Tiana came up beside Alex and wrapped her in a hug. Together they watched as Regina carried the baby carrier over to the sofa and then proceeded to slowly undo the restraint.

"He's so cute," Juju said, peeking down at him.

"Of course he is," Regina said as she lifted him out of his seat, looking him over carefully, taking in every inch. He was frantically sucking on a pacifier, but the minute he was sitting in her lap it popped out of his mouth. "Oh, look at you smiling at me. What a flirt. Do you get that from your daddy?"

"Yes, he does," Alex said, smiling at Jake. He sat down beside her on the other sofa and grabbed her hand.

"Let me hold him," Tiana said, sitting by Regina.

"Not yet, I'm not done." Regina smiled at the sweet little face in front of her. "Am I, Nathan? I'm not done telling you how handsome you are."

Tiana looked over Alex and Jake. "Can you stay for supper? We've got plenty."

"Only if you're sure. We don't have to. I know we just showed up unexpectedly."

"Your momma is acting crazy like we may not have enough food in this house," Regina cooed at Nathan. "Isn't she? Yes she is." She turned to Juju. "June, go get Papa and tell him to get on in the house."

Juju ran off, so Alex waited for everyone to join them. The minute Leon stepped into the living room his eyes widened. "Alex, what are you doing here, girl?"

She stood up and went over to hug him. "Brought you a visitor."

"I see that," Leon said as he sat down next to his wife. "Look at that," he said, smiling at Nathan, who lifted a hand and batted it at him. Leon chuckled and grabbed his tiny finger. "So this is Nathan Cooper. He sure is handsome."

"Isn't he?" Regina said, bouncing him on her knee.

"We have some exciting news," Alex said.

"What's that?" Tiana said.

"Well, the reason we're here, in Atlanta, is because I had a job interview."

Regina stopped bouncing her leg and peeked around Nathan. "Where at?"

"It's a natural energy company. And, well, they offered me a job."

"Are you going to move here, Aunty Alex?" Juju asked, rushing over to her.

"We are," Jake said to the little girl. "In two months."

Regina's mouth fell open. "You can't be serious."

"We are," Alex said, biting back a smile. "Jake can do his job remotely, so he agreed to move here for me." She grabbed his leg, loving how he reached down and laced their fingers. He hadn't even hesitated when she'd mentioned the idea.

"Does that mean I get to be your Grammy Regina all the time?" she said to Nathan. His face lit up with a giant grin. "I think you like that idea, don't you? And someday I'll tell you about the man you're named after. He's special. Just as special as your daddy for giving you such a beautiful name."

That night, back in their hotel room, Alex pulled out her journal.

Day 125 since Nathan's birth
Life has been crazy lately, but so good. Nathan slept through the night for the first time last week, and

although I know this trip will probably mess up our schedule a little, at least I know he can do it. Getting to know his personality has been the greatest joy, and watching Jake be a father . . . I can't even describe how much I love it. Every night when Nathan wakes up, Jake gets out of bed, goes to get him, and brings him to me so I can nurse him. Sometimes I listen to them together on the baby monitor and cry because I know that this was exactly what my life was supposed to be.

That makes me feel a little bit guilty. But I know that loving Nate was part of my journey. It was part of my destiny. Meant to be. Because it was through you, Nate, that I connected with Jake in a way that is deeper than anything I've ever experienced. I love that he knows how much I loved you, and that he respects it. Loving you, and being loved by you, has made me a better person.

I'm still afraid. I think I'll always be afraid, but I just try to keep seeing every single day as a gift. Jake was right—love is worth it, and loving him and our baby is worth the risk of whatever could happen. If anything, I know how strong I am, and that I can survive.

Alex glanced down at the man sleeping beside her in the hotel bed. Next to him was a tiny body, rapidly sucking on a pacifier, with his teeny fingers wrapped around his daddy's pinky. She knew she'd have to lay Nathan in his travel bed, but right now, she felt like she could watch the two of them sleep like this forever.

I think I'm going to give the journal writing a break. Maybe I'll come back to it, I'm not sure. In the meantime, I intend to feel the same way, every day, as often as I can: happy and grateful.

Catch up on the
Whiskey and Weddings series
by Nicole McLaughlin

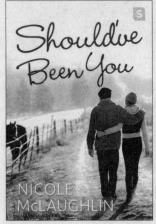